THE FRACTURED MAN

A Q.C. DAVIS NOVEL

LISA M. LILLY

SPINY WOMAN PRESS

All that I did for you, you said you'd owe me
Whenever I lost my way, you said you'd show me
Call if I needed you, you always told me
Then when I called you, you said you didn't know me

All that you said you'd do, none of it mattered
The whole and the parts alike fractured and shattered
Vows that you made, you rewrote so soon after
And your words of wisdom, they're nothing but chatter

- Fractured and Shattered

$$1$$

____

THURSDAY, MAY 15, 12:03 A.M.

Once you've lost a person you love, a call in the middle of the night means only one thing.

This one woke me from a dead sleep. I flailed for the phone and whacked my knuckles on the oval table next to my bed. The phone clattered to the floor.

I scrambled to retrieve it from under the bed. My mother's phone number showed on the display. Her number is one of the few programmed to get through my nighttime Do Not Disturb setting, but she never calls me during the night.

She rarely calls me at all.

Sitting cross-legged on the hardwood floor between the wall and my bed, I answered. It was chilly outside for mid-May, and the draft from the sliding glass doors blew across the condo onto my bare legs, but I had no desire to move.

If you're already on the floor, there's nowhere to fall.

"Is it Dad?" I said.

It was the only reason I could think that he wouldn't be the one calling with bad news.

"He's fine," my mom said.

Maybe Dad was too upset to come to the phone. Which made me think of my grandmother, my dad's mother. She's in good health but in her late seventies.

"Gram? Kendra? The kids?"

"Nothing's wrong," my mom said.

I let out my breath and rested my back against the metal bedframe and box spring. I'd covered our whole family. My mom's anxiety keeps her from sleeping, so by itself her being awake this late meant nothing. Except that it hadn't occurred to her that I'm normally asleep by ten-thirty and calling at midnight would scare me.

"So you're calling at midnight to, what, say hi?"

"Caleb called. He's trying to reach you and keeps getting your voicemail. He says it's important."

"Caleb?" I wound my fingers into my long, tangled hair. My brain conjured an image of *The Alienist*, a book I'd read in high school and loved by Caleb Carr.

"Caleb," Mom said.

Nothing in the way she said it changed. But as I climbed into bed it sunk in. "Oh."

I hadn't heard from him in over a decade, but Caleb was my best friend from fourth grade through the middle of college. A short, skinny kid good at making me laugh, after his parents divorced, he and his mom moved into a rambling three-story Victorian a few blocks from where I grew up. Gram knew his mother from church and insisted she bring him over to meet me because he, too, liked acting.

I scrolled through the missed calls listed on my phone. An unfamiliar number had tried three times in the last fifteen minutes. My phone hadn't rung because I'd set it on Do Not Disturb.

"Why'd he call you?"

"He remembered I'm always awake all night," Mom said. "He needs to talk to you."

My mom still used the same flip phone, and cell phone number, she had for the last fifteen years. Mine had changed, and my law firm website lists only my office landline.

I drew my knees to my chest and wrapped my free arm around them. "Is it his mom or dad?"

Caleb and I had spent so much time in each other's homes that we felt like members of each other's families. Ironically, both our parents had seemed more interested in the child not their own.

"He didn't say. I'm tired. I'll text you his number."

She hung up without waiting for me to respond.

———

Thursday, May 15, 12:10 a.m.

You can use social media to stay connected, or you can use it to stay away. Caleb did the latter with me.

Over our junior year of college, Caleb became busier and busier. When I texted, he answered, but days later. If I left a voicemail, he responded on social media saying he missed me, things had been crazy, we'd catch up soon. But on the same date I'd see photos online of him drinking pale ale at Kitty O'Shea's on Michigan Avenue, eating chocolate chip pancakes at the Artists Café, or enjoying Manhattans in the lounge of a storefront theater. Before the opening of a play I'd asked him to see with me.

I stopped checking his feeds. A couple years after college I got off social media altogether. All it did was make me feel bad, and once I stopped acting I didn't need it professionally again until I opened my own law firm.

So I had no idea what was happening with Caleb now. The last thing I'd seen was that he moved to L.A.

I made chai tea with whole milk and honey while waiting

for my mom's text. When it came, it included only the number, the same one that had tried calling me earlier.

No question about how I was, which I didn't expect via text. But also no apology for frightening me, which I'd thought might have occurred to her.

With a lot of therapy I'd accepted, more or less, that my mom's depression and anxiety made it hard for her to step out of her own head. Exhausted and wired after being jarred awake by a ringing phone, though, my acceptance at the moment was definitely less.

I dialed Caleb.

"Q.C.?" he said when he answered.

"Quille," I said. His mistake told me he'd never looked me up online at all. Once I stopped acting, I stopped using Q.C. Davis. My law firm is Quille C. Davis LLC, and my occasional social media posts identify me as Quille, not Q.C. "What's going on? Your parents okay?"

"Mom's good. Dad's on Wife Number 4, but our relationship has improved exponentially."

Exponentially seemed like an oddly formal word for an after-midnight call. Maybe Caleb at thirty-four years old was a formal person. But his parents were all right, and I couldn't think of anyone else we knew in common after all these years.

I set the mug on the steamer trunk I use as a coffee table and shifted to a more relaxed position on the couch. "So what's going on?"

"My friend died."

A memory from last year flashed through my mind. The image of Marco's dead body, which I'd been the one to find. I huddled in the corner of my couch. "Oh, no. I'm so sorry."

"He was my mentor," Caleb said. "And boss, sort of. He was the one who — he hired me. Trained me. Believed in me."

"Are you okay?"

"The police are asking questions. I might need a lawyer. Which you are these days, right?"

"Not that kind. But I share office space with a criminal defense attorney. I'll text you her info. She's who I'd call if I were in trouble. She's a singer, too."

The last part had nothing to do with law, but Caleb loved singing, so he might feel more comfortable having something in common with her. I still wondered why he'd called at midnight. But Danielle always complained about clients calling her after they talked to the police instead of before. I supposed I should be grateful Caleb was calling now rather than from the police station.

"I want to connect with you, though, too," Caleb said. "In person. Tomorrow morning? Or this morning, I guess it would be."

I rubbed my forehead. A stack of litigation files sat in my office, cases where I'd already gotten as many extensions as I could. In the early part of the year I file taxes for actor and artist clients, which means in late April and May I'm busy playing catch up on everything else.

Carving out time for Caleb when he hadn't gotten in touch in all these years, and now only called because he needed something, didn't sound appealing.

But a potential murder investigation was scary. People want to talk to someone they know, not just a lawyer with expertise. And he'd been there for me often enough before college.

"Come to my office at eight-thirty," I said. If he was still acting, he kept a late schedule. But there was a limit to how much I'd rearrange my day out of the blue.

"You got it. And Q — Quille —can't wait to see you."

2

Thursday, May 15, 7:13 a.m.

My condo is one of the many brick warehouses and printing factories in my neighborhood that have been converted to loft space. My office is in a similar building a few blocks away. The area is known as Printers Row. I've loved it ever since I first walked through it to meet Caleb at Columbia College where he studied music and theater. It's especially beautiful in late spring. The trees, planted in grates in the sidewalk, are full of leaves and all the potted flowers the businesses put out are in bloom.

On Thursday morning I picked up an Earl Grey tea at the café on the ground floor of the building where I have my office. I took a big gulp in the elevator, hoping it would wake me up, and scalded my tongue and throat.

The suite was empty.

I didn't usually get in before 7:30, but I had no idea how long Caleb's story was likely to go and I had a legal brief to finish and file with the court. After flipping on the lights, I looked over the changes my virtual assistant had made for me the night before. She works from her home in South Carolina after she puts her kids to bed.

I spotted a mistake in reasoning I'd made, so I reworked the last third of the brief. My tea cooled, its lavender and vanilla notes filling the air as I revised, printed, and reread. Other people came in as I worked, and the air conditioning cycled on. It's set automatically by the building and goes on whether it gets above seventy degrees outside or not.

I ignored it other than pulling on my blazer.

The bell at the front desk rang. I glanced at the time on my laptop. 8:20. I didn't expect Caleb yet. When I'd known him, he'd been ten to fifteen minutes late for everything, including auditions and rehearsals. He still got cast because he was good, but not as often as he might have, even in student films.

We don't have a receptionist and my office is right off the reception area, so I poked my head out the door.

And there he was.

Had I passed him on the street I wouldn't have recognized him. He wore narrow-legged light gray chinos and a crisp mint-green collared shirt, open at the neck, and loafers. With tassels. Other than on stage, I'd never seen Caleb in formal or business clothes even when his dad took us out to eat somewhere nice.

I must have looked as different to Caleb as he did to me, if not more so. His wardrobe had been casual but had flattered his lean build and dark hair. In contrast, offstage through my teenage years I'd worn mostly faded, loose-fitting jeans I got at thrift stores and oversized, stretched out T-shirts. Now I wore what I thought of as a variation of my office uniform: low heels with skinny jeans, a white tank top with a gold and silver twist necklace, and a charcoal pinstriped blazer. I'd spent a few extra minutes smoothing my hair into long waves.

While Caleb and I had never been romantic — we weren't one another's type — I'd still wanted to show how much I'd changed while he'd been gone.

However different his look was, his scent was still the same. A blend of coconut, lime, and some spice I've never been able to identify that makes me think of vacation. Though I'd meant to shake his hand as if he were a new client, when he reached out his arms I stepped forward and we hugged.

When we moved apart, he surveyed me. "The professional look really works for you, All Eyes and Hair."

"You don't look bad yourself, Tiny Boy."

Caleb shook his head. "It's a wonder either of us stayed in theater."

The nicknames came from a director who'd spent more time critiquing our appearances than our performances. After having been a fairly cute kid, that year I'd become an awkward twelve-year-old. Skinny with braces and medium-length hair that bushed out all over the place, the director's barbs about my bony arms, oversized eyes, and unkempt hair made me cry.

Caleb, always the shortest and skinniest kid in the class, told me that one day he'd be taller and I'd become a beauty but the director would always be a no talent jerk. Caleb even hunted down awkward childhood photos of some of my favorite actresses.

"The play, though," I said.

It had been one of my favorites, written by a Chicago playwright who went on to win multiple grants and awards.

"Exceptional," he said. "And our one time acting together. I'll never forget it."

I ushered him into my office and shut the door. Danielle, the criminal defense attorney, was out at court all day today. My desk stands kitty corner from hers along one of the windowless interior brick office walls. I sat and spun my desk chair so I faced Caleb. He sat in one of two green vinyl visitor chairs next to the closed door.

"How serious are the police about you? Did they ask you to come into the station?" I said.

"Not yet. But when they questioned me at the scene, they said they'd follow up."

"Danielle said she'll try calling you tonight. She'll give you good advice."

"Thank you. It means a lot." He folded his hands together and leaned forward. "You must be wondering why it took a murder for me to get back in touch."

"It crossed my mind," I said.

"I take full responsibility. I fractured our relationship. That's past, but I want to remedy it now."

He sounded like he was reading from a script.

"Remedy it how?" I said.

"I've thought a lot about it. Why I disappeared on you." He unclasped his hands and made a small spreading gesture with his arms. "I was jealous."

"Jealous? But you — "

"Yeah, maybe that's why I recognized it."

My first boyfriend had been an actor. As I got more and more paid acting jobs, the relationship started falling apart. I didn't make the connection, but Caleb did. And he was right.

I'd never imagined Caleb felt jealous of my success at acting, though. If anything, I'd felt jealous of him. How easily he fit in with other people. How much more fun he seemed to have no matter what he was doing. And how often my mom pointed out that his personality was like that of my middle sister, the original Q.C. She'd been blond and bubbly and laughed all the time. Or so I'd been told by everyone who'd known her.

"But you disappeared after I decided to quit theater," I said.

"I couldn't believe you were walking away from it." He sat back in his chair, his legs sprawling. "And I knew any minute my dad would start saying I should be sensible like you."

"I wasn't being sensible. I was doing what I wanted."

I'd loved acting and had felt proud of earning my own money at it as a kid. But the longer I did it the more disappointed I'd felt when my mom didn't react to, or sometimes so much as notice, my successes. Whatever I did on stage, I'd always been less of a star than her lost child would have been.

At the same time, the business classes I'd taken so that I could better manage my acting career turned out to be fun. I especially liked accounting. Numbers meant something. They were predictable. When you got the right answer, the books balanced. Later I found that in law I could bring together my love of performing with my business skills.

Caleb nodded. "I knew that. You knew that. But my dad never would."

"That wasn't my fault."

"It wasn't. But you know, with my friends at Columbia, I felt like a god. Half of them were never going to be actors anyway. They were killing time until they went into their parents' businesses or got into grad school or started selling insurance. They thought I was amazing."

"I thought you were amazing."

"I know." He met my eyes. "I was messed up, and it was terrible to do that to you."

"It made me feel — it reminded me of my mom. Like the only thing interesting about me was my work in theater."

"It so was never about you, Quille. I wanted to blame you, blame my dad, blame everyone but me for what I didn't like in my life. It took me a long time and a lot more mistakes to take full responsibility for myself. Vincent, my friend who's gone now, helped me see that I needed to do that. And I don't blame you if you don't forgive me. Or if you forgive me but don't want to help. But if you could, it would mean so much to me."

3

Thursday, May 15, 8:59 a.m.

In the suite's narrow kitchen, I made myself a cup of tea from the Keurig machine and filled a glass of water from the tap for Caleb, who waited in my office. It gave me a moment to think. I'd offered to make him coffee, but he'd said he didn't drink caffeine anymore.

I didn't know how I felt about him coming to me for help. Or what I could do for him other than sending him to Danielle. But I knew how hard it was to deal with loss. I wouldn't send a stranger away in that circumstance without at least listening.

So I'd do that for Caleb.

He stood at my windows, looking down at Dearborn Street. "Neighborhood's a lot busier."

"Wait until you check out south of Roosevelt." I handed him the glass. "So tell me more about your friend."

He set the glass on a coaster on the credenza next to Danielle's printer and settled into the vinyl chair again. "Vincent Lenzi. He introduced me to Seminar and was my mentor from then on. More like a dad, really. But a good one."

"What kind of seminar?"

"No, no. Seminar. With a capital S."

He took out his wallet and pulled out a business card. His phone number and email address appeared on it in small type under a single word: Seminar, printed in bright green ink. The S was twice the size of the remaining letters and had extra swirls at the top and bottom. The color and flourishes might make it a trademark or some other type of protected logo. The company name itself struck me as too generic to be memorable.

"What is it?"

"An educational personal growth program. Founded by Scott Gary."

He said the name as if I ought to know it, but I didn't.

"He used to be a psychiatrist, but he left the profession when he realized he could help more people and create global change by working with groups rather than individuals."

I made a note to look for Seminar's website and see if that exact language appeared. "And how did you meet Vincent?"

"My dad sent me to him a couple years after I graduated. He's a business coach. You were right, BT double-V. Took me six years to get my degree."

I'd always found his way of saying By The Way annoying. But at least he sounded more like the Caleb I knew.

That it had taken him six years to get his bachelor's degree didn't surprise me. He'd regularly dropped classes after the official drop date, leaving him short on credits at the end of every semester. He'd ribbed me about sticking with classes I disliked, but my partial scholarships didn't cover the full tuition as it was. I couldn't afford extra years. It was different for Caleb. His dad hadn't liked him majoring in theater, but he still paid the bills.

"And after? When you moved to L.A.?" I said, then

clamped my lips together. Too late. I hadn't meant to show I'd checked on him at all. But he didn't seem to notice.

"Mostly storefront theatre. A lot of auditions. No musicals. Never quite got there despite all the voice lessons."

While Caleb's voice had a warm quality, and he could project, he didn't have a wide enough range for most lead roles in musical theater. He also had trouble singing harmony. A baritone, he could sing a duet with me because I'm a soprano and our parts would always be far enough apart. But when he sang with a tenor, alto, or bass, he drifted off key, struggling not to sing the other person's part. As if he couldn't help joining the voice with the range nearest to his rather than go his own way.

"Did Vincent have theatre contacts?"

"No, no. He did business coaching for Fortune 500 execs. He suggested I move to Austin. Audition for corporate films. Eventually I did, and he was right. I got work."

"Enough?" I said.

"Not once I hit thirty."

Caleb's dad had agreed to help support him while he pursued acting, but only until Caleb turned thirty. Which had seemed forever away when we were in college. Now we were both thirty-four.

I flipped a page on the legal pad. "So what'd you do?"

"Accepted a job offer from a company whose corporate films I was in. It was sales. Commission only. My dad agreed to help out a little longer so I could get on my feet. And my manager suggested — strongly — that all new salespeople go to Seminar."

"The manager was in Seminar, too? Is this a bigger organization than I'm thinking? Because I've never heard of it."

My phone pinged five times in quick succession, my scheduling app reminding me of tasks I'd planned to do today. And I still needed to finish my brief. Federal court allows until midnight to e-file, but leaving things to the last minute is a recipe for stress. If you have a computer glitch, or the court does, at best you're stuck writing a motion asking the court to let you file late. At worst you're not allowed to file at all.

"No, the sales manager knew Vincent from Seminar. That's part of how I got the job offer."

"So you don't work for Seminar, you take courses there?"

He held up his hand to forestall more questions and took a long drink of water.

With a prospective client at that point I'd share my hourly rate and explain that I charge a twenty-five-hundred-dollar retainer. That repelled people hoping to chat my ear off for free, get my thoughts, and then call the next lawyer on the Internet in the hope of more free advice.

It also meant people who did hire me got to the point faster. When you realize rambling for half an hour will cost you over a hundred dollars, you cut to the chase.

Caleb crossed one leg over the other and stretched his arm across the back of the chair next to him. "I work at Seminar now. But I started by taking part in an Event. Not a course. There are no courses. My first Event led to exponentially exceptional change for me."

Exponential, exceptional — he really was talking out of a corporate handbook, complete with emphasis on words like Event so they sounded as if they were capitalized.

"So Seminar helped with your salesperson job?" I said.

"Yeah. I kept taking part in Events, and I did better each year at work. Then Seminar offered me a position, and I love it. But now I not only lost my friend, my mentor, I'm afraid people at Seminar will blame me. For Vincent's death."

Caleb's shoulders drew together and his whole body seemed to fold in on itself.

"Blame you? Why?"

"Because the police questioned me."

"The police must have questioned a lot of people," I said.

"Yeah, but they spent a lot of time with me. I was at the offices late Sunday night. The night he was killed."

"Who else was there?"

He told me the names of two men and one woman. I printed them neatly on my legal pad so I could hand it all off to Danielle if she ended up representing Caleb. "Did you see Vincent that night?"

"Yeah. Around seven we ate dinner as a group in a conference room. He went to a back office to prepare for the Event starting on Monday."

"That was the only time?"

"Yeah. But I heard him arguing with someone. A man, I'm pretty sure, about a half hour before I left."

"Which was when?"

"That I left? Around ten."

Caleb told me he'd been working down the hall in the kitchen, which was at the opposite end of the suite from Vincent's office. When he passed by to get to the supply closet, he heard Vincent yelling and another man shouting back. Vincent's door was shut, so Caleb didn't see who it was, but he was sure it was someone in person, not on a speaker phone.

"Did you recognize the other man's voice?"

"No."

"Would you have noticed if it was an unfamiliar voice? Someone who wasn't supposed to be in the office?" I said.

He rocked his chair again. "Probably. I guess."

"And are you sure one of them was Vincent? Or did you assume because it was Vincent's office?"

He stared at the ceiling. "Before you asked I would have said yes, definitely Vincent. But you're right. Maybe I assumed."

It probably had been Vincent, but I'd learned in my law practice and life that assuming can be dangerous.

"What were they saying?"

"I don't know. The insulation's really good, and the doors are thick. It's hard to hear much from outside an office."

"You tried?" I said.

"Not then." He glanced down at his hands. "A couple different times the month before. When I was wondering how I was doing at Seminar. Didn't press a glass to the wall or anything. But paused a few times out of sight to see if I could overhear. I never could."

"So how can you be sure Vincent wasn't on the phone?"

"Their voices, they sounded about the same level. Not like one person right there on the other side of the wall and the other on a speaker."

I still didn't see why Caleb thought the police might be focusing on him. What he'd overheard explained why they spent extra time talking to him.

"Do you have something to gain from Vincent's death?" I said. "Or would other people in Seminar think you do?"

"I'm not in his will if that's what you mean."

"Are you in line for his job?"

"It's not like that in Seminar. Promotions are based strictly on performance."

"But there needs to be an opening for someone to move up, doesn't there?"

"No. It's more that positions are created for talented people."

That might be the party line, but any business can only support so many people at the top. Seminar might be different from the small and medium-sized companies I usually represent, but I doubted it was that different.

"Who found him?" I said.

I'd found Marco's body. While I hadn't been a serious

suspect, the detective spent a long time questioning me. I still dreamed about that night and answering questions while the techs carted Marco's body out. Except in the dream we sat in the living room with Marco still lying on the couch, white faced, his body stiff.

"His wife," Caleb said. "She came into Seminar's Chicago office suite Monday morning and found him on the floor."

"How'd he die?" I said.

"No one's saying. People at Seminar talk about Now, not Past."

Like Event, he spoke the two words as if they were capitalized. More buzzwords.

"But it was only a few days ago," I said. The idea that no one was talking about a recent sudden death confused me.

"It's still Past."

"So?"

"You can only live an exponentially excellent life if you focus on what you can do and change. What happened before can't be changed. It's Past."

I rubbed my hands over my arms. This bot version of Caleb unsettled me. If I stripped away the buzzwords, though, his point sounded a little like what my therapist in college encouraged me to do as I struggled to deal with my feelings about the original Q.C. and my family. But I couldn't imagine my therapist telling me to stop speaking of something traumatic two days after it happened.

"Could Vincent have died of natural causes?"

Caleb shook his head. "The police didn't think so. And they said there was a big gash on the back of his head."

My laptop trilled, a signal that someone I'd marked as a priority emailed me. Right now, the only people in that category were parties in an unfair competition lawsuit. We had a court hearing tomorrow.

"Danielle can help you with the police issues. What is it you're asking me to do?" I said.

"Can you find out if people in Seminar suspect me?"

I looked up from my notes. "How? The only person I know in Seminar is you."

"You found out what happened to your boyfriend last year."

I set my pen down. Nothing about my being involved in Marco's death investigation had been in the news. And I hadn't posted anything on social media, which it seemed clear Caleb hadn't been checking anyway. "How do you know that?"

"Your mom told me. I called her last summer looking for you. She said to give you some time because of what happened to Marco."

I was at the same time pleased my mom felt concerned about my emotional state and frustrated she'd never mentioned that my best friend from childhood had called.

"She didn't tell me."

"Don't be mad. I told her I'd call you in a couple months. But my moving got delayed until mid-January. Between getting all my stuff here and sorting it out with my girlfriend — ex now — and settling into my new position at Seminar, I just didn't have a chance."

Caleb had always been more forgiving about my mom's absence from my life than I was. He said at least my parents didn't go out of their way to make me miserable.

"How would I get these people who don't talk about anything to talk to me?"

"Come to a Seminar cocktail party with me. Tomorrow night. I can't ask anyone about Vincent because as a Seminar Coordinator I can't dwell on Past. But you can. And people will talk to you because you're my friend."

"Then they'll talk to the police."

"They won't." He reached out and took my hands. His fingers felt cool. "But if you say you're interested in learning more about Seminar and ask how Seminar helps them deal with it all, they'll answer. It's something the cops can't do. And it won't take long. 6:30-8:30. I'll take you out after for dinner. We can catch up. If you're not busy."

"You seem more worried about what your Seminar friends think than the police," I said.

He ran his hand through the front of his short, dark hair. "Seminar's the first thing I've succeeded at. First thing my dad doesn't think I'm wasting time doing. So, yeah, maybe it's whacked, but it matters what these people think. Especially the founder. Please, Q."

"Quille," I said. Q is what people who've been in my life forever sometimes call me if they have trouble switching to Quille. After all his years away, though, I wasn't willing to let Caleb use it.

"Quille. I'll get used to it, I promise."

I opened my calendar, but it was only to stall for time. I had plans with the guy I'd been seeing the last few months. But he'd understand if I cancelled to help an old friend.

"You really think I can find out something helpful in one night."

"It can't hurt. All the powerful people in Seminar will be there. Including Vincent's wife."

"But she won't be there, will she? With her husband having just died?"

"Sure she will. She's hosting."

4

———

When I got to the Daley Center courtroom the next morning, it was deserted except for the judge's clerk. I'd worked late preparing for the hearing, and no one called to say it wasn't going. The clerk said the judge was out on an emergency. It had been a cold, rainy spring in Chicago, the result of a frigid winter that kept Lake Michigan iced over through late February. I couldn't help wondering if the emergency was the first sunny Friday with a temperature above sixty degrees.

But it was a beautiful walk to and from court, and it freed some time to research Seminar.

No one in my office suite had heard of it, but a few colleagues said they'd ask around. I found a single Wikipedia entry for Dr. Scott Gary. No initials were listed after his name, making me doubt Caleb's claim that he was a psychiatrist. I'd dealt with quite a few medical doctors in my tax and law practices. I'd yet to meet one who didn't include M.D. on every piece of paper, email, or webpage.

The article also said nothing about a medical degree. It

listed a Bachelor of Arts in sociology from the University of Iowa and an honorary doctorate in Communications from a private college in Austin, Texas.

Gary worked as a counselor in the early 2000s. Before that he was a partner in a nutritional supplement company that promoted vitamins and powders that supposedly boosted brain function and the immune system. That nutritional supplement company's website included the usual disclaimers about no studies or government agencies approving its claims.

The company site no longer listed Gary as a partner, if it ever had. Wikipedia gave his current occupation as founder of Seminar, a private educational self-improvement corporation with its main headquarters in New York, New York. A note at the top asked for verification and sources.

Seminar itself appeared to have no Internet presence. Either that or the name was so generic that any results relating to it were buried on the hundredth page of my search results.

A strange choice for any business to make either way.

———

FRIDAY, MAY 16, 6:24 P.M.

After the sunny start to the day, it rained most of Friday afternoon. The skies cleared just before I left my office to meet Caleb at the downtown residential high rise on Madison Street where Vincent had lived with his wife.

Had I paid more attention to the address before I got into a cab, I would have realized the Lenzis' condo must face Michigan Avenue, making it among the priciest real estate in Chicago. Its lobby was small but had marble floors, overhead chandeliers, and a gas fireplace flanked by sleek leather couches. The doorman buzzed us through glass double doors.

"It might get a little salesy," Caleb said as he hit the button for the 35th floor.

"I thought it's a sort of memorial for Vincent."

"It is, but also people are invited who are thinking about going to Events. They're sort of like week-long courses where you apply Seminar concepts."

"Are people going to try to sell me on taking one?"

The doors slid open to a wide hallway with deep orchid carpet and muted lighting. All the doors lining it had matching brass door knockers.

Caleb pointed to the right. "Not sell you. But everyone at Seminar is really excited about it. So anyone new, they want to tell you how it changed their lives. That's why they'll talk to you when they wouldn't to the police."

"It's okay." We walked down the hall. "Plenty of people call my firm trying to sell me things. I'm used to it."

A woman with reddish-blond hair artfully piled high on her head opened the door a few seconds after Caleb knocked. She wore a navy sheath dress with a matching tailored jacket, a string of cultured pearls, and what looked like a two-carat diamond ring. Faint lines around her mouth made me guess her age as early forties, but her skin overall looked dewy and fresh.

I felt for the seam on my skirt, afraid it had shifted as I'd gotten out of the cab. My outfit would be fine at a Chicago Bar Association cocktail party: a short, flared skirt with a tiny checkerboard pattern, navy tights, a fitted rose-colored T-shirt that matched a thread running through the skirt, and a short-cropped blazer. But compared to this woman, my short skirt plus my chunky onyx and silver necklace and flats left me feeling as if I looked both too young and too casual.

I told myself that was good. People speak more freely around someone who seems non-threatening.

"This is Karla Lenzi," Caleb said. "Karla, Q.C. — Quille Davis."

"Welcome, Quille."

As Karla shook my hand her last name registered with me. I realized this was likely Vincent Lenzi's widow.

Before I could express condolences, Karla said, "Scott won't be here. He got tied up with some business on the West Coast."

"Really? I wanted Quille to meet him."

"Another time, I hope," Karla turned away to answer another knock at the door, and Caleb and I walked into the wide living room.

Its dark hardwood floors gleamed. The lacquered tables and curved furniture looked like genuine 1940s art deco. The floor-to-ceiling windows gave the entire space the appearance of being suspended in mid-air over Michigan Avenue. North of the Chicago River the street is known as the Magnificent Mile for its designer stores and the historic sandstone Water Tower.

But here I could see the landscaped gardens of the Art Institute, the fountains at Millennium Park, the silvery, serpentine bridge across Lake Shore Drive, and the vast, blue lake itself stretching to infinity.

The living room flowed into a dining area with a long, twelve-seat table and a marble breakfast counter at the far end. Bottles of wine, rows of glasses, and a chrome ice bucket sat on the counter, and a glass-fronted refrigerator held more drinks below.

Plated appetizers and bite-sized desserts filled the dining table. Caleb poured me a glass of Pinot Noir and took a small green bottle of sparkling water for himself from the fridge.

About thirty people stood in the living room. All ages,

backgrounds, ethnicities, and genders seemed to be represented, and I didn't need to worry about my outfit. People wore everything from business suits to T-shirts and leggings. They all seemed to be gesturing as they talked.

I'd been at wakes where people eventually got to laughing, but I'd never seen this level of merriment and excitement.

"Let me introduce you to Richard Messerly before things get busy." Caleb took my hand and drew me through the crowd. A small group stood near a gray stone fireplace. Rows of pillar candles burned in place of a fire, scenting the air with vanilla. Caleb spoke into my ear. "He was there that night."

I nodded. I'd memorized the names.

Caleb tapped the shoulder of a man with long limbs, the faintest glints of silver in his russet brown hair, and a bottle of Goose Island Pale Ale in one hand. In the other he held a plate of appetizers that he set down to shake hands with me.

He stood about six feet, roughly four inches taller than me. "Caleb's talked about you a lot, Q.C."

"It's Quille," Caleb touched my elbow. "I have a few things I need to help out with. Do you mind?"

I shook my head and turned toward Richard as Caleb stepped away.

"So you used to be an actress?" Richard studied my face, and a line formed above the bridge of his nose.

I'd seen the look before the rare times I told people I used to act. Usually they were trying to figure out how a woman with my only slightly prettier than average looks could succeed. Because of my long, dark hair and large eyes, if I spend enough time on makeup and hair styling some people consider me striking. But I'm not magazine cover material or movie star stunning.

"Stage actress," I said. "But I haven't acted professionally for a long time now."

He took a long drink of ale. "Oh, right, I remember. Caleb said you flitted around a lot."

I nearly choked on my wine. "Flitted?"

"He didn't say flitted. But you quit acting in college because you thought you wanted to be an accountant, then quit that after a year or two for law school, right? Then didn't like the big firm you went to?"

"That's not what happened." I gripped the stem of my wine glass so hard I was afraid it would break and scanned the room for Caleb. Maybe I could stab him to death with my eyes. But he'd disappeared.

Richard bit into a stuffed mushroom and the other half crumbled on his plate. "Hey, nothing wrong with trying different things. But if you focused all that energy you could maximize your success."

"I'm maxed," I said.

"Everyone, could I have your attention?"

It was Caleb's voice cutting through the din. Everyone quieted and shuffled around. Caleb stood near the hallway that led to the back half of the condo. He had his arm around the broad shoulders of a young man with a crew cut who wore new-looking khakis and a buttoned-down white shirt. "This is Kevin, and he'd like to say a word about how Vincent enhanced his life."

Kevin smiled, showing uneven teeth that seemed incongruous with his starched shirt. He wasn't one of the people Caleb had told me was at Seminar the night of Vincent's death or was important in Seminar. I listened with half an ear, fuming about Richard's comments.

In the United States, you need a four-year bachelor's degree before you can go to law school. Pretty much any major in undergrad will work. A few of my fellow law students majored in criminal justice, but I'd met ones who majored in everything from fine arts to sociology to physics. Business, political science, and communications backgrounds were pretty common, too. A lot of people go straight through from college to law school, but many work anywhere from a year to a decade or more in other professions before deciding to go to law school. Danielle was a Chicago cop for years before she went to law school at night and became an attorney.

"And because of Seminar, you're looking at an ensign in the United States Navy," Kevin said.

The room burst into applause.

Kevin made a slight bow, bending at the waist. I took another sip of wine, confused. I was pretty sure the story had started with Kevin washing out of basic training three months ago. I didn't know much about naval ranks or rules, but I knew ensign was an officer position.

That trajectory seemed impossible.

"If you're thinking it's impossible," he said, "that's exactly why I'm here. To tell you to stop thinking things are impossible! You're with an exceptional group of people, and you'll learn to get around all those blocks you're putting in your own way. Thank you."

The second round of applause died out.

"Maxed how?" Richard said.

5

———

Friday, May 16, 7:10 p.m.

"My clients like my accounting and business background. They followed me from my old firm. My practice was in the black after six months, about half the average time it takes."

I took a gulp of wine to make myself stop. I sounded defensive, the way I would if his take on my life were true.

More important, I didn't need to justify myself to this man. It also wouldn't help me learn about Vincent, which I still meant to do despite that I wasn't feeling very charitable toward Caleb right now.

"What do you do?" I said.

"I'm a lawyer, too. I was a poly-sci major," Richard said.

"Really? And my career path surprises you?" I said. "You must have had classmates with business backgrounds."

Now I was sure he'd purposely goaded me. Caleb might genuinely not understand how law worked. A lot of people don't realize a law degree is a doctorate that takes years beyond college, especially if they're familiar with other countries where law is an undergraduate degree. But as a lawyer himself, Richard knew.

"I struggled to find my footing in college and beyond," Richard said. "But you're correct, and I take full responsibility for my mistake in assuming you did as well. But what made you quit acting?"

A young woman in a tuxedo appeared with a tray of appetizers. Richard picked out a variety of them.

I took a small white plate and filled it with a couple crab puffs and skewers of chicken dipped in sesame sauce.

"Long story," I said.

"People's stories are what Seminar is all about." Richard arranged some prosciutto on a triangle of cheese and took a bite.

"I thought Caleb told me Seminar isn't about the past."

He finished eating and frowned. "Caleb's wrong. We look at Past to gain useful information. Sometimes it's useful so we can understand our choices. So it might help you to tell me."

"I understand my choice," I said.

"If you did, don't you think you'd be comfortable talking about it?"

I needed to move the conversation on to Vincent before I accidentally spilled what was left of my red wine on this guy's white shirt. "I talked about it plenty at the time in therapy."

"Therapy can be wonderful. I'd never tell anyone not to go. But an Event with Seminar is worth years of therapy."

A blond-haired woman wearing a long colorful wrap dress and red sandals with three-inch heels slipped in between us and put her arm around Richard's waist. She smiled at me. "He's pitching you the one Event with Seminar is worth five years of therapy thing, isn't he?"

I smiled back. "I think he was about to."

She held out her hand to shake mine. "Olivia. Fellow potential recruitee."

"Is that what I am?" I said.

"That's what all the guests are, yeah?" Olivia said.

"Shh. You'll scare her off." Richard wagged a finger at his partner, but he did it in a playful way. His body language seemed more relaxed in Olivia's presence. "We don't recruit. But we are enthusiastic about the way Seminar exponentially enhanced our lives, so it's hard to keep quiet."

Olivia waved at the rounded chairs near the fireplace. "Let's sit. They're killing me, these new shoes I've got on."

"Excuse me for a minute," Richard said. "I need to talk with Karla."

Olivia set her martini glass on the round table between us and grabbed a plate from the appetizer tray as the waitperson passed by again. "Figured a rescue was in order, yeah? Before your eyes glaze over from the Seminar Speak."

Like Caleb, Olivia spoke in capital letters, but at least it was in jest. Probably.

"Is that an official term?" My chair was wood, with a high back and no cushions. It was surprisingly comfortable, though. It felt like it conformed to my body.

"Nah, my term," Olivia said. "Lots of jargon here, right? The first time I went to a Celebration I hardly followed what everyone was saying."

"Is Celebration a buzzword too?"

"Anything big that happens, yeah, they have a Celebration. Someone finishes their first Event, there's a Celebration." She raised her martini glass as if in a toast. "Someone gets promoted at work thanks to Seminar: Celebration."

"Someone dies?"

"That too."

"Did you know Vincent?" I said.

"Met him once. You?"

"No."

"Really?" She set her glass down without drinking. "I thought you must have done."

"Why's that?"

She flattened her spine against the chair back and folded her arms over her chest. "Most people spend months meeting people, hoping to get invited to a Celebration at the Lenzis. Yet here you are."

"Is that a big deal?" I said.

"It's a sign you'll be invited to your first Event."

"And how much does that cost?" I said.

"Not sure. Haven't been invited yet, have I? But Richard tells me around eight hundred dollars or so."

"Not cheap," I said.

It was also, in my view, an annoyingly manipulative sales technique. Seminar had people competing to be "invited" to pay eight hundred dollars.

Olivia brushed a wisp of hair out of her eyes. "Not to make too much of Richard's therapy analogy, but if you divide that out by the hour it's a great deal. Five nights, average of about three hours per night. About sixty bucks an hour, right? A lot less than therapy."

I'd paid eighty-five dollars every two weeks for a forty-five minute session, with my student health insurance paying a fraction for a limited number of sessions. On the other hand, that had been one-on-one with a trained professional, not in a group led by I wasn't sure who.

"It's a good point," I said.

"And a good investment."

"An investment should earn you money," I said. "I used to be an accountant."

"But it does. For a lot of people, yeah? Seminar doubles their income. Or triples it. The Events more than pay for themselves."

"That can't be true for everyone."

"No, and I'm not counting on it." She leaned toward me, her woodsy perfume overriding the vanilla scent from the candles. "But I have another motive, yeah?"

"What?" I said.

"Feel closer to Richard."

"Do you not feel close?" I said.

"Sure I do. But Seminar is so much of his life, right? He's all the time at Celebrations. Coordinating Events. In meetings."

"And you're not invited?"

"To some Celebrations, sure. But there's a balance. You need to get to know people in Seminar before you're invited, but once the offer's extended if you don't take it you aren't a welcome guest, right? Which makes sense. Otherwise people might keep coming to Celebrations just for the spread." She waved at the dining table with its rows of appetizers and the drinks beyond it. "Though most Celebrations aren't this elaborate, yeah? My first was in a Starbucks."

"Was it at least a fancy Starbucks?"

She laughed. "Very. That multi-level one near Chelsea Market in New York. Richard and I are from there."

"You said you only met Vincent once. But I take it Richard knew him pretty well?"

"Oh, yes. Talked about Vincent all the time, didn't he? That's who introduced him to Seminar."

"Caleb said that too. He mentioned he and Richard were both in the office the night Vincent died. That has to be so disturbing for them."

Olivia dipped a large, pink shrimp in cocktail sauce. "It would be for me. But Richard's been so calm. It's a pretty good example of how well Seminar works, yeah? If it can help him through something so traumatic."

"Do you know if the police have any idea what happened?"

"No idea." She spread her hands wide. "Thought Caleb might know. He was closeted with the police for almost twenty minutes according to Richard."

Maybe people were wondering about Caleb. That Richard had been timing it, and told Olivia about it, suggested he might feel suspicious of Caleb. Or maybe he had a personal reason to be happy they spent more time questioning Caleb than him.

"They didn't spend that long with Richard?" I said.

"Five minutes, he said. He never saw Vincent that night. They were working on opposite sides of the suite."

I sipped a little more wine. "Caleb seems very happy working for Seminar."

"He does seem to be skyrocketing to the top, doesn't he?" Olivia said. "Richard can't quite figure it out."

"Is it unusual?"

Olivia gave a tiny shrug, making her dangling gold earrings catch the candlelight. "Caleb's come so far in three years. Richard admires him. And maybe he's a little jealous, yeah? I told him maybe Caleb has something on Scott Gary. Knows his secrets."

I didn't doubt the founder of Seminar had some. One thing you learn early as a lawyer is that everyone has something they'd rather not talk about. It might mean nothing to anyone else, but they'd like it to stay private.

But Caleb had made it sound like Vincent was the one who paved the way for him.

"Something on Scott Gary? Not Vincent?" I said.

"Neither. It's a joke. Kidding. But it took five years before Richard got to Coordinate an Event, right? Caleb's doing it for the first time next week."

I didn't know what Coordinate meant in the world of Seminar, but Olivia obviously thought it was important. "Is that because Vincent died?"

"I'm pretty sure Caleb was on the schedule before that, wasn't he?"

I wanted to draw Olivia out more on the subject. But the

light outside was shifting to golden and rose, signaling sunset sometime soon, and I'd only talked to one of the three people on Caleb's list. A few moments ago I'd seen Karla break away from the dining area and head toward the back of the condo.

"Would you excuse me for a few minutes?" I said to Olivia.

She said of course. I headed for the hallway, hoping to catch Karla alone.

6

——————

FRIDAY, MAY 16, 7:46 P.M.

Just beyond the entrance hall an arched doorway led to what looked like a Chef's kitchen with a restaurant grade stainless steel stove and two sinks. Another marble counter divided it from a family room area with oversized couches and chairs around a large flat-screen television. Copper pots and pans hung above the counter, so gleaming and carefully arranged by size that I wondered if they actually got used.

Karla stood in the kitchen area fitting wine glasses onto prongs on the top shelf of the dishwasher. Her rigid posture contrasted her hair, strands of which hung around her neck in uneven sections.

"Can I help?" I said.

She nodded.

I poured white wine out of a half-full glass and set it on the rack, following Karla's placement. "I'm so sorry for your loss."

Karla shook her head as if to dismiss my words, but her chin trembled. "Vincent enhanced my life exponentially. He enhanced Seminar. It's all a reason for joy."

I didn't know what to say. Her response sounded more like she was parroting what she'd been told to say, not what she felt. But from losing Marco, and from growing up in a family shadowed by death, I knew there were as many ways to grieve as there were people. Maybe Seminar Speak was her way.

I emptied another glass. "It must be hard hosting a party, though, so soon with Vincent gone."

Her mouth jerked into a facsimile of a smile. She paused with a transparent green goblet halfway to the dishwasher. "I'm fine. It's Past."

Her eyes darted sideways toward me, but I got the impression she was checking the doorway and hallway beyond me.

"But still a loss." I reached across the dishwashing rack and touched her upper arm. "I found the man I loved dead last year in his apartment. We were about to move in together. It took a long time to deal with it. I'm only now starting to feel like myself. It doesn't mean it's that way for you, I know. But if it is, it's okay. It's normal."

Her shoulders dropped and her feet flattened. She lowered her arm and rested the goblet on the counter. Tears trickled out of the far corner of her eye. She made no move to wipe them away, and she looked again at the hallway. No one was passing through now, but if anyone did, she'd be seen.

"Why don't we sit?" I guided her toward a leather counter stool on the family room side. I sat next to her, shifting toward her so my back was to the hallway. I felt fairly sure I blocked her from the view of anyone outside of this room, but if she leaned to one side she could check the hall whenever she wanted to.

"It was awful finding him," she said. She spoke in a low voice. I shifted my stool closer to hear better. "I couldn't take it in. I felt sure he was still alive."

"I thought Marco was a mannequin at first. It had — he'd

died almost twenty-four hours before, so there was no way I could have seen him and thought he was still alive. So my brain, what I saw, for the first second, I thought it couldn't be him. I refused to believe it."

She rested her head in her hand. "It's been so hard."

"How could it not be?" I said.

"But it shouldn't be. Vince would tell me it doesn't matter what the Event is, big or small, Past is Past. Somehow this time I can't feel it, though. It's like I'm slipping down a Step. Or ten."

It took months before I really believed in my heart that Marco was gone. Sometimes I still grabbed my phone to text him when something happened. Or wanted to get off the L at his stop and felt like I should find him in his apartment. It was hard. But I didn't have the added burden of feeling deep down there was something wrong with me because I still felt that way.

I filled a glass with water from the dispenser in the fridge and gave it to her. She swallowed it down in two gulps, and I refilled it and sat next to her again.

She took a sip and pushed it away. Her shoulders rounded, and her string of pearls sagged toward the countertop. "I should be better. I made so much progress. I can't admit to everyone that I'm stuck in Past."

"How long were you married?" I said.

Voices and laughter filtered in from the living room. I found it interesting that both Karla and Caleb expressed more concern about how others in Seminar saw them than grief over Vincent's death. It could be unique to Seminar, or it could be avoidance, a strategy I was familiar with. Sometimes I thought I'd been determined to find answers about Marco's death because it put off feeling it.

"Eighteen years," Karla said.

"How did you meet?"

"I was in college. He was an adjunct professor. Taught a one-credit client development course. Romantic, huh?" Karla sat straighter and smiled, and it looked genuine, not forced. "Vince tossed out a group invitation to a Celebration after the class was over. I was the only one who went."

"Because Seminar interested you? Or Vincent?"

She touched the ends of her reddish hair. Her cheeks flushed, giving her some much-needed color. "Oh, definitely Vincent. I had a crush on him. It's the only reason I went. And signed up for my own Event for the same reason."

"Did that mean you got to spend time with him at it?" I asked, thinking of Olivia and Richard.

"Oh, no, not at the Event. I was disappointed, but now I understand that. You never spend much time at the Event with the person who invited you. But he took me out when it was over to hear more about it. We've been together ever since." Her body crumpled again. "Were."

I couldn't grill her about the death or Seminar. She probably wouldn't register that I was doing it, but it was wrong. Caleb's worries didn't trump a grieving woman's feelings.

Instead, I tried to think what I could do for her. After Marco's death, a lot of people asked if they could help me, but I hadn't known what to ask for. I'd appreciated when people offered something specific. But I didn't know Karla well enough to guess what she needed.

"Can I help you clean up tonight? Or take you out for a cup of coffee sometime this week or next? Just for a change of scene."

Her hands shook as she drank a little more water. "I — coffee might be nice." She squeezed my hand. "I shouldn't feel this way, but it was nice to talk about Vincent. I don't know about coffee, though. I probably won't have time. So much to do."

"In case you do." I fished a business card out from my

purse. "I won't be offended if you're too busy and never get in touch."

Just as I held out the card, I heard someone clear his throat behind me.

Karla's face paled. I realized she had a few freckles across the bridge of her nose, as they now stood out against her white skin.

"You ladies all right?" Richard said. "You look so serious."

"Fine." Karla snatched my card and stood. The ghastly smile returned. "Lovely, in fact. Quille was just offering me some legal advice. In case I need it for the estate."

Richard put a hand on the small of my back and propelled me toward the door. "I need to talk with Karla. And Caleb is looking for you."

"Sure," I said.

I glanced at Karla as I left, but she kept her eyes fixed on Richard's face. She held her body so still it reminded me of the way rabbits freeze when you step too close.

My law practice didn't involve estates, but Richard had asked a lot about my accounting background. I hoped that was enough to support Karla's story about why she'd taken my card.

And I wondered why she thought she needed one.

$$7$$

Friday, May 16, 8:03 p.m.

I ducked into the bathroom toward the back of the residence. With a large marble sunken tub, separate shower, make up counter, and double sinks, it was nearly as large as the studio apartment I'd lived in during law school.

Before exiting I fished three Advil from my purse, cupped my hand under the faucet for water, and downed them in one swallow. A dull ache had started in the back of my head as I'd been talking to Karla, and the tightness at my temples told me I was a few short steps from a migraine.

In the living room again, I took off my blazer. The room had become hot with so many people inside.

Caleb was engrossed in a conversation near the dining table. I interrupted and dragged him behind the marble counter serving as a bar. "What's the deal with making me sound like some sort of flake who can't stick with anything?"

He glanced around, but no one stood near us. "I needed to come up with something. For everyone invited, we have to say specifically at least one thing we think Seminar might be able to help you with. We've been out of touch so long all I knew to talk about was your career."

"So if you wanted to invite a friend who's doing great, you couldn't?" I said.

"No, no, that's not it. But no one's life is perfect. People just want to have an idea where you might want to improve so they can try to help with it. I'm sorry. Wasn't one of my better ideas. Have you learned anything?"

"Some. But I still need to talk to the other man who was there. Frank Hernandez?"

He gestured toward a bearded, beefy man standing near the glass doors to the balcony. Before he could bring me over there, another guest said he needed Caleb's advice on dinner plans.

I walked over and introduced myself to Frank. Rather than shaking my whole hand, his thick fingers closed over mine for an instant and let go. It struck me as an oddly weak handshake for such a large man.

"I was about to step out on the balcony for some air," he said.

The cool lake breeze made the skin on my arms prickle, but it felt good. I lifted my heavy dark hair off my neck for a moment and took in the view. Rose gold hues tinged the clouds and the lake. The sound of a bass drum thrummed from some open window near us, but the horns, sirens, and squealing brakes from the streets below sounded far away.

"Caleb says wonderful things about you, Quille."

"That's nice to hear."

I noticed he'd picked up on how I'd introduced myself rather than calling me Q.C.

"As soon as Vince started talking about expanding Seminar into Chicago, Caleb said he'd love to come back here. That he had a friend he wanted to get back in touch with."

"So Seminar is new to Chicago?" I slipped my blazer on again. I'd appreciate the cold lake breeze when July and August rolled around. Right now, though, it made nights too chilly for bare arms.

"We opened our office a few months ago. But Vince and Karla have made their second home here forever, so in that sense we've had a presence."

With the expansive living and dining area, separate family room, high end kitchen, and what looked like doors to multiple bedrooms, the Lenzis' condo must cost upwards of two million. I wondered if Vincent had been one of the people who'd multiplied his income through Seminar. Pretty good advertisement for it if he had, though I'd had plenty of clients who "owned" multiple properties that were underwater or mortgaged to the hilt.

Either way, the impression of wealth probably was the point of hosting parties here for potential recruits.

"Where's their main home?" I said.

"New York. Where Seminar started."

New York. One of the few cities, along with San Francisco and Los Angeles, that made Chicago real estate look reasonable. Someone could be inheriting a lot. According to Caleb, Vincent had two daughters from a previous marriage. Caleb had never met them, though, and didn't know their names.

The balcony was surprisingly small. Frank bumped my elbow as he pulled a skinny cigar and a pack of matches from his pocket. "Sorry." He nodded at the cigar. "Do you mind?"

I inched sideways. "Not at all."

I'd been thrilled when Chicago expanded its indoor clean air ordinance in 2008 to ban smoking in bars as well as restaurants. Going out to listen to music, or to sing in the a cappella trio I belong to, no longer meant a sore throat and reeking of smoke when I got home. These days I didn't mind breathing near a burning cigar, pipe, or cigarette occasionally.

I felt almost sorry for smokers in winter who stood shivering in ten below windchill, sucking on cigarettes the required fifteen feet from public building entrances.

Frank lit his cigar. A sweet, smoky tobacco scent filled the air. "When did Caleb get in touch with you?"

"The other day."

I wondered if Caleb had told people something different. The conversation with Richard had made it seem like it. I hadn't agreed to lie for Caleb, and the "flitted" still irked me. But if this guy was important in Seminar, I didn't want to tank Caleb's chances to advance by saying the wrong thing.

"But I guess he stayed in touch on Facebook or some social media?"

"I'm not online much," I said.

He cocked his head. The waning sunlight gave a reddish tint to his beard. "But you have your own law firm, don't you? Wouldn't you need an online presence?"

"Seminar doesn't have one."

"We're word-of-mouth. Ensures people are vetted."

I buttoned my blazer as the wind grew stronger. "I have a website. But I get most of my business from referrals. Former clients, accountants. Lawyers and actors I used to work with."

The website was basic. If a person or company was thinking about hiring me, it'd show my experience and give them a sense of stability, but it wasn't designed for strangers to find me.

If Frank had done some research of his own about me, he wouldn't have learned very much.

"So why would you come to this with Caleb when you haven't seen him in so long?" Frank said.

He studied me, as if he were trying to figure something out about Caleb based on my response.

8

<hr>

"Caleb was sort of my lifeline when I was a teenager," I said. "I was home schooled so I could focus on acting. I was comfortable in the theater world, but not so much with kids my own age."

Frank nodded. "I could see Caleb being the perfect guy to know for that."

In high school Caleb, outgoing and a bit of a chameleon, was an ideal bridge between me and kids I never would have met otherwise. While he didn't go out for any teams, he played well enough in gym class and intramural games that people wanted him on their side. He knew everyone in band because he played saxophone from junior high through freshman year. And the brainy kids and the teachers liked him around because he always asked their opinions and listened when they gave them.

"He was," I said. "When did you meet him?"

"Three years ago. In Austin."

"Did Vincent Lenzi introduce you?" I said.

"In a way." Frank shifted his cigar to his left hand. "I

helped out at the first Event Caleb took part in. Vincent Coordinated it."

"Which means?"

"For an Event? That's who gives an overview at the first session and later guides everyone through interactions. You'll see. I'm sure you'll be invited to take part in one."

I decided not to mention that I planned to decline.

"You said for an Event. Is there some other time someone Coordinates?"

"Every Celebration has a Coordinator."

"Wouldn't that be the host?"

Frank puffed on his cigar. The red tip glowed. "In a pinch. But usually the roles are separate. Like tonight. Karla's the host, so she ordered the food and drinks, oversees the caterers while Caleb Coordinates."

"Caleb?"

"Vince would have done it. But now it falls to Caleb."

His tone sounded neutral, but that he mentioned Caleb taking Vincent's place made me wonder if he'd been dwelling on that point.

"Because?"

"What do you mean?" he said.

"Why does it fall to Caleb and not you?"

"Vincent left instructions as to who would take over different parts of his duties if anything happened to him. Caleb succeeds him in quite a few areas."

I wondered if the police knew that. And I made a mental note that Frank, unlike Olivia, attributed Caleb's leading the next Event to Vincent's death.

"Did Vincent think something would happen to him?" I said.

"No, it's just part of our succession plan."

I wasn't sure if I could draw much from that. My liability insurer requires me to have a document naming another lawyer to take over my firm's cases if I become incapacitated or die. It's to make sure no legal matters get left undone, harming the clients. Insurers for other types of businesses must have similar requirements. Though, as I understood it, Vincent wasn't the head of Seminar, Scott Gary was.

"What does the Coordinator do at a Celebration?" I said.

"Makes sure everyone has a good time, meets enough people. A lot of guests are like you, they only know the person who brought them. That can be awkward at any gathering. With a Coordinator, everyone mingles with everyone else. No one sits in one little group."

It was a good idea, assuming that was the real reason for it. I'd had parties where my theater and musician friends started out in one corner, my finance friends in another, and my lawyer friends on the deck. I always made an effort to bring people together, and everyone had a better time.

But the formal planning, and that Caleb hadn't told me about his role for tonight, made me sure it had more to do with recruiting the guests. No matter what Richard said.

"Seems like Caleb's doing great at Seminar."

Frank tilted his head. "Not sure what you mean."

"He's been working for the organization for a while, and he seems to love it. And everyone seems happy with his work."

"Did he tell you it was work?"

"He said it's a paid position." I turned toward him. "Does 'work' have some kind of specific Seminar meaning?"

Frank shook his head and puffed on the cigar. "No. But most people don't call it work. It's more of a vocation."

Great. I'd violated some unspoken Seminar Speak rule.

"Caleb didn't use the word work. But you feel like he's doing well?"

Frank's eyebrows rose. "You worried about him?"

He was avoiding the question, which might be answer enough, or he suspected I had some ulterior motive.

As with clients and witnesses, I decided telling the truth, as much of it as I could, was the best route. I've found most people match truth with truth.

"A little. He seems to enjoy Seminar more than anything else he's done." I carefully avoided calling it a job or profession, assuming those words sounded too much like work. "I hope that Vincent's death won't change that. It seemed like they were close."

"Vincent enhanced a lot of people's lives."

"How well did you know him?"

"Very."

"I'm sorry for your loss."

He waved the hand with the cigar. The red tip swirled. "You can't live life looking in the rearview mirror. It's Past."

"So you feel fine about his death? Just like that?"

I was beginning to think these people weren't human.

"Not fine, no. Vince was a big part of my life. But we can't control death. Feeling devastated by it does nothing for the person who's gone. Isn't it better to focus only on how that person enhanced our lives?"

"I don't know if it's better to do that right away," I said. "I spent a lot of time in therapy trying to stop controlling my emotions."

And despite that therapy, I still struggled after Marco's death to let myself feel the pain rather than push it aside and think about anything and everything else.

"It's not about controlling," Frank said. "It's about choice. I choose to focus on what I feel good about. That's what I can do something about."

"Did you and Vincent get involved in Seminar at the same time?"

"He got involved with my nutritional supplement

company first. Became a partner. He promised Seminar could help me with the business, and it did."

"Are you still running it?"

"Yep. On my own now that Vincent's gone."

I asked the company's name so I could check on it later. Public records might give me a hint at whether Vincent's share of the business reverted to Frank on death.

I pulled the sleeves of my blazer down over my wrists. As twilight descended, the evening was becoming chillier. I didn't want to stay out much longer, so I decided to just ask my next question.

"Did you talk to the police about Vincent's death?"

He stubbed out the cigar on the brick railing. "Why do you ask?"

It could have been a hostile question, but his tone sounded more like he was curious.

"Someone I loved died last year. I found him. I had to talk to the police. All of it was overwhelming. I couldn't imagine being at a party a couple days later trying to recruit people for my business."

I looked out at the gardens below as I spoke. The trees loomed like jagged shadows. I didn't like using Marco's death as a wedge. It had been different with Karla. I'd felt sharing my experience might help her feel less alone. This was pure manipulation.

But I didn't want to say it had shaken Caleb, as already I sensed that was a non-Seminar thing to say. And I couldn't see how else to explain my interest.

"But listen to yourself." Frank poked the stubbed-out cigar toward me. "You can't imagine it. Exactly. But if you could imagine it, you could do it, and you could feel better. Right away, not after a year of grieving."

I rubbed my hands over my arms. I hadn't said Marco's death happened a year ago.

"And that's what Seminar helps with?"

"That's one thing." Frank tilted his head toward me while holding the rest of his body still. His eyes bored into me. "Hasn't Caleb shared his Seminar experience with you?"

"He told me about it," I said. "I'm not big into the self-help industry."

"Did he tell you it was self-help?"

My fingers tightened on the railing. Usually I was better at reading people and grasping the rules of a new world. It was part of acting and lawyering. If you don't understand how a witness is using words, you can miss key facts. But maybe it wasn't me. Maybe Frank would take issue with anything I said because he wanted to see Caleb in a negative light.

Or he wanted to distract me from the fact that he hadn't answered my question about the police.

I tucked my hair, which was flying about in the wind, behind my ears. "Again, my word. What would you call it?"

"It's like having your own one-on-one business development coach."

First therapy, now business coaching. Seminar was one-size-fits all.

"I'm sure I misunderstood Caleb."

He nodded. "You should ask him more about it. It's made a huge difference in his life from what I've seen."

"So how does it work? You were there when Vincent died, maybe talked to the police the next day, and you just, what, imagined yourself feeling better?"

Frank gazed out over Grant Park and the lake beyond it. "It's not quite that simple, but in a different way, it is. Seminar can show you."

I decided to use a little manipulation of my own.

"What happened that night? If it's not too painful to talk about."

"It's not. I was working in my office. It's three away from

Vincent's. Said goodnight to him on my way out. He was bent over a stack of reports. Gave me a quick wave, went back to his work, and I left. Poor Karla found him in the morning. About half an hour after I got in I heard her scream. Ran up there. I told the police all of that."

"The police didn't grill you? Because they grilled me when Marco died."

"They asked more questions, but I had nothing else to tell them. What's Past is Past."

I could imagine how that had gone over. The detective who'd handled Marco's death investigation hadn't been, in my view, the strongest card in the deck but he would never have let that answer put an end to his questions. Still, I could see why Caleb thought anyone outside Seminar wasn't likely to get a lot of answers.

"And where does the imagining part come in?"

"After I talked to the police, I imagined the coming week and how I wanted to feel. What I wanted to get done. And I sat down to finish work for the week's Event. Because that was Now. If I started thinking about how Vincent might have died, conjuring mental pictures, I purposely changed them."

"How could you do that?" I'd relived the moment of finding Marco's body so many times in the months after his death. I still dreamed of it and woke sweating and shivering.

"I see it as a cartoon. Or speed it up so it was comically fast. Once I pictured him jumping up off the floor, laughing, and telling me it was a Halloween prank."

Maybe that worked better if you hadn't really seen a horrific thing.

"Do the police think there's something suspicious about the death?" I said.

I wanted to know if Caleb was the only one to whom the police gave that impression.

"Who knows? You can't spend energy on what other people think of you. It's a waste."

"I've got to think about it a little," I said. "No one hires a lawyer they don't trust."

"Well, sure, professionally. But I mean where it can't affect you."

"What do you think happened? Did Vincent have enemies?"

"No enemies. I told the police that. He was Whole."

"Whole?"

That must be another buzzword. I'd have to ask Caleb for a dictionary.

"Everyone has fractures in their psyche. You go through life, parts of you fracture off. Sometimes to protect yourself. Sometimes because you let someone else chip away at you. Seminar helps you retrieve your fractured parts. Become Whole again. You should take part in an Event. All these questions you have, this obsession with death. You're fractured, I can tell."

9

"Isn't Frank exceptional?"

The instant I'd stepped back into the condo a middle-aged woman with jet black hair had approached me. She had a tattoo of the Yin and Yang symbol below her right collarbone and wore earrings made of a series of turquoise, pearl, and shell-pink beads that danced in the light.

Frank smiled, thanked the woman, and headed for the dining area.

"He is," I said. "How long have you known him?"

"I met him at a Celebration a friend brought me to last year and he was amazing. It was as if he read my mind, and I knew I had to sign up for an Event. I'm SaraBeth, by the way."

"Quille. Read your mind how?" I unbuttoned my blazer. The warmth of the room felt intense after the cold wind on the balcony.

"He talked to me for fifteen minutes, asked three questions, and knew right away I'm a visual artist. Even though I never said that."

I replayed my interaction with Frank on the balcony. He

hadn't shown any particular insight about me. But he had commented on my lack of social media presence.

"Were you at least posting your artwork online?" I asked.

SaraBeth tugged at her earring. "Just on Instagram. And Pinterest. But I never listed artist in my profiles before Seminar. I never felt confident enough to identify that way."

"Did you know Vincent?"

"He invited me to my first Event. Karla and I are on the board of the Museum of Mexican Art together."

"His death must be devasting for her. And his daughters."

"I'd think. But I've never met them. The older one lives in Manhattan."

"What about the younger one?"

"Gina." SaraBeth leaned close and whispered. "She dropped out of Seminar. She's Hostile."

The way she spoke made me feel I was hearing still more buzzwords. It seemed no one here could speak without jargon. Or maybe I was looking too hard for it and seeing it in everyday words.

"To Vincent?"

"To Seminar." Her eyes darted around the room. "It must have been awful for him. A family member who's Hostile."

"But Vincent still talked to her?"

She drew back. "Of course. We're not some kind of cult."

"Of course," I said. "I didn't mean it that way."

She angled her head toward me and lowered her voice again. "Though if Gina were just uninterested that'd be fine. But she constantly badgered Vincent about it."

"Badgered him how?"

"Sending him links to negative articles about self-help organizations. Finding what she said were academic studies that contradicted what she'd learned at her Events. Trying to talk other people into quitting and demanding their money back."

I asked SaraBeth if she knew Caleb, but she'd only met him tonight and hadn't heard anything about him before.

"I hope he does as well as Vincent at Coordinating Events. That first one is when I realized I should leave my day job. Though I didn't do it until Vincent steered me toward the intermediate Artist's Path Event. Now I'm finally starting a real journey to where I want to be. Who I want to be." She bounced a little on the balls of her feet and laughed. "At fifty-nine. Isn't that something?"

"It's wonderful." Her enthusiasm reminded me of how a lot of my actor friends felt about theater. I'd enjoyed it, but by the time I reached college I hadn't felt that way anymore, which was part of why I'd gone another direction. It's a tough business, and if you don't love it with all your heart, I feel like you'll be happier earning your living another way. "Frank mentioned Seminar being almost like business coaching. Do you think so?"

"Oh, yes. I'm scheduled for the Intermediate Build Your Business Event in May. It's in Austin, but I'm sure it's worth the trip."

"Is it expensive? The Event itself?"

"About two thousand dollars. All on my credit card, but it's a good investment."

Like the comparison to therapy, it sounded like investment was a talking point. I hoped, having quit her day job, this woman could afford it. And wondered if anyone blamed Vincent enough to want to hurt him if they spent too long paying off Events.

"I hope you get a good return," I said.

Her forehead creased. "What do you mean?"

"On your investment. I have an accounting background. It's a term for how much you make compared with how much you invest."

SaraBeth folded her arms over her chest. "Not all return has to be in money."

"That's true." It hit me that I might be thinking about Seminar too narrowly. At fifty-nine, spending to increase her overall happiness regardless of financial return might make perfect sense for SaraBeth. Though the accountant in me hoped she'd secured her retirement first.

Caleb appeared at my elbow. "Making friends I see."

———

FRIDAY, MAY 16, 8:48 P.M.

Gibsons is one of a group of bars and restaurants where Oak, State, and Rush Streets come together in Chicago's Gold Coast north of downtown. The area is known as the Viagra Triangle, a name that comes from the abundance of fiftyish and up men visiting Chicago for conventions or business trips. They flock to the clubs and restaurants eager to impress younger women with their platinum cards or expense accounts or both.

It's also a big tourist destination.

Tonight people stood two-deep around the bar, and diners filled every high-top table near it. What I could see of the restaurant seating area was jammed, too. Waiters wearing black pants and green vests squeezed around leather booths and crowded tables with practiced skill.

Our group stood near the open archway between the entry hall and bar area. Caleb and I had planned to get dinner alone after the party, but three Seminar people, including SaraBeth, came out of the building while we were debating restaurant choices. One person had driven in from Milwaukee and was excited about Gibsons, having heard it was the best steakhouse in Chicago.

It was one of the best, but it definitely wasn't the place to go on a Friday night without a reservation. Our only hope was eating at the bar if anyone ever left. I wished I'd talked less and eaten more at the party.

The sounds of voices and music made it hard to hear one another and started a dull throb in my head despite the Advil I'd taken. A man wedged himself between Caleb and me and told me about his online men's clothing business. He'd expanded it and customized it based on what he learned in Seminar's Build Your Business Event. He mentioned concrete strategies he'd applied. He also said that he'd been in a small group Caleb led at an Austin Event and everyone had been inspired by him.

A waiter edged past us balancing a tray of martinis. A few minutes later a noisy group of six left the table behind us. The people hovering around them swooped in, so it didn't give us a place to sit, but we moved closer to the bar.

I shuffled around SaraBeth, who wasn't too keen to talk to me again after I'd questioned her spending.

"Why didn't you tell me you were Coordinating tonight's party?" I said into Caleb's ear.

"Who told you that?"

"Frank. Why? Is it a secret?"

"No, no, not at all. We just don't usually tell people about different roles until they've attended a couple Events."

"How many Events are there?" I said.

"The roster's always evolving."

He said he hadn't heard of the succession plan. But if Frank had mentioned it to the police, it could explain why they'd suggested they might need to talk to Caleb again. He also didn't know anything about Vincent's daughters beyond that there were at least two.

At last, five people left the bar and in one motion all of us slid onto their vacant stools before the glasses were cleared.

"What happened to us catching up?" I asked Caleb after

we'd gotten settled. I sat at the end of the bar, away from the other Seminar people. Still I needed to repeat myself twice before he heard me.

"Really sorry about that," he said. "It felt rude to exclude the others. But I take full responsibility. And dinner's still on me."

It had been a while since I'd eaten red meat, and Gibsons served a perfect wet-aged bone-in filet. Alone it cost more than I usually spent on a dinner for two, one of several reasons I rarely came here. The others were the noise and the crowds.

The bartender brought me a whiskey sour and Caleb a Perrier.

"I've got to tell you something," Caleb said. "I didn't hire your friend Danielle. My dad insisted I go to a lawyer he knows. But please tell her again thank you for talking to me."

I hadn't seen Danielle today, as she'd had a bench trial in a DUI case. She must have called Caleb on a break.

"You're telling me you woke me at midnight to get a referral, but you're going to a different lawyer?"

"I'd rather go with your friend. I'm sure she's Exceptional. But Dad's paying the legal fees, so he's got final say."

Whoever pays the lawyer's bill usually influences which lawyer gets chosen, so it didn't completely surprise me. But it was rare for Caleb to go along with what his dad wanted. Maybe this was the "exponentially" better relationship at work.

Still, I felt more than a little annoyed with Caleb. When the bartender asked about food, I ordered the bone-in filet.

"You could pay yourself," I said after the bartender disappeared.

"I am paying."

"For the lawyer."

"Yeah, but why when he's willing to?"

It was one thing that hadn't changed. When Caleb had complained about his dad's interference in his life in the past, I'd always suggested he take less money from his dad. A suggestion that never went over well.

"If your relationship is so much better, why didn't you ask him for a referral in the first place?"

His dad initially made money by creating one of the earliest car-sharing services. When a larger company bought him out, he switched his focus to other industries and started investing in real estate. I felt sure with all his different companies he knew plenty of lawyers.

"I had to think about it before I decided to tell him I might need a criminal defense attorney. Our relationship's better, but his temper hasn't changed."

The steak when it came was cooked a perfect medium-rare, though eating at the bar meant constantly bumping elbows and having people behind us jockeying for position. Somewhere in the course of the meal the third Seminar tagalong switched places with Caleb. She proceeded to tell me in detail about her classroom teaching and that she hoped Seminar would help her improve her career path.

I listened, but if the noise drowned her out I didn't worry too much about catching every word. She barely knew Caleb and told me she'd never met Vincent. And I'd heard enough about Seminar's wonders for one evening.

My head was pounding by the time the group started ordering dessert and another round of drinks. I downed another two Advil and slid off my bar stool.

"I'm going to grab a cab home," I told Caleb.

He grasped my wrist. "Please stay. We've barely talked."

"I don't think we're going to tonight." I gestured at the people jammed into the entryway near the host stand. "It's not getting less crowded or quieter."

"Let me settle up and we'll take a walk."

I swigged more water and stepped outside. The car horns and the rush of traffic was nothing compared to the din inside. The relative quiet and cool air eased the throbbing in my head. My shoulders dropped. I straightened my neck to ease muscle tension and slowed my breathing, imagining the pain being drawn up and out the top of my head.

By the time Caleb appeared I felt a little better. And I had plans the rest of the weekend, so I might as well share what I'd learned with him tonight and be done with Seminar.

10

—————

Friday, May 16, 10:32 p.m.

The wind died down, so we decided to walk to Caleb's dad's row house. It was in the Gold Coast about half a mile away. His dad had owned the house since the divorce and lived there on and off depending on his business needs and marital status. When Caleb started college, his dad refused to pay for a dorm, but he allowed Caleb to live in the row house rent free. Caleb was staying there again now.

The neighborhood quieted only a few blocks from Gibsons. The air, still slightly humid, smelled cleaner and less like auto exhaust thanks to recent rain. We crossed Chestnut near State Street where the modern-looking Sofitel Hotel rises gracefully toward the sky. I told him that Richard had noticed how long the police spent with Caleb and his quick rise in Seminar.

"His partner, Olivia, implied you might have something on Scott Gary. Like you were blackmailing him. She claimed she was joking, but she said it."

"That's crazy."

I told him what Olivia had said almost word-for-word.

While I don't have a perfect memory, I'm pretty good with remembering people's words. It had always helped me as an actor.

It also helped me find a missing woman and stop a murderer the previous December.

"Maybe," I said. "But if she's not the only one who thinks you're 'skyrocketing' for no obvious reason, I'm betting someone mentioned it to the police."

We passed a car dealer that sold cars whose prices topped that of most people's homes. I'm not much of a car person, but we paused to peer in at the silver Bentleys and sleek Lamborghinis. I wondered what could possibly make them worth the price beyond the status of simply owning one.

"I don't know why anyone would question me succeeding," Caleb said as we walked on. "In Seminar, everyone values success. Feeling great. Doing great. It doesn't have to be fast, but faster is good. We don't believe in Limits. So if it usually takes five years to become a manager somewhere, you might start seeing yourself as a manager right now, even if you've been at the company a week."

"Positive thinking?" I said. We'd reached Dearborn Street, and we paused at a Don't Walk sign.

"It's so much more than that," Caleb said. "But you've probably heard enough tonight about how great Seminar is."

"Uh, yeah."

The Walk sign blinked on. Caleb stepped into the crosswalk without looking, never wise to do in Chicago. A midsized sedan that had swerved into the cross-lane to make a left darted around the turn, ignoring the red light.

I grabbed Caleb's arm and yanked him back to the curb. The sedan whizzed past, showing no sign the driver saw either of us.

Caleb shivered. "Thanks. Lived in Austin too long, I guess. Forgot what it's like here."

"It was only a little red, no reason he'd stop," I said.

The city's been retiming traffic lights and Walk signs to account for all the drivers who hit the gas when the light turns yellow, but it seems to have only worsened the practice. That and drivers who hug or jump the curbs on turns make alertness key. For all that, because so many people walk in the city I still find most Chicago drivers are more aware of pedestrians than in LaGrange, the near west suburb where Caleb and I grew up.

"Did you talk much with Karla?" Caleb said.

"No." I decided not to mention the business card I'd left with her. If Caleb and I stayed in touch after tonight I didn't want him hounding me about whether she'd called or what she'd said about him. "I did ask Frank how you were doing. He sidestepped the question. More than once. But I'm not sure if it was because he didn't want to answer or he thought it was weird I was asking."

"He might not have wanted to talk with an outsider. He's right up there with Vincent in the organization."

We passed the Newberry Library. The park across from it took up an entire block. Despite its unlovely name — Bughouse Square — it was filled with wrought iron benches, flowers, and leafy, overhanging trees. The smells of wet ground and tree bark reminded me of when Caleb and I walked each other home along the tree-lined streets of LaGrange. I had lived in an apartment building behind a row of retail businesses, so our path had been half trees and grass and rambling houses and half aging and sometimes quaint brick stores.

Often I'd walked him home and then, not ready to stop talking, he'd walk me home, and on and on until Gram finally yelled out the window for me to get inside.

"So Frank's opinion matters to your career?"

"The one who matters most is the Founder. Scott Gary. After that there was Vincent. But Frank, too."

An outdoor light blinked on as we mounted the concrete steps of Caleb's dad's house. It was on the corner, last in a row of similar tall, narrow brick homes all over a hundred years old. The outside looked better than I remembered. The bricks must have been tuckpointed recently.

The long entry hall inside smelled of lemon furniture polish and opened on one side to the living room. A staircase with an old-fashioned wood bannister flanked the other side.

When Caleb flipped the switch for the living room light, nothing happened. "Ugh. My dad. He's still got everything on these timers."

"He never changed them?"

Because Mr. Jackson had sometimes left the row house vacant, he'd always kept at least one light in each room on a timer that turned it on and off at set times so it looked like people were home. To work, the light had to be left on at the switch. If you accidentally turned it off, you'd have to reset the timer to get it back.

"He refused," Caleb said. "Wife Number 4 doesn't want to live in a smart home, so he won't upgrade to put it all on an app."

"But she doesn't live here."

"And yet."

Caleb flipped on the stairway light. The dark hardwood floors, similar to those in the Lenzis' condo, gleamed. From memory I knew that the end of the hall led to the kitchen and attached dining area. The back door beyond that led to a small porch and stairs down to ground level. The patch of grass and single tree between the house and garage would barely have been called a yard where we'd grown up, but in the Gold Coast where buildings nestle against one another any small plot of land is coveted.

The row house's second level had two guest bedrooms, one of which Caleb's dad used as an office, and the third a master bedroom and bath.

"Hey," I said. "Does it still have the —"

"Yep, wanna see?" Caleb grinned. "Wife Number 3 used it to record some kind of podcast about knitting, but she cleared out two years ago. Hold on, I'll grab some wine."

The first time I'd been at the row house I'd been eleven years old. Caleb took me to the master bedroom and showed me the walk-in closet, which was wide and long. I thought it was neat all by itself. It was triple the size of any closet I'd ever seen.

Caleb, though, hurried past me. He pushed aside Wife Number 2's evening gowns and fur coats to show me a solid door. Behind the door was a windowless bonus room about eight feet by eight feet. Orange crates of vinyl records lined two of the walls, but it was otherwise empty, making it a perfect hideout for two middle school kids.

The albums were still there, but eggshell foam had been added to two of the walls and industrial-looking carpet to the floor, probably to help soundproof it for the podcast recording Caleb had mentioned. Caleb brought in floor pillows, a bottle of Malbec, wine glasses, and two boxed waters. The only light was a standing brass floor lamp in the corner by the crates.

Caleb twisted off the top of the wine bottle. "Bottom line, do you think this police investigation makes people in Seminar suspicious of me?"

He poured two glasses of wine and pushed one across the carpet toward me. We sat against the wall opposite the orange crates, legs stretched in front of us. The foam cushioned my back.

"The only one who mentioned it was Olivia. And once it's over, people will forget," I said.

I opened the water. It always strikes me as strange when people in Chicago buy packaged or bottled water. Lake Michigan tap water tastes better than most of it, and there's rarely any proof on a water bottle that what's inside is any cleaner or safer. More good marketing, I supposed.

"But it can take a long time, can't it?"

"Yes." I sipped the water. It had a slight aftertaste that made me think of well water. "Is it the investigation that's throwing you? Or Vincent's death?"

"Both."

"But which one more?"

"The death is Past, and the investigation's Now. Vincent taught me to focus on Now. But I think more about the death."

"Vincent meant a lot to you."

He twirled his wine glass and watched the wine slosh inside. "I'd never have gotten this far without him. He guided me. Helped me figure out which Events to take. What to volunteer for. How to present myself to the Founder."

"All the kinds of things your dad never did."

He ran his hands through his hair. "Yeah. So what if without him I screw it all up?"

"Is that what this is about? You won't," I said.

"I hope not. But you have no way of knowing that. We haven't seen each other in so long. Which is entirely my fault."

I wanted to say more to reassure him, but I had gotten an uncomfortable vibe from both Olivia and Frank. They seemed to be looking for something wrong about Caleb, maybe because he'd been Vincent's favorite. And if Olivia felt that way, it seemed to me it must flow from things Richard said to her in private.

I shifted and adjusted the pillow so I could sit straighter. "Seminar's founder, does he know you well?"

"Pretty well. I get the impression he thinks highly of me because Vincent did."

"So he should be in your corner."

He tapped his fingers on his knee. "Unless he thinks I had something to do with Vincent's death."

"Why would he? You were there that night, but so were three other Seminar people, including Vincent's wife. Plus possibly someone else arguing with Vincent. Maybe you won't do as well in Seminar without your mentor. But why would anyone, including the police, be more suspicious of you than of anyone else who was there? What aren't you telling me?"

He sighed. "I've got a record."

11

Caleb moved around to sit cross-legged across from me. "It's part of why I didn't want to tell my dad I needed a lawyer. I went through a rough time in L.A. Too much partying. Got in a bar fight. The other guy pulled a knife."

"A fight. You?" I'd never seen Caleb so much as yell at anyone.

He looked down at his hands. "Yeah. I know. Can't remember it that well. But the guy was kind of big and lumbering, and witnesses said it looked like he didn't know how to use the knife. It was more like a pocket knife and he was as messed up as me. Probably more. Apparently I grabbed the knife from his hand and stabbed him in the stomach with it."

I crossed my arms over my midsection. "How bad was he hurt?"

"Stomach fat protected him a little, but I nicked his intestines. He almost died from shock. He needed two surgeries, but he survived."

That was attempted murder territory if a jury believed Caleb acted intentionally rather than in self-defense.

"Did you go to trial?"

"Plea bargain. Dad hired me a really good lawyer. He tracked down the witnesses who thought I didn't know what I was doing and said the other guy started it. I pled to lesser charges, got a year of intensive probation with drug and alcohol counseling and pee tests. Finished with no problems. But it's there on my record. A felony for a violent act."

Having a good lawyer never guarantees getting a better plea bargain or winning a trial. But a lawyer known for trying cases and who understands the law and penalties inside and out gives you a much better shot than one with little experience handling felonies or an overburdened public defender. It's one of the ways our court system favors people with money.

Caleb had been lucky.

"At least he survived," I said. "And you didn't go to prison. You don't remember doing it?"

Marco had been a recovering alcoholic. He'd told me blackouts signaled a serious drinking problem.

"It's hazy," Caleb said.

"But you're not drinking like that anymore," I said, thinking of the sparkling water he'd stuck with until we'd gotten here.

He waved at the wine bottle against the wall. "Obviously I still like a drink now and then. But once I got into Seminar that need to obliterate myself went away."

"So your background is why you're so worried about the police focusing on you."

"Yeah." He sipped the wine. "No one else there that night has a record."

"Do they know you do?"

"Nope. Which is another problem."

I drew my knees up toward my chest and rested my arms on them. "Isn't it Past, though, or whatever? Why would they care?"

"It's Past, but I was embarrassed about it, so I didn't tell anyone. Didn't deal with it in Seminar. You're supposed to take full responsibility for everything by the Intermediate Events. No internal conflict. No secrets."

"Everyone can't possibly share everything." I wound the ends of my hair around my fingers, wondering how much conflict it would cause if they did. Or whether anyone else took advantage of knowing people's secrets.

"Maybe not. But that I didn't say it would make them suspicious." He shifted so he lay on his side on the carpet, his head propped on his elbow. "You see what I mean about the police and Seminar people not talking to them? And how hard it would be for police to make sense of it if they did?"

I drank some of the Malbec, my first taste of it. I'd already drunk a glass at the party and a whiskey sour at Gibsons, double my usual limit. Alcohol makes me sad if I'm not careful, though sitting here with Caleb in our hideaway was fun. It was where I'd had my first drink ever — peppermint schnapps he swiped from his mom's house mixed with Pepsi. It tasted awful, but we'd been twelve and had felt as if we'd gotten away with something major.

"It's a lot of jargon to wade through," I said. "And no one seemed to want to talk about anything but Seminar."

"You think you could do better? Than the police?"

I set the wine glass down on the carpet. "What?"

"Everyone will talk to you even more than they did tonight if they think you're becoming devoted to Seminar."

"But I'm not."

"Yeah, but you still know how to act, right? Isn't that a big part of being a lawyer?"

"Not exactly. Being comfortable talking in front of people

helps. Remembering lines. But a lot of what I do is in writing."

His eyebrows rose. "Really? I thought lawyers spent all their time in court."

"Only on TV."

"But I know you haven't forgotten acting. So you could pretend. Take part in an Event. No cost to you. Just so you could try to find out more."

"Wouldn't the no cost part tip people off?"

"I'll pay for it. Or, actually, Mom would. She's really worried about all of this. And you know she has a ton of faith in you."

Caleb's mom and I exchanged holiday greetings and occasionally emailed for years after Caleb moved. She sent a beautiful card when Marco died.

"But eight hundred dollars? Or whatever it costs? She wants to spend that?"

Caleb's mom was a grade school teacher, and I doubted she earned a very high salary. It didn't feel right for her to pay my way. But I'd never choose on my own to spend that kind of money on a self-help course. And things were busy at the moment. I expected to work a few evenings a week for the foreseeable future. A five-evening Event would take time away from my practice as well as cost a lot.

"No question," Caleb said. "Don't worry about it. It'll be a weight off my mind, and hers, to have you on my side. And if you find something out, I can tell the police about it as long as my lawyer says it's okay."

"She could hire a private investigator. A real one."

"Which would cost more. And how's that person going to get invited to an Event, which is the only way to get to Frank, Richard, and Scott Gary?"

I stretched out on the floor, my head on the floor pillow. The alcohol was having an effect, and I'm not much of a late night person. Reason 101 why theater hadn't been a good fit for me. "What's Scott Gary got to do with it? You said he wasn't there that night."

"Yeah, but he's the founder. If Vincent's death had to do with Seminar, he must know something."

"And he'd talk to me?"

"He's always there the last day of the Event. He'll definitely talk to you. Please, Q? Your mom told me the police were clueless about Marco's death, and you were the one who found out the truth. That's what I need."

I stared at the popcorn ceiling. The lamp light made concentric circles on it in one corner. "My mother said that?"

My mother had known I'd helped with the investigation into Marco's death, but only because I'd gotten hurt doing it. She'd never asked me for details. My dad had, so he'd probably told her. But I was surprised she'd listened.

"She was really impressed. And proud."

"I know she didn't say that."

"No. But I could hear it in her voice."

I thought Caleb was reading into it what he wanted, though my mom and I had grown a little closer after Marco's death. And in the same way I saw Caleb's parents as more complex people than he did, and saw more of their concern for him, maybe he saw something in my mom that I couldn't after all the years of feeling I disappointed her by not being everything she was sure the original Q.C. would have been.

"Either way, I can't count on the police," Caleb said. "I need someone I trust to find the answers. And I feel like I owe it to Vincent."

I sat and opened my calendar app on my phone. Some of my litigation projects could be pushed down the road another week. And if I worked on the weekend, I could get enough done that I didn't need to work any weekday evenings. My plans with myself — to unwind by reading or watching Netflix a couple nights — were the only ones I'd simply need to cancel. Which wasn't a small thing. I needed to decompress from tax season and its aftermath.

But this was Caleb.

"I'll come to the Event," I said. "But I can't promise I'll find answers. And if I don't in a week, that has to be it."

He hugged me. "Thanks, Quille. I told Mom we could count on you. I owe you."

"Big time," I said, echoing another of our childhood exchanges.

"Biggest time. I'll email you a form to sign up."

12

"Let me get this straight." My friend Lauren scooped tomato sauce and melted goat cheese onto an oval slice of herb and garlic bread. "You've got a new guy in your life, who was taking you to that dusty little theater you love last night, and you cancelled? For an old 'friend' who didn't so much as text you for twelve years?"

"We were good friends as kids," I said.

We sat at a high top table in the bar area of Tapas Valencia, one of my favorite South Loop restaurants, along with my friend Joe. He, Danielle, and I sing in an a cappella trio together. Joe's also a financial advisor, and one of his clients had hired us to sing later that night at an anniversary party in a semi-private space in the back of the restaurant.

Because it was in a sense a client event, Joe had dressed more formally than he did for most of our singing jobs, wearing a crisp collared shirt open at the neck, a navy sport coat, and jeans. I wore a bright red dress that hung about mid-thigh over black leggings and sandals.

"Who just stopped hanging out with you for no reason," Lauren said.

She wore jeans tapered exactly the right amount for this month's trends. Her designer sandals were a year old but unmarred by a single scuff, and her sterling silver butterfly necklace from Tiffany's set off her fitted navy tank top and shiny blond hair. Her date was meeting her here later. I suspected she'd twisted his arm to attend, as 1960s and 70s classics weren't really his idea of great music.

"No reason that made sense at the time," I said. "He kept telling me I was making a big mistake getting away from acting, messing up my life. I thought that was why he disappeared. And it kind of was, according to him."

"You're right." She wiped her mouth with a cocktail napkin and pushed her plate to the side. "That makes absolutely zero sense. I wouldn't stop being your friend if I disagreed with you about a life choice."

Joe polished off the last piece of toast, careful not to let the cheese or tomato sauce drip on his crisp white shirt. "Because Quille's only half right."

I met Joe when I got my first paid part in a play at Red Orchid Theater, a storefront theater in Old Town. I'd been ten, the same age as his little brother, and he was eighteen. Gram tagged him and his then-girlfriend, who was the female lead, to look out for me. We'd crossed paths in theater every other year or so until he quit to get his MBA at Northwestern. He'd given me a lot of good advice when I was navigating my career path away from theater.

"Which half?" I said.

"The half where it happened when you quit acting. But he was mad because it messed up his life, not yours." Joe swapped out his plate for a clean one from the stack by the window. "You cancelled on Ty? And he's not coming tonight? Thought he was the next love of your life."

"It's a little early to know that," I said, surprised by the hint of sarcasm. I'd been seeing Ty since late January. I'd known Marco not much longer than that when we'd decided to move in together, but Joe knew how unusual that was for me. "And he's at his sister's all day today. Helping her and her husband move. He's driving back in early tomorrow."

Joe passed Lauren and me clean plates from the stack. "I just meant you seemed really excited about him that night we all met."

"I am," I said.

Lauren pulled the plate of garlic potato salad over between us and spooned some onto each of our plates. "This Caleb was an actor too?"

"Yeah, and he was good," Joe said. "But he didn't do much of his own legwork. Tagged along to Quille's auditions a lot, followed up on tips from her Gram."

"And I tagged after him for everything else," I said. "Anyway, he told me what happened. He was jealous, and he didn't know how to handle it."

Joe raised his eyebrows but didn't say anything.

"You never liked him?" Lauren said.

Joe poured himself more wine and held onto the bottle for a moment. "Everyone likes Caleb. He fits in everywhere. Like water. Pour him into any container, and he'll take its shape."

I tasted the Rjioja he'd ordered. "You say that like it's all bad," I said. "I learned a lot from him about making friends and fitting in."

The wine was fruity and dark with a slight chocolate aftertaste, making it automatically a new favorite for me. But I don't like to drink more than a few sips before I sing. The alcohol is too dehydrating. I had no desire to sing two sets of ten songs each with a parched throat.

That Joe had ordered a bottle had surprised me, but I

thought he might be drowning his sorrows. He'd recently ended what seemed like a pretty serious relationship. And the woman he dated after that had just told him she was moving for work to Los Angeles.

"You didn't need nearly as much help with that as you thought you did," Joe said.

"Sure, because you and the other older actors were really nice to me. Big surprise, it wasn't so easy with kids my own age."

"It's seriously decent of you to want to help," Lauren said. "And he asked the right person. Just be careful."

I ate a bite of the garlic potato salad, enjoying its tanginess. It's one of my favorite Tapas Valencia dishes. I gestured toward Joe. "Why didn't you tell me you thought Caleb stopped hanging out with me because I couldn't help him with acting anymore?"

"I tried. But you got so upset, like I was saying he'd never wanted to be your friend. And it was when you were going through all that therapy. I figured better to let you deal with it your own way."

"He apologized," I said. "He wants to make things right."

"After you help him or before?" Joe said.

"At least he knows he was a jerk," Lauren said.

Joe took a stuffed mushroom cap from the plate. "He gets minimal credit for that. I knew he was a jerk twelve years ago."

Outside on the street, a cab pulled up and Danielle hopped out. I waved at her through the glass and turned back to Joe and Lauren. "So what about this Seminar thing? Either of you heard of it?"

———

Sunday, May 18, 6:50 a.m.

Despite not getting to sleep until midnight, partly because I'd been texting with Ty after our show, I woke up early Sunday morning. I decided to take a walk through Dearborn Park. It's a quiet neighborhood a few blocks south of where I live. Stately old trees arch their branches over the streets. Most of the homes are townhouses with brick patios and rooftop decks.

I like walking. It helps me stay in shape without running which, in my view, the human body was never meant to do unless being chased by a person-eating tiger.

It also helps clear my head.

As I passed the park behind Dearborn Station, an old train station converted to a retail and office building, I inhaled the smell of trees and spring flowers.

Joe's comments about Caleb kept running through my head. But Joe had been negative about a lot of things since his break up with his longtime girlfriend. And whatever ulterior motives he might have had, Caleb saved me from being really lonely as a kid. I met him right around when my oldest sister went away to college. And while I'd had friends other than Caleb in grade school, staying close was hard once they were in high school and I was doing independent study. Only Caleb went the extra mile to include me. It seemed like a fair enough trade for me taking him along to auditions.

I paused to watch a tennis game in the park near Roosevelt Road, then retraced my steps, ending at Café des Livres in the building where I work. Ty was driving straight there from Michigan to meet me for breakfast. I didn't expect him until about nine, but I'd brought my iPad to do some research first. The more I knew about Seminar the better use I could make of my time at the Event.

The whole café smelled of dark hot chocolate, frying

bacon, and fresh bakery. I sat in an armchair near the book-shelves and fireplace in the back corner.

On my iPad I tried once again searching for information about the blandly-named Seminar, but I got pages of unrelated results no matter how I tried to narrow it. The business of self-help seminars was thriving in Chicago and all over the Internet.

Next I tried narrowing it by people. I found nothing about Richard Messerly in connection with Seminar. Seminar plus Olivia Medford, Frank Hernandez, or Caleb Jackson also retrieved nothing. I found an Instagram and other social media accounts for Karla Lenzi. She mentioned Seminar now and then. All vague and positive about how it enhanced people's lives.

I held out more hope about finding something about Gina Lenzi, Vincent's supposedly hostile daughter. People always tend to speak out more, especially online, when they're unhappy.

The first four pages of search results for her name, Seminar, and Chicago showed mostly unrelated Gina Lenzis, annual reports for universities, and listings for corporate conferences, some of them long over, throughout the city. But a blog snippet on a social media site appeared in the middle of page 4 that looked promising. I clicked through and found Seminar: My Father's Folly.

The blog's low rank and that I hadn't found it during my original research suggested Gina wasn't drawing much traffic.

"*Bon matin.* Earl Grey or Chocolate Chai?"

Carole Ports, the café owner, set a small plate with a warmed chocolate chip scone on the tall oval table next to me. She wore her trademark colorful scarf over a black blouse and flowing skirt. Her bobbed black hair was threaded with silver strands that, on Carole, made her look more striking rather than older. She'd turned sixty the year before.

"I was going to wait for Ty. But you convinced me," I said. "Earl Grey."

"*Maginifique.* Lovely that you're still seeing him."

"Not sure 'seeing' is the word. Our schedules have not matched well. Today's the one day we could carve out in the last two weeks."

"But tax season is over, *non*? That should make it easier."

"He's in the middle of a major deal. And I just agreed to help an old friend with an issue that will keep me pretty busy."

Ty was a commercial real estate broker responsible for bringing together investors from opposite coasts. Most of our conversations lately were by text. My planning to attend an Event that would book my evenings the following week wasn't going to help.

Carole waved a hand. "It is not bad to start slowly. You've both been through much. Relax. Take your time. But tell me, this issue, I hope it is not like mine was?"

Helping Carole search for a missing neighbor had gotten me in the crosshairs of a murderer during the winter holidays. She'd been beside herself about endangering me. She hadn't let me pay for anything at the café since then, though I kept telling her it wasn't necessary. Carole was like the mom I'd never had. If Caleb felt about Vincent the way I did about her, I could see why he was so set on proving he had nothing to do with Vincent's death.

"It might be a little," I said. "But I'll be careful, I promise."

The front door jangled. Three women in yoga outfits entered. Grace Place, a community center/church across the street, offered yoga early Sunday morning. Carole met them at the counter where they told her how much they liked the new instructor.

On my iPad I scrolled through Gina Lenzi's blog. It didn't allow for comments and had only a few entries.

While the blog included her name in a header, she didn't name her dad or anyone in Seminar. Instead, she used nicknames. I supposed that might have been some comfort to Vincent if he'd seen it. People in Seminar, though, would most likely be able to read between the lines.

The first entry was dated early in January of this year.

Seminar Madness

Dear Old Dad finally decided I could take part in one of his precious Seminar "events."

Yes, the one-week introductory course is called an event. As if 50 humans or however many sitting in creaky chairs in the Thompson Center's auditorium is something to make a big deal over.

(By the way, state of Illinois, one thing I agree with D.O.D. on. Sell that monstrosity! I worked in three different offices there. All it does is leak when it rains and cost a gazillion to heat and cool. Tear it down. Make a park. No wait, you'd just sell it to some developer who paid off the right alderman so let's keep it. At least it's different looking.)

It was a big favor, supposedly, from D.O.D. to me to be invited to attend.

Because what do you do with a daughter who never lives up to her potential? Or, let's be honest, who you never thought had potential?

Of course he's been after Big Sis forever to join up. (I know, I know, Seminar humans, if any of you are reading you'll say no one joins, there's no such thing as membership. But you have to be invited to attend so what is that but membership?)

No doubt because Sis is a plastic surgeon with the required 2.2 kids (counting the flock of guinea pigs as the .2) so she checks all the boxes. Unlike the loser English major/dental hygienist daughter.

I switched over to my search results. Knowing Gina was a dental hygienist helped me narrow down the many profiles I'd found under the same name. She almost had to be the Gina Lenzi who was about my age and lived in River North. I didn't feel positive, though, because that neighborhood north of the river is so expensive. Most of the residential buildings are newer high rises with prices double that of Printers Row where I live.

My condo is a thousand square feet plus a small sleeping loft I added above my bedroom area. In River North, half that square footage costs a third again more to buy. I'd bought because the numbers made sense. I wanted to stay in my neighborhood for at least five years, usually the point where buying becomes cheaper than renting overall, and I had enough for a down payment because I'd lived with Gram and worked through college, worked two years at an accounting firm before law school, and had minimal student loans when I graduated.

If Gina were like most people our age she rented, but that wouldn't make River North any cheaper. The lowest rents I saw for one-bedrooms were over two thousand dollars a month. A search of entry level salaries for dental hygienists in Chicago suggested Gina earned between fifty and sixty thousand dollars a year. It couldn't be easy to get by on that. She'd be spending half her take home pay on rent.

Her reference to her plastic surgeon sister helped me find Tina Lenzi, M.D. Dr. Lenzi was board-certified, which a medical school website told me meant six years of specialized training. I noticed most of the services her Manhattan office offered now fell into the cosmetic surgery field. A little more research told me cosmetic procedures were done to enhance appearance and plastic surgery was reconstructive to correct injuries or deformities. I wondered if Dr. Lenzi started out in plastic surgery and switched.

A little more digging gave me a guess at why she might have done that. Reconstructive surgery is more difficult and getting reimbursement requires going through insurance. Patients pay for cosmetic surgery out of their own pockets. That means the doctor's office doesn't need to jump through hoops to get reimbursed. It sounded like a more lucrative and less stressful practice.

Gina's next entry was only two days after the first. Another followed it a day later.

How To Treat Your Daughter Seminar Style

Speaking of my new career, what do you think D.O.D. said when I got my hygienist certificate? Are you thinking Congratulations?

NFW. He said, well, finally maybe you'll support yourself.

Nice.

I ask you Seminar humans (I guess you are technically still human), is that Seminar-approved language? At the very least I'd think you'd have some super chipper happy way to say your adult child disappoints you on a regular basis.

Anyway I told him what is the point of your Make The Most Of Yourself powerhouse organization or whatever it is if it's only for people who are already doing fabulously. Seriously, how much help does Big Sis need? It's like she's genetically programmed to succeed.

To which he says, well, your sister doesn't need me to front her travel expenses and tuition. This was back when I would have had to fly to Austin or New York to attend. Now that it's opened a home base office here in Chicago he has no excuse.

Also, tuition. Like it's a university and you get a degree.

Lavender, vanilla, and citrus steam filled the air as Carole poured tea from a small china pot into a sturdy mug. I hadn't heard her approach. She left the pot, which had the café's fleur de lis design on the side, touched my shoulder and headed back to the counter where more people had lined up.

It was nearly eight-thirty. Ty would be here soon.

Why He Finally "Invited" His Deadbeat Daughter To Seminar

Okay, okay, I can hear you saying if you think Seminar is so stupid why did you ask D.O.D. if you could attend?

Because he pretty much thinks anyone who's not in Seminar is useless. With the exception of Big Sis who's never wanted anything to do with it. But he says she naturally adopted all its principles because she grew up hearing about it.

What tipped him over is I pointed out that he spends more on a dinner at one of those "fine dining" restaurants than it costs for one event. (Like Everest in the financial district. I looked at the menu online. Cheapest meal for two if you get a halfway decent bottle of wine — and who could survive dinner with D.O.D. without a bottle of wine or two — is over $600 and he never gets the cheapest meal. And from Karla's Instragram I know he orders caviar every time they go there.)

I guess I should be honored he finally decided I'm worth the price of dinner.

I sipped the tea and ate a few bites of the scone. Gina's anger at her dad and asides about Seminar people definitely could be called hostile, but I wondered how many people read the entries. At the Celebration, SaraBeth had mentioned being on a board with Karla. I wondered if Karla told her about Gina or if SaraBeth found the blog. Or heard about Gina some other way.

The next entry included a harsher critique, starting with the title **Seminar Wants Your Money.**

13

Seminar Wants Your Money

Seminar humans, stop reading if you want to avoid everything negative like a good Seminar-ite (my word not Seminar's) should do.

But if you happened on this blog because you're right now thinking of paying money to Seminar do read. Please.

So, the event (I refuse to capitalize everything the way that Seminar humans do):

You're not allowed to sit with anyone you know. Which, who cares, I didn't know anyone except The Henchman, and he was running it. And was doing this thing where he was determined to act like he barely knew me.

Which it turns out is a thing. People at events pretending.

Also a thing: focusing on now. A word Seminar humans capitalize but I refuse. Now is a freakin common word. Like all the other ones Seminar uses.

I think it's to make people feel like they're talking in a secret code when they're in the outside world.

Oh, almost forgot. Talking about Seminar anywhere except in the groups is forbidden for the week. And no drinking at all. Any time during the week.

Like I followed that rule.

I started a document and created a column of Seminar terms I'd heard and what I thought they meant. In another column I typed the nicknames Gina was using.

The Henchman might be Frank Hernandez. He seemed to be the most important person at the cocktail party. I supposed it could be Richard Messerly, but I hadn't gotten the impression he was that pivotal to Seminar. It also might be Caleb for that matter, but I felt like Gina was writing about someone older than herself. I sent Caleb a text asking if he could find me a list of employees and of people who helped run Events. Because The Henchman could be someone I hadn't met.

Dear Old Dad and D.O.D. were obviously Vincent. Based on social media posts and queries of a subscription database I use for my law practice I confirmed that Vincent had been married twice. Once to Gina's and Tina's mother, who died in her late forties a few years after she and Vincent divorced, and then to Karla. Karla and Vincent had no children. They'd married six months after his divorce became final.

Whether or not the divorce stress contributed to whatever condition caused her mom's death, Gina might very well think that it had.

Her next entry was two and a half weeks later, not the next day.

It's An Honor Just To Be Asked

Meant to post sooner but work got crazy busy. Three

emergency root canals this week. Who waits until they are screaming in pain to go to the dentist?

My boss takes all the emergency patients when other dentists are closed because she's still getting established. Maybe she should go to Seminar to learn better ways to market.

Finished my second event all of an hour ago. I'm more hostile.

First is this idea that not just anyone with a spare thousand dollars (or two or three) can come to an event. Oh, no. A Seminar human has to invite you.

To be invited supposedly you need to be someone who shows potential for, aspires to be, or is in the top ten percent. Of what? Not clear.

So if you're a lawyer it could be you're in the top ten percent of lawyers in your area of law. But who measures that? How? For example, a lawyer who does real estate closings, how do you prove you're in the top ten percent of that? How hard is it to do a closing? From what I've heard the paralegals do all the paperwork.

The Henchman mumbled something to me once about some magazine about super lawyers (is that like superheroes? Is he the Thor of lawyers?) and walked off.

If it's top ten percent emotionally I fail that. But half the humans I saw there do too. They came to Seminar to improve their emotional control. So I guess they fit in the "aspire" category.

Maybe that's how D.O.D. got me in. I can hear him now. "My daughter Gina is such a loser but she aspires to be in the top ten percent of losers, and maybe she'll go somewhere from there."

Need wine. More tomorrow.

(I know, I know, I haven't been any better at sticking with blogging than anything else. If you came here for information on Seminar, you're probably disappointed. So feel free to email me or use the contact form and I'll tell you anything you want to know.)

The smell of coffee overpowered that of my tea as a big guy in a sports jersey dropped into the armchair next to me and plunked a giant white mug on the table between us.

The next blog entry had posted the morning of Vincent's death at 10:43 a.m. It seemed to have been written before Gina heard the news.

Why I Went Back

I know you've been wondering (I'm pretending someone is reading this) why I went back to another event.

(1) I'm an idiot and (2) The Henchman convinced me I hadn't given it a fair shot. He said the next event, which was all about relationships, targeted what I need.

So in case you were wondering about relationships, yes, there's an event for that, which, ugh, is actually what the Seminar humans say.

There's an event for everything.

No official list I know of because events come and go. But here's the ones I've heard of:

•empowering event (everyone's first one, basically an overview of all Seminar principles)

•relationship event

•business event

•physical fitness event

•mental fitness event

•charitable living event

•cure hunger event (right, I know, hunger is not a disease, not like you could develop a vaccine or something but that's what they call it)

•executive event

•intermediate, advanced, and expert versions of all of
the above

The entry stopped there. It was the last one. The abrupt
ending and timing made me wonder if Gina got the call
about her Dad at that moment. If so, she'd still hit publish,
but maybe before she knew what she was about to hear.

I set my iPad on the coffee table in the center of the
seating area and finished my scone. Gina Lenzi had lost both
her mother and father. She'd invited readers to email her
about Seminar, but I questioned whether she really wanted
that now.

14

Sunday, May 18, 9:12 a.m.

We moved to a marble table near the front window along Dearborn Street when Ty came in.

"So what was it your old friend wanted?" Ty said.

I explained as he stirred a third spoonful of honey into his chocolate chai tea. One of the first things Ty and I bonded over was our mutual dislike of coffee, though he wasn't quite as much of a tea drinker as I was. Thus the copious quantities of honey.

When I mentioned Seminar, Ty dropped his spoon. "Seminar? You're sure?"

"Yes. Why?" I said. "What do you know about it?"

Despite its lack of web presence, Seminar seemed to be all over the place. Somebody there knew how to get the word out.

A waitress set two slices of bacon, extra crispy, and a plate of whole wheat cinnamon toast in between us.

"The founding partner at the firm in Minneapolis was big into it. He used to live in Austin, and he said it's what got him to start his own firm. After going back there for some kind of training he started conducting his own Seminar-like encounter sessions on Saturday mornings. Optional but not if you get what I mean."

"Oh yeah."

The accounting firm where I'd worked after college and before law school held a cocktail party the first Friday evening of each month. It was optional, too, but if you missed it one of the partners always pointed it out.

"So you attended?"

"Once." He spread his hands wide. "Had to. Couldn't be the only one who didn't show."

I nodded. Ty had told me he was often the only Black man at any firm or business dinner, especially in Minneapolis. For good or bad, everyone noticed whatever he did. He also heard people refer to him as the token African American, though his family had come here from Jamaica two generations ago.

"What was it like?" I bit into the bacon. Perfectly cooked to a crisp with a faint, smoky maple flavor.

"Mike pushed people to talk about their most frightening experiences so he could use Seminar techniques to help deal with them."

"What's that got to do with real estate development?"

"Nothing." Ty broke a piece of cinnamon toast in half. "Not in any direct way. Or any way I could see. But supposedly these traumatic experiences fragment a person, and you lose pieces of who you are. Some thing or another like that. So reimagining them in a healthier way makes you whole, and a whole person is better able to connect with other people."

"Frank Hernandez — one of the higher ups Caleb reports to — said something about that. So the idea is if you connect better with other people you put more deals together?" I said.

"Yeah, but nothing helped anyone connect better at that

session. Mike zeroed in on a newer broker. Got him talking about his father. The guy's sweating, gripping his chair, and practically weeping as Mike shoots all these questions at him. I tried to stop it, but short of yanking Mike or the broker out of there physically there was no way to derail it."

"No one else tried?"

"Everyone froze. In shock. I finally stood and said this is not part of my job. Asked the broker to leave with me. But it was like he was glued to that chair. Found out later he ended up sharing that his dad sexually abused him. He'd never told anyone before."

"Is it — was it — did it maybe help him to stop keeping it inside?"

"No idea. He never came back to work. My assistant said Mike tried to convince him that it never happened, that he'd made it all up in his own head."

"That's awful."

Outside the window a pedestrian stepped into the bike lane. It's oddly situated between the curb and a row of parked cars, and it goes both ways. The car traffic beyond the parked cars is one way heading north. The man looked right only for northbound traffic. A bike from the opposite way swerved around him, almost hitting a parked car. The biker and the pedestrian shouted at one another and kept going.

"Sounds like I better keep my guard up," I said.

"Your guard up? What do you mean? You're not buying into this thing are you?"

"Not buying. Well, Caleb's mom is. She's paying for me to attend an Event. That's what they call their week-long courses."

"Why would she do that?"

"She thinks it'll help Caleb to have someone there on his side. Or on the inside if you prefer. Because the Seminar people are so immersed in it, Caleb's sure they won't talk to the police, and he's afraid either Vincent's murderer won't be found or he'll be tagged with it. Not formally, but that people in the organization will keep believing he was involved and never trust him."

"Jesus, Quille." Ty rubbed his chin. "You almost got killed in December. That wasn't enough for you?"

"I hurt my arm," I said.

"It could have been so much worse."

"You're not wrong," I said. "But I'll be careful."

"And there's psychological risks. This Seminar thing is nothing to mess around with. If you'd seen that guy, you'd know what I mean."

I took half a piece of toast. "You said that wasn't a Seminar Event. Who knows if this Mike person understood Seminar or was doing what he was supposed to do."

Ty placed his hands on either side of his plate, making the table shudder. "If things weren't so crazy now — if you can wait a week, take the next Event or whatever you call it, things'll be slower and I can go with you."

"And protect me?" I squeezed his hand. His fingers were warm. "You know I'm pretty good at taking care of myself, right? Been doing it forever."

He collapsed back into his chair. "Ah, I'm sorry. You're right. But it's, what, barely more than a year since Marco's death? Plus there's everything about your sister and your parents. A bunch of self-proclaimed gurus playing at group therapy could do a lot of harm. There's nothing wrong with a friend at your side to help you through."

"And I appreciate it. But you've been thinking that deal will come together since Valentine's Day. You don't know when it'll close or what'll come up next. And anyway, introductory Events aren't held all the time. If I miss this one it'll be another month."

As if to prove my point, Ty's phone rang. "Sorry," he said.

While he talked, I wrote an email to Gina Lenzi. I considered pretending to be someone else to make it less likely anyone would connect me to Caleb and figure out why I was asking questions. That worked for me when trying to find out what happened to Marco. But with the pain Gina must be in at the loss of her father, I didn't want to mislead her unless it was absolutely necessary to protect Caleb's confidences.

Dear Gina,

I'm so sorry to hear about your father's death. A friend who recently asked me to take part in a Seminar event told me about it.

I found your webpage when researching the organization.

Your blog says you're willing to talk with people about Seminar. If you still are, I'd like to talk by phone, or I could meet you for coffee anywhere in or near downtown.

I understand completely if this is a bad time or you don't want to talk to a stranger about Seminar. You can look at my firm website (link below) if you want to know more about me before responding.

Quille C. Davis

When Ty got off the phone I told him about Gina Lenzi's blog and showed him my draft email. He was all for me contacting her.

"You'll find the right thing to say that doesn't upset her more," he said. "And it'll give you a heads up on what to watch out for."

Before we left the café I reread the email and added "and to disturb you during what must be a hard time" at the end of the first sentence and my cell phone number. Then I hit Send.

15

———

Sunday, May 18, 11:02 a.m.

Ty and I spent the rest of the morning and all afternoon on his boat. He took us first through the North Branch of the Chicago River, then out on Lake Michigan. In all the time I'd lived in the city I'd never been out on the lake, only looked at it from the shore or Navy Pier. The skyline looked beautiful in all directions, and the expanse of water to the west and the boat's rocking made me more relaxed than I'd been in days.

We'd just gotten back to my building when Lauren texted that she had some information on Seminar. She lives only two floors down so I told her to come over.

Ty disappeared into my bathroom to take a shower, and I opened a bottle of Chardonnay. I'm not usually a fan of white wine, or any wine before dinner, but it sounded cool and crisp after so long in the sun.

Lauren knocked on the door as I was filling glasses of ice water to go with it. We have keys to each other's places, but she always knocks if she knows Ty's over.

She dropped her tote bag on the floor by the counter. It was my current favorite of all her bags. Marc Jacobs grained leather in evening blue, it stood straight on the floor because of its flat base and structured sides. I loved my leather shoulder bag by Frye. I'd gotten it for half price six years ago at Nordstrom Rack. But next to Lauren's, its weathered leather and classic style looked a bit dull.

"People love it or hate it." Lauren set a yellow bowl of her homemade guacamole on the counter. "Figured I'd bring an appetizer since I'm interrupting your date."

"Seminar?" I said. I got out some chips from Trader Joe's. I'm not a big fan of their brands, but Lauren likes them, so I keep them for her. "How many people heard of it?"

She slid onto one of my counter stools. "Two clients and one other real estate agent so far. One attended when he lived in San Francisco. Hated it. Says they mess with people's heads and high pressure you into bringing people in."

"What'd you do, spend the last twenty-four hours calling and texting people?"

"Almost. Gave me something to do at that open house. Which drew all looky-loos."

I sat across from her. "So what about the other two?"

"One went in January. Here in Chicago. Says she got totally unblocked. She's a physical therapist and she hated the clinic she worked at. It prompted her to quit and partner with a chiro she knows. They started their own practice and it's going gangbusters."

"Because of Seminar?"

"My guess? She absolutely was on the verge of making a break, but needed a last push and Seminar gave it to her. The other guy went to classes, events, whatever they're called, for years when he lived in Austin. Since then he's been doing some online course that's got similar concepts, but he's seriously unmotivated to go it alone. He was thrilled when I told him Seminar now gives courses here. Might call and sign up."

She scooped guacamole onto a chip. "Seminar ought to give me a commission."

"I'll tell Caleb that."

"Joe find out anything?" Lauren filled her wine glass and mine.

"I don't know." Joe is more apt to email than text, and I hadn't looked at email since leaving the café. I took out my phone and checked. "Says he contacted almost two dozen clients today. No one heard of Seminar."

"Wrong income bracket maybe," Lauren said.

Joe's clients are high net worth individuals, defined as people with five million to twenty-five million in assets to invest. When I was in college I thought of a million as high net worth. Joe shocked me when he told me a million dollars wouldn't be enough to retire on by the time I hit sixty. Like me, Joe came from a family that struggled financially and he paid his own way through school, so I knew his estimate wasn't based on outsized income expectations.

"Did he seem off to you last night?" I said.

The sound of the running shower cut off, and I heard cabinet doors banging from the bathroom.

"He definitely doesn't like your friend." She drank some wine. "Also, I'm seriously starting to think he has a thing for you."

"Joe? No. You're imagining things. I was a kid when he met me."

"Right, Quille, but that was, what, thirty years ago?"

I calculated. "Closer to twenty-five."

She ate another chip. "My point exactly."

It had crossed my mind when Joe and his girlfriend split that it might relate to me, but only in a roundabout way. She'd rarely come to see us when our a cappella trio sang. She claimed she didn't like the old songs that made up our repertoire. But I often thought she didn't like sharing Joe with anyone. If Lauren was right, she hadn't liked sharing him with me.

I shook my head. "I don't see it."

The shower turned off and Ty, one thick white towel around his waist and another around his neck, gave a quick wave to Lauren and disappeared into my walk-in closet. He kept a few changes of clothes there.

"Nice," Lauren mouthed. Aloud she said, "Are you going to ask your brother-in-law about Seminar?"

I piled guacamole on a chip and sighed. "I should."

My oldest sister's husband had started one business after another over the years. Unfortunately for his family, none of them paid off. That and his lies to my sister had brought them to the brink of a divorce after I uncovered one of his major falsehoods. It had been at her request, but she never quite forgave me for being the messenger.

"Text him," Lauren said. "That way if he doesn't know anything you don't need to talk."

As I sent the text, Ty emerged barefoot wearing a pair of jeans and a gray fitted T-shirt. "Hey, Lauren. Are you talking Quille out of this Seminar thing?"

"She can't skip it now," she said. "Caleb's mom already paid, right?"

"Probably."

He sat with us at the counter and told her about his experience in Minneapolis and his concerns. "If I were going to be in town, I'd go with her. Moral support."

"I'll go," Lauren said.

I ate the last of the guacamole. "What?"

"To the Event."

"Don't you have showings this week?"

She shrugged. "A few. That new agent I've been helping out owes me a favor. I'll get him to cover for me. And probably be late to the Event or whatever it's called a few times."

"Lauren is good at talking to people," Ty said.

"I seriously am."

"But you got hurt last time you helped me get information," I said, despite that the argument hadn't worked on me when Ty tried it.

"Yeah, so much that I totally went skiing three days later. I'll be fine."

"I'd love to have you along. But it's over eight hundred dollars."

She shrugged. "Business expense. Based on what everyone said, and on that condo Karla Lenzi lives in, I'll make it back in no time with all the potential buyers. Maybe she wants to sell."

———

SUNDAY, MAY 18, 6:39 P.M.

Ty and I had been planning to go out to dinner, but we both felt wiped out and decided to get Lou Malnati's pizza. Its South Loop location is only about six blocks from my place, and we could have eaten there. But it's always crowded and loud, and I'd had enough of that Friday night.

While he ordered online, I texted Caleb that Lauren wanted to attend the Event with me. By the time we got back with a butter crust, sausage, and extra cheese stuffed pizza Caleb had emailed Lauren a form to sign up. As I suspected, though she hadn't attended a Celebration, Seminar wasn't turning down her eight hundred dollars. Though I supposed that could be because, if Olivia Medford was to be believed, Caleb was on the rise and his vouching for someone meant an automatic invitation.

He called and asked if I could find out the name of Lauren's former client who might return to Seminar.

"Why? Do you get a commission?" I said. "Because if you do, you should take Lauren to dinner."

"No commission. But it's never bad for people to know someone returned to Seminar partly through me. Plus it makes your interest seem a lot more legitimate. With you bringing another person, maybe two, no one's going to wonder if you're really into Seminar or what you're there for."

16

MONDAY, MAY 19, 6:21 P.M.

My auditorium chair squeaked as I twisted to peer over my shoulder at Lauren, who mimed a yawn. She sat three rows behind me and to the right. Seats had been assigned when we checked in. So far tonight I'd seen only two people from the Celebration. Richard Messerly, who sat on stage now with Caleb, and Richard's partner, Olivia, who sat in the front row. I hadn't had a chance to talk to any of them. A helper in a green T-shirt had escorted me immediately to my assigned seat.

Everyone was crammed into the first twenty rows of the center section. I couldn't text Lauren because the people in green T-shirts collected all our electronic devices before we entered the auditorium. And after we signed a waiver that we couldn't hold Seminar responsible for any loss or damage.

The evening had started with Caleb taking the stage precisely at six p.m. to introduce himself and Richard. They sat on folding chairs, and Richard spoke about tax shelters. He gave the impression he and Caleb needed these vehicles because of Seminar. Listening carefully, though, neither ever said he earned enough or amassed enough assets to fall into the tax brackets that would justify the legal fees to create those vehicles.

I couldn't help shaking my head when they moved on to corporate structure, insisting every business needed to be a C corporation no matter how much or little you earned. While I don't help people form companies, I knew enough to form my own and to understand my clients'. No one structure is right for everyone.

My jaw clenched as they veered back to estate planning, rambling about avoiding the "death tax." In Illinois you need to leave at least four million dollars to trigger any estate tax, which is the formal name for it. For the federal estate tax the threshold is higher — $11.8 million these days. About two out of a thousand people who die will leave estates that need to pay estate taxes. It wasn't something that kept me up at night.

Richard segued to putting assets into a trust to avoid losing them if you or your business got sued. If there were other lawyers or professionals in the room, they must have spotted the flaws in the entire presentation, but no one spoke.

I waved my bright green placard, following Seminar protocol to be recognized and allowed to speak. Even if I had come here because I truly wanted to be part of Seminar this whole presentation would set me on edge. When Richard pointed to me, I stood and introduced myself by first name only, also following Seminar rules.

"Richard, if someone's earning the median wage and has less than $300,000 in assets including the equity in a home, wouldn't it be cheaper and easier to get a decent umbrella insurance policy than pay to create a trust?"

Richard frowned. "This is a general discussion, not specific advice."

"I just don't understand why we spent so long on asset

protection and tax issues that apply to maybe .2% of the population."

"Quille's a bit new to Seminar." Richard looped his arms out in wide circles. "Does anyone want to tell her what she needs to do?"

At least half the crowd answered something in unison that I couldn't quite understand.

"Image expo what?" I said, wondering if it was some sort of trade show.

"Imagine Exponentially," Richard said. "You're thinking small. You came here to Exponentially Improve your life. Stop stopping yourself on Day One."

Caleb, still sitting to one side, nodded. "Good point. We're always happy to have constructive comments that help everyone else along, Quille. But there's no place for negativity or limitations here."

There also was no place for realism, apparently, but I sat. Caleb chiming in suggested he needed me to stick with the program, not poke holes in it. I placed the placard on the floor and worked my hands under my thighs to keep myself still.

Monday, May 19, 7:17 p.m.

There were no breaks.

After Richard finished Caleb spoke the rest of the night. He talked first about how Seminar took him from being a struggling actor who depended on his dad for rent money to an in-demand industrial film actor to a Seminar Coordinator in three short years. He spoke well, his voice and gestures conveying his enthusiasm. Next he explained some Seminar concepts. He did all the things a speaker should do. Moved around the stage, used well-defined gestures rather than waving his hands randomly, varied his volume and tone.

But I kept slumping lower in the chair, then forcing myself to sit straight and stay awake, then slumping again. I'd taken a deposition that afternoon. The concentration needed to listen carefully to every answer and ask follow up questions while still checking off the topics on my outline always made me tired.

I also didn't hear anything all that new. My self-study in high school included in-depth research and multiple papers on psychological theories. My therapist told me later it was because I was trying to fix my mom. The Seminar concepts I'd heard so far were what my Gram would call a mish-mash of pop psychology and all those theories.

Caleb paused and smiled.

Maybe it was something about the way the light hit, but for the first time I noticed how much whiter and straighter his teeth were than when we were kids, and he had good teeth then.

"So here's what I ask you before we say goodnight," he said. I sat straighter, grateful I'd be released soon. "We've covered a lot without giving you a chance to put it into practice. Which I promise we will tomorrow. Remember, no smoking, caffeine, or drinking this week, and no mind-altering substances. You need your brain and body clear. And please don't tweet, don't talk, don't post about your experiences. Yet. Wait and see what you feel and think tomorrow and the next day and the next. Especially because we have a special guest for you later in the week. From San Francisco, the founder of Seminar, Scott Gary, will join us and will meet with each of you individually."

A murmur spread through the room, and everyone seemed to come awake. Or maybe, like me, they couldn't wait to get out of the auditorium.

When I got my phone, hope that I'd get something done tonight returned. Gina Lenzi had texted me at seven-forty-five p.m. She suggested we meet that night.

MONDAY, MAY 19, 8:15 P.M.

"I was right with you," Lauren said as she typed on her phone. We stood outside the Thompson Center. "But I figured both Caleb's invited guests saying the emperor had no clothes might be too much."

I zipped my leather jacket. The wind felt cold again today. "I shouldn't have said anything myself."

Though we'd waited fifteen minutes outside the auditorium doors, Caleb had never emerged. I'd texted with Gina and agreed to meet her at 8:30. Lauren was headed to River North to buy the agent covering her showings this week a drink.

The restaurant where I was meeting Gina was a block east and two blocks south. The fastest way was through Daley Plaza, which stands kitty corner to the Thompson Center. The Daley Center takes up half the block and houses state court houses and the Cook County Law Library. The rest is plaza.

The Picasso, a fifty-foot tall cubist sculpture, stands in the center of it. During the day, kids slide down its base, which is on an incline. At night it looks like a giant black bird looming over the empty expanse, massive wings folded and straight metal rods in place of a body.

I cut across the plaza on a diagonal. On the Dearborn side a flame burns endlessly as a memorial to veterans. Most nights lone people sit separately at tables near it. They keep their bags of possessions close around them and have never bothered me.

The surrounding blocks have foot traffic from the stage theaters and restaurants in the area, so it's usually a safe enough place to walk at night. As always in Chicago, though, I kept my eyes and ears open for anyone behind, ahead, or on either side of me. A few people left the Thompon Center around the same time Lauren and I did, so at first I assumed whoever was walking behind me was another participant cutting through the plaza. But as the footsteps gained ground, and the person stayed directly behind me despite plenty of room in the vast plaza, I felt less and less sure about that.

I took a large step sideways and swung around.

"Go on ahead around me," I said, meeting the eyes of the middle-aged white man behind me. He wore a long-sleeved golf shirt and khakis and carried a backpack over his shoulder.

"Sorry." He made a gesture as if tipping his hat, passed me, and angled toward Washington Street on the south edge of the plaza.

Once he reached the street and crossed I continued on my way, striding faster than before. The man might have absent-mindedly gotten too near me, but he hadn't seemed at all startled when I stopped and turned. Instead, he'd apologized, suggesting he knew he was following way too close.

I shivered. Probably a garden variety pickpocket, but I'd been mugged once and ended up in the emergency room after cracking my head on the concrete floor of the Pedway. I had no desire to repeat that experience.

17

As I descended the stairs at Trattoria 10, I inhaled the scents of fresh cooked garlic and oregano. The restaurant is underground on Dearborn Street, and I love eating there in the winter. The lack of outside walls, doors, and windows keeps it warm and shielded from the icy winds. And its soft lighting, adobe-style off-white walls, and archways make you feel you're dining outdoors at night in a villa in Florence.

As the weather turns warm and the sun appears more often, I prefer restaurants with an outdoor view or, better, outdoor seating so long as the bugs aren't out in full force. But Gina had suggested this as a meeting place, and I wanted it convenient for her.

The polished wood bar stood on the long end of a rectangular room near the stairs. Gina sat at the bar, a quarter-full glass of wine and half-empty bottle of Chianti near her right hand.

I recognized her from her blog photo. She was a thirtyish white woman. Her shock of dyed black hair was shaved at the sides and moussed at the top so it stood straight except at the forehead where it dipped toward her eyes. What looked like a diamond stud but might be cubic zirconia glittered in the right divot of her nose. Her clothes contrasted the rest of her look. Her dark denim leggings hung loose at the ankles and her T-shirt dress tented over her. A swirling glitter design across the chest made it look like a sparkly tarp.

Her face, only slightly rounded, suggested her oversized clothes were making her look larger than she was.

"Already started," she said after we introduced ourselves. She waved at the half-empty bottle. "Hope you like Chianti."

I sat on a stool next to her. "I like all red wine."

I'd offered to buy her a drink, not an entire bottle, but I'd manage. The early part of the year had been busy for me, but not very profitable. Actors and artists can't afford big tax preparation bills. The litigation work I'd done over the past few weeks paid much better, but it's usually sixty to ninety days between doing the work and getting paid. All of that means I budget a lot more carefully during the first half of the year than the second.

The bartender poured wine for me. It tasted dark and a little dry for my taste, but not bad. I asked him for ice water as well.

"So you're not following the Seminar no drinking rule, I see." Gina raised her glass. "A girl after my own heart."

"I'm not much for people telling me what to do," I said. It was true, and I suspected it also might resonate with Gina.

She grinned. "Me either. Who's the friend who roped you in? Might know him."

"Caleb Jackson. He said your dad was his mentor."

"Huh. Never met Cool Cal myself."

"Did your dad talk about him?"

"Oh sure. Made a point to tell me how excited Cool Cal was about Seminar. Not like me." She drained her glass, then emptied the wine left in the bottle into it.

"I'm sorry if this is hard for you," I said. "Maybe I shouldn't have contacted you."

"What, just because D.O.D.'s dead? You didn't off him, did you?"

I wondered how much the alcohol was affecting her or if she always said whatever came to mind. "No. Do the police have any idea what happened?"

She'd raised the topic, so I figured I could ask a few questions.

"Not that they told me. Good thing I've got an alibi or I'd probably get blamed."

"They asked for an alibi?"

Of course they had, but I hoped she might say something more.

"They didn't say 'alibi.' I'm being dramatic. That's what D.O.D. would say. But they asked where I was. Overnight at a guy's place. He lives in Germantown."

Gina held up the empty bottle and waved to the bartender then glanced at me. "Okay with you? I'm not driving."

"Me either," I said.

"Great."

After she ordered I asked where Germantown was and she told me it was a Wisconsin town near Milwaukee.

"It's on and off with him," she said. "Lucky the night my dad got killed it was on. Once the cops talk to him, case closed on me."

I didn't say so, but it might not be as clear-cut as that. When Danielle defends a client, an alibi from a lover or family member is never quite as good as one from a stranger or someone less close to a suspect. Caleb had said the building that housed Seminar's Chicago office required a sign in on the weekends, and all exits but the one directly across from the front desk were locked. But if anyone could get past a guard and into the suite, I'd think it'd be someone in Vincent's family. Which meant the police probably were looking closely at Gina.

"You don't know if the police talked to him yet?" I said.

"Haven't talked to him. We don't hook up that often."

Hook up or not, I would hope the guy would have called her if he learned from the police that her dad died. But maybe not.

"Is there anyone the police suspect?" I sipped my wine. I felt simultaneously grateful Gina's drinking might make her less likely to wonder what my questions had to do with Seminar and guilty for feeling grateful about that. "If you don't mind talking about it."

"Don't mind, but no idea. He was so horrible to so many people. Oh, wait, no, mostly horrible to me. And Karla. Nice, huh?"

"Nice" could refer to her dad treating her or Karla badly. Or both. I found it interesting that she used Karla's name and not a nickname. It might mean she felt closer to Karla or liked her better than her dad or other people in Seminar. Or that she didn't think her important enough to give her a nickname.

"What do you mean horribly?"

"Yelling about everything. Telling me I'm worthless. Telling Karla that, too, probably. Never spent much time with the two of them together."

The bartender appeared with the second bottle of Chianti and two glasses of ice water. He asked if we wanted food. Gina shook her head No, but I ordered a plate of Italian cookies. The sugar might counteract my fatigue and the wine's effects. Or just leave me both wired and exhausted when I finally got to bed, but I thought it would be good for Gina to eat something, too.

"What makes you say your dad treated Karla badly?" I said.

"The woman barely speaks. You meet her? All she ever did was laugh at his jokes, tell him he was brilliant. Couldn't say two words unless he said them first. Then she'd look at him like she was waiting for him to pat her head and say Good Girl."

I pictured the elegant, overwhelmed woman I'd met. It was hard to imagine her laughing, but she was grieving.

"Was his relationship with your mom different?"

I'd need to bring this back to Seminar soon. Wine or not, Gina was going to start wondering about me.

"Oh, yeah. They had real knock down drag out fights."

"Physical fights?"

"Screaming. Like, all the time. He married Karla so he'd have someone who'd go along with everything. Step to the Seminar drumbeat."

"So Seminar is all about enhancing lives," I said, "including relationships, but it sounds like your dad wasn't very good at it."

She poked her finger at my chest. "Said perfectly. Except he'd always tell me we had a great relationship. I just needed to learn to recognize it. Stop telling myself negative narratives about him. Something like that."

"At least my mother never tried that on me," I said. "It must make it harder that he's gone. With so much unresolved."

She downed nearly half her glass of wine in one swallow. "Well, it was never going to resolve, so there's that."

"Was his relationship with Karla better than with your mom?"

"For him? Sure. I mention that he cheated on her? Last year. Big Sis told me Karla bought his story that it happened once when he was superstressed. They took some couples relationship event and that was it."

So Vincent yelled at Karla a lot and cheated on her. That must interest the police as well. I doubted Caleb was their main focus despite his record, though it probably felt like that to him.

"Did you tell the police that?"

"They didn't ask. And I didn't want to mess up Karla's life more. She'd never hurt Dad. She was crazy about him."

I didn't think the two things were mutually exclusive.

A noisy group of middle-aged people in business suits clattered down the stairs and gathered at the far end of the bar.

"You know no one from Seminar so much as texted or sent me an email since D.O.D. died," Gina said. "Nice, huh? Not even Cuz."

"Cuz?"

"Frank Hernandez. You meet him? D.O.D.'s cousin. In Seminar almost as long as Dad. Known me since I was a kid. Something isn't it? Your dad's dead but don't feel bad. It's all Past."

"I met Frank, but I didn't know he was your dad's cousin," I said.

Frank had said they were very close, but not that they were family. Caleb also hadn't mentioned that.

It made me wonder if Frank was inheriting anything. With a second marriage, it's less likely people own everything jointly with a current spouse. Or leave everything to the spouse. I made a mental note to look at the probate court records for Vincent's will. If I was lucky, it had been filed in Cook County and would answer some questions.

The bartender set the cookies in front of us on his way to the end of the bar to deal with the new arrivals.

"Could it be no one contacted you because of this whole

Past concept I keep hearing about?" I said. "Vincent's gone so there's no reason to talk about the relationship?"

"You got me."

"This woman the other night, SaraBeth, called you hostile to Seminar. It's what made me look online to see if you'd posted about Seminar."

"Huh." Gina tapped her fingers on the bar in an uneven rhythm. "Don't think I know her. But hostile's one of their buzzwords. What'd she say I did?"

I relayed SaraBeth's comments.

"I told one person, the one next to me at the second event, that we both ought to ask for a refund. Not a whole bunch of people. And I sent D.O.D. one article. Like three years ago. Must've been Karla."

"What about her?"

"Bet she's been talking about me. She hates it when everyone doesn't live and breathe Seminar. Was royally pissed when Cuz's wife stopped taking events."

"She did?" I said. That was a surprise, and another thing Caleb hadn't told me about and Frank hadn't mentioned. For all its positive talk, Seminar sounded as full of conflict and dissatisfaction as any other company.

"Zipporah," Gina said. "Used to be diehard. Frank never talks about her or brings her around since she quit Seminar. Nice, huh? No one would tell me what happened. But I sort of miss her." Gina nibbled at a flat cookie shaped like a star.

"And your sister's not in Seminar?"

"Nope. You have sibs?"

"Two older sisters. One died before I was born," I said. "I was named for her. And all my life I heard how amazing she was."

It was something I told almost no one, but I felt like I owed it to Gina to share something of my personal life when she was spilling so much of hers. The few times I've had too much to drink and rambled, I've felt embarrassed after, especially if the other person was a lot more reserved.

"That sucks," Gina said.

"I worked through it. Mostly. With a lot of therapy."

"Well, Big Sis called Seminar a haven for WannaBes when I told her I was going."

"That's mean."

Gina shrugged. "Yeah, but once I went, I kinda agreed. She said if people spent half the time working that they do in Seminar they'd have more success."

On the basis of the first night alone, I agreed. But I wasn't sure that was enough to judge the program. I wound my hair around my fingers, thinking about what else Gina had written in her blog. "You said something about people pretending?"

"Sure. They all want to show how great Seminar works for them. It's like an in-person social media page. Everyone's living an excell — expo — whatever exceptional life but you. Wow. Maybe I'll slow down." She took a piece of almond biscotti.

I rested my elbows on the bar and filed the information away in my mind to consider in case it somehow connected to Vincent's death. Maybe a disgruntled participant got angry over money spent on never-ending courses without the promised success. The trouble was, there were far too many maybes for me to feel like I was doing much beyond wasting Caleb's mom's money and my time. But one week in my life was a small enough favor in the big scheme of things.

When I asked, Gina said she didn't know of any formal complaints against Seminar, like through the Better Business Bureau, or lawsuits. It was something I could check online, but state courts and state agencies are all separate. Meaning I'd need to sign into and search a different website for every single one. If there had been something major, I hoped she might have heard of it.

I also asked her who The Henchman was.

She swung her legs back and forth, making her barstool wobble. "Richard Messerly. D.O.D. always raved about him too. How dedicated he was. Unlike me. Moved from New York, left his law practice, came here to help start Seminar in Chicago."

Gina seemed to take any good thing Vincent said about anyone as an indirect criticism of her. It could be an example of what he'd meant by her creating narratives about him. But the idea must have come from somewhere.

She finished another glass of wine.

After that her answers to my questions morphed into rambling that reminded me of her blog posts only less structured. She told me Vincent met Seminar's founder, Scott Gary, three years after Gary started the organization. Before that, Gary worked as an individual life coach. Gina also thought he'd been a pharmaceutical sales representative, though she wasn't sure.

I tried asking more about Vincent's relationships with Scott, Richard, and Frank, and also about why there seemed to be no women or people of color at the top in Seminar, but she kept returning to her own relationship with her father. Not surprising with just losing him, and I listened without interrupting though it didn't tell me much that was helpful.

"Fair was a thing for Dad when it came to how people treated him," she said as she finished the last of the wine. "Didn't care when it came to how he treated me. Just said life is what you create. Create it. See it say it whatever. So that's what he thought of me. And you know what? Even in death he screwed me. Promised me my condo but now I have to go to Karla for everything."

She talked more about her dad's will, but it wasn't making

a lot of sense to me. I asked if she or her sister inherited any part of Seminar.

"Nope. Gary owns all of it. Too bad. Must generate a ton of cash."

"Through the Events?" I said. "I saw that long list on your blog."

"Yeah, cash cow. People stay forever. Take event after event. Like an addiction." She gestured toward the empty wine bottle. "I should talk. But these humans. Can't say a thing without Seminar words."

"I definitely noticed that." I glanced at the time on my phone. It was nearly ten. I had an early conference call, and Gina said she needed to leave for work at eight.

We asked for the bill, which Gina insisted she'd split with me, saying it wasn't fair for me to pay for two bottles of wine when she'd drunk most of it. While we waited for the bartender to come back I asked if she thought Frank's wife would talk to me.

"Uh-uh. No idea. Haven't seen her in years. Kinda miss her."

"Does it cause problems for Frank? His wife having left Seminar?"

She shrugged, tipping the bar stool a bit. I reached out a hand, but she grabbed the bar and steadied herself. "It's not like a cult. She just stopped coming to family things. Maybe sick of Seminar talk."

Everyone seemed to protest that Seminar wasn't a cult.

I finished the last cookie. "Caleb. Could he be friends with me if I'm not in Seminar?"

It had struck me that it could be he wanted to reconnect, but felt he could only do it if I were part of Seminar too. It probably wasn't his only motive for asking for my help, but it might be part of it.

"Sure. He could. Long as you don't come out against it like I did."

"And if I did?" Not that I was planning to, but I was curious how deep the rifts ran between Seminar people and those who opposed it.

"At first? He'd call you every day, trying to change your mind. Invite you to dinner. Bring Seminar people along."

"Seriously?"

"When they want people they pull out all the stops." She shifted, bumped her water glass. "You know what's crazy? Spent the last five years trying to convince dear old Dad I was Seminar material. Then I do, and he dies. Just like him. Nice, huh?"

I insisted on riding with Gina in the cab to her place before turning back toward mine, though we lived in opposite directions from the restaurant. She told me she often drank this much. But it was bad enough I'd picked her brain after her dad's death. I didn't want something happening to her because of it.

18

———

Tuesday, May 20, 9:48 a.m.

Wills are a matter of public record. A look at the online docket told me Vincent's had, in fact, been filed in the Circuit Court of Cook County. I finished my morning conference call early, and by ten a.m. I stood at one of the worn counters in the Probate Division on the tenth floor of the Daley Center. The tiled floors there are scuffed, and the air smells of the thick, sticky finger paste I remember from kindergarten. My favorite clerk wasn't in, so I gave my form to the skinny guy with red-framed glasses who always seemed rather put out to be asked for anything. That the will had been filed here told me the Chicago condo must have become Vincent's principal residence.

The clerk meandered along the metal shelves while talking on his cell phone, occasionally glancing in the general direction of the crammed-together brown accordion files. I took out my own phone and texted Caleb. I've found bringing other work at all times is the best way to stifle impatience at the Daley Center.

I told Caleb I wanted to talk to Zipporah, Frank Hernandez's wife, and asked if he knew how to reach her.

He texted back right away.

bad idea she will tell frank

But she used to be part of seminar could get good insight

never heard that you sure

Gina lenzi said

We had a back and forth about when and why I'd talked to Gina Lenzi. I asked again about Zipporah.

frank will think strange if she tells him you asking questions

I'll say I'm asking because thinking of going to an intermediate event

just wait talk to more people at the event

I took a breath before responding and consciously loosened my grip on my phone. I'd only been a lawyer for eight years, but already I was tired of clients trying to tell me how to handle cases. And this was a non-client I was helping as a favor.

Will do that too Want to talk to Scott Gary But want to hear from more outsiders Also hard to talk at event

told you small groups will B better

You can always leave it to the police if you don't like my approach

I hit Send and regretted it. There was no way I wasn't going to help Caleb, so I didn't like threatening.

But a minute later, as the clerk finally handed me a thin manila folder that already smelled of dust and had bent corners, my phone buzzed.

ok sorry but what do I say to frank if he asks why you asking questions

Remind him I'm a lawyer say you know what lawyers are like

I hate trading on lawyer stereotypes. Like any profession, the way "lawyers are" is as different as any one person to another. But people's views are formed by popular culture which loves to glorify lawyers or hate them or both. Might as well make good use of it.

———

TUESDAY, MAY 20, 10:15 A.M.

At the Starbucks on Washington Street across from City Hall I got a chai latte with an extra shot for more caffeine. Squeezed onto a seat at the counter along the window I breathed in the sweet, spicy scent as I read a photocopy of the will.

It made no mention of any shares Vincent held in his cousin Frank Hernandez's business. There might be a separate agreement that governed death of a shareholder. It listed no specific assets other than personal items like clothes and watches.

I'm not an estate lawyer, but it looked to me like what's called a pour over will. A lot of wealthy people create trusts while they're alive and transfer property into them. It keeps the assets private, as trusts aren't in the public record.

If set up the right way, it also avoids the estate tax Caleb and Richard spent so long talking about. And it simplifies the handling of the estate. A pour over will names an executor but typically directs that person to put any assets, except perhaps a few personal items, not already transferred to it into the trust upon death.

This will named Karla as the executor. Based on what Gina had said about now needing to go to Karla, I guessed Karla must be the trustee as well.

Gina's comment suggested that Vincent had owned, or at least co-owned, Gina's condo. Also that if Gina knew about the trust before her dad's death, she'd all the same believed, until she saw the will, that her condo would remain separate from it.

Caleb texted that if I insisted on contacting Zipporah he wouldn't try to stop me, but he didn't have a phone number or email for her. I doubted Frank would provide it if I asked. I returned the will to my shoulder bag. Without the trust, it didn't tell me if anyone benefitted from Vincent's death.

On my phone, I searched the Internet for Zipporah Hernandez. Like me, she kept most of her social media accounts private. Or non-existent, I wasn't sure which.

At last I found a professional listing on Linked In. She was an account manager with a mid-sized ad agency in Austin, Texas. Her photo showed a Black woman with a wide face looking directly into the camera. Her gray-streaked hair was gathered on top of her head and held by a violet band. She wore a red blazer over a collared white shirt.

I started an email to her business email address and then deleted it.

Sometimes talking is better.

———

TUESDAY, MAY 20, 10:35 A.M.

Back at my office I tried Zipporah's line and got voicemail. But I had some luck in another way. I share the office suite with a dozen other people, most of them attorneys. I'd emailed all asking for connections to Seminar. The suite landlord responded while I was calling Zipporah's number.

I longed to head down the hall to ask questions right now, but instead I asked him if we could talk in a couple hours. I needed to do some legal work first. For the next hour I scrambled to finalize answers to interrogatories — written questions the parties exchange as a lawsuit moves toward trial. The case involved a client accused of violating trade secret laws and poaching employees of the plaintiff.

My clients, the two partners of the firm, hadn't done so, exactly, but some of their choices when they'd started their own company walked pretty close to the line. Both had to sign the answers and swear they were true. They were so bad about returning my calls and emails that we were already two months behind. We had a court hearing tomorrow on the other side's motion to require us to answer.

I spent forty minutes arguing with them about what they could and couldn't say based on the information they'd given me and another twenty on digital files they claimed they'd only recently remembered existed. Finally we reached language we could all live with, and I emailed them documents to print, sign, and have notarized.

While I waited for them to send me one more file to review, I tried Zipporah's line again. This time I left a voicemail: "You don't know me, but my name is Quille. I live in Chicago, and a friend is encouraging me to get involved in Seminar. I heard from a mutual acquaintance that you used to be devoted to it and changed your mind. I can't go into detail now, but it would mean a lot to me if I could talk with you for just a few minutes."

It was nearly three when I emailed and snail mailed the Interrogatories to the other side and told him we were still getting some electronic documents together to send him the following week. I also reminded the clients by email that they needed to sign an affidavit saying they were turning over everything the other side asked for. That drew an email telling me there actually was one more laptop to check.

Some days I have more trouble with my own clients than with the other side.

I hung up and looked for Sam, the red-haired bicyclist and attorney who rents the suite from the building and subleases to the rest of us. I found him in the suite's kitchen. Most of us call him Mensa Sam, though not to his face, because of his habit of shoehorning a mention of his membership in the high I.Q. society into every conversation. He'd probably be flattered if he knew about the nickname.

I dropped into a chair at the end of the long lunch table that doubled as a conference table in a pinch.

"Bad day?" he said.

"Clients," I said.

"Root beer? I bought more Dang!"

"More sugar is definitely welcome."

Unlike some landlords, Sam rarely bought lunch for the office or did anything to say thanks for being good tenants. But he'd been on a gourmet root beer kick lately, ordering different brands over the past month for all of us to try. Dang! was caffeine free, so I wasn't in danger of it keeping me awake later on top of the chai.

I popped the bottle open and took a sip, savoring the slightly sweet but not too sugary taste and fizz. I rarely drink soda, so when I do I especially enjoy it. "So you know someone who's a Seminar Drop Out?"

"If that's what they call someone who used to go to their sessions and quit in disgust. It's this woman I met years ago at the D.C. regional Mensa gathering. She used to live in Austin, Texas, and paid a whole lot for these sessions or classes or whatever they are. Sounds like a whacked out group."

"In what way?"

"The founder claims he's the most intelligent man who ever lived and he's got the secret to complete fulfillment or wholeness or something." Sam opened his own bottle of root beer and joined me at the table, turning two chairs to face each other so he could stretch his long legs onto the second. He must be planning to leave soon, as he was already in his black spandex biking clothes.

"That fits with what I've learned so far."

Sam snorted. "The most intelligent man who ever lived? My friend said he failed the Mensa test."

"How does she know?"

"Apparently it's a big deal in the Mensa grapevine. So what's the guy like?"

"I haven't met him. Yet." I drank more of the root beer.

"Probably not that smart. If he really were, he wouldn't need to run around telling people he's the most intelligent man ever."

I refrained from making any comments about kettles and pots. "Why did your friend leave Seminar?"

"Oh, also, there's some scandal about the guy," Sam said. "I didn't get details, but she said she'd talk to you." He handed me one of his business cards with a name and phone number on the back. "She doesn't want you to email or text. Worried about people forwarding things. She said call. It's a landline. And she wants you to call from a landline."

"Is she worried about someone listening in on cell phones?"

"Probably. Hackers can intercept them. You think she can help your case?"

"No case. This is personal research for a friend."

"Because she sounded a little paranoid. Probably not the best choice if you're looking for a witness."

"It's personal," I said.

"Also, she's in Austin and pretty broke, so it's not like she can travel here for a deposition or trial on her own dime."

I often wonder how Sam ever wins a trial, he's so bad at listening to the answers to his questions. But most of his cases settle, so maybe it didn't matter.

I stood. "No depositions. No trial. But thank you very much for the info. I owe you one."

"Next tax season I'll take you up on it."

I couldn't tell how serious he was, but if he needed a favor, I'd reciprocate. Sam had gotten on my nerves when I'd started sharing an office with Danielle, particularly his tendency to not listen to any side of a conversation but his own, but he'd grown on me a bit. He was always willing to answer questions about personal injury law or tap into his networks of contacts. And after I'd referred him a case of an actor friend who'd been hit while riding her bike along Lake Michigan he'd finally realized I was a lawyer, not only an accountant. He'd sent me a new tax client at the end of last year.

It had turned out to be a pretty good relationship after all.

———

Tuesday, May 20, 4:55 p.m.

Dinner was a power bar, an apple, and the rest of the root beer at my desk while I finished researching a motion due next week. I'd gotten no answer at Mensa Sam's friend's number. I'd left a voicemail with my office landline. Leaving the cell number wouldn't have done me much good anyway, as I was headed straight to Seminar from the office.

She called half an hour before I needed to leave.

19

TUESDAY, MAY 20, 5:12 P.M.

"Sam vouched for you, so I'll tell you what I know," Sam's friend said after introducing herself as Angela. She refused to give me her last name, and she hesitated so long before saying the first that I felt sure she'd made it up on the spot. "But you gotta promise you won't say you heard any of this from me."

"I won't," I said.

"First, and this isn't the worst of it, but it's what I know the most about — Seminar bankrupted my son. Literally. Because of Attending and Spending."

"What's that?" I said, though I could guess.

"Scott Gary's big strategy. My son — I won't tell you his name, not even his first. I don't want to get him in trouble with them again. But he kept rising in Seminar. Telling me he's progressing, moving up the Steps, they call it. After a while I figured out that just means taking course after course."

"Courses meaning Events?" I said. "Or something else?"

"I don't know events. Courses. This was six, seven years

ago. A course took a week. Every night for a week. Plus some party after to celebrate finishing. You had to bring someone who might sign up for a course. Someone new to Seminar."

It sounded pretty much like the Event/Celebration format Seminar used now.

"Why did he take so many courses?"

"We lived in Austin at the time. He took one every other week. As soon as he finished one, they'd start pushing him to take the next. And then they got him to pay for a year's worth in advance. Discounted from what he'd pay by the course, but expensive. He maxed every credit card he had, and he had eight. Eventually couldn't make all the payments and filed for bankruptcy."

"Is he back on his feet?" I said.

"Barely. He still has student loan debt. Can't get rid of that in bankruptcy."

"Did he have debt problems before Seminar?" I said. "Besides student loans?"

Most of my clients who ran into credit problems didn't do it in isolation, absent some sort of major medical emergency or damage to their home where the insurance wasn't enough. The son might have spent on clothes or cars or gambling if not Seminar.

"He had some balances on his cards. But they pushed him over the edge."

"Do you know how much he spent total?" I asked.

"Over two hundred thousand dollars," she said.

I dropped my pen. "Two hundred thousand." I calculated in my head. "How is that a discount?"

"It includes about six months of courses before he bought the one-year package and two months after. He tried for five years to pay it off. On most cards he owed more at the end than when he started."

I guessed he'd been making minimum payments on all the cards.

My first accounting teacher made us all calculate the results of doing that in a hypothetical scenario and they were daunting. If my Gram hadn't already drilled into me the dangers of debt for anything other than an asset you're expecting to increase in value, that exercise would have put me off revolving credit card debt.

"And what was his income? If you don't mind my asking."

"He made less than forty thousand a year. Those credit card companies had no business giving him all those cards."

I shook my head. People have to be responsible for themselves, but I think credit card companies share some blame, maybe more blame, when that sort of thing happens. Whoever issued the later cards to him hadn't looked closely at his total available credit compared to income or hadn't cared. They'd probably collected more than enough interest in the long run to make it worth it despite the bankruptcy.

As for Seminar, while companies don't have to make sure a person can afford their services, it seemed like a personal growth company ought to pay attention to that.

I looked at the notes I'd been writing.

"Why are you worried about getting your son in trouble by talking to me?" I said.

As Sam had said, paranoid might be a better word. Not sharing her number or name, not talking or texting on a cell phone. But she might have good reason for all those behaviors, and if she did, Caleb had gotten mixed up in something very dangerous.

"They hounded him day and night to take more courses when he stopped. Showed up at his work."

"Threatening him?"

"No. But his boss got tired of the phone calls and people waiting outside the building. He got fired."

I wished I could talk to the son myself. If he hadn't wanted to admit to his mother that he wanted to keep taking courses, or if he'd gotten fired for some other reason he didn't want to admit, he might have exaggerated the pressure on him. But I had to think if he'd really spent that much someone was doing the hard sell.

"You mentioned two things. What was the other?"

"While my son was attending, he met another young man whose friend also took tons of courses and ran up his credit cards. But he decided to fight them. Reported them to the state."

"Texas?"

"No, New York," Angela said.

"But this was someone your son met in Austin?"

"Yes. The person my son knew moved to Austin from New York. That person knew the young man — I think it might have been an old roommate — who made the complaint in New York. Anyway, a month after he reported Seminar, he disappeared."

I circled New York on my legal pad. I prefer writing notes rather than typing because people can hear keys clicking over the phone and think you're not listening. "Disappeared meaning what?"

"Abandoned his apartment and everything in it. Never said anything to his family or friends, just packed a single bag and took off."

"And you don't think he just wanted a change of scene."

"My son's friend didn't think so. He thought someone from Seminar did something to him. Killed him, kidnapped him, scared him enough that he took off. Which is why I'm so careful."

The time on my laptop said 5:32. The Thompson Center is a mile from my office, so I needed nearly twenty minutes to walk there. During rush hour a cab would barely be quicker than walking.

"Had he ever taken off before? The roommate?"

"I don't know," Angela said. "And before you ask, I'm not asking my son for his friend's information. It may be paranoid, but I'm not risking anything being traced back to him."

She wasn't sure, but she thought this all happened about eight years ago and that the man who disappeared had lived in Queens. At least it gave me a starting place to look for state-specific complaints against Seminar. I wished I knew if Angela's son's friend really knew the person who disappeared. He might have heard about it from someone else who knew someone else whose friend disappeared. An urban legend.

Maybe.

Tuesday, May 20, 6:02 p.m.

Frank Hernandez took the stage less than a minute after I slid into my seat. Since Scott Gary wouldn't be here until Friday, and I'd already talked with Richard and his partner a lot at the Celebration, I'd asked Caleb to be sure I got in Frank's small group tonight. The large man wore a sport coat in light caramel over an olive green buttoned down shirt and khakis. The stark fluorescent lighting made him look a bit pale and ill, but that type of lighting flatters no one.

No dry facts and figures tonight. Instead, Frank introduced a short, round woman in a flowered dress and flat shoes.

Her voice trembled as she said, "When I came to my first Event, I hadn't spoken to my father in thirty-three years."

Only half-listening as the woman on stage explained how she'd taken full responsibility for her father having thrown her out of the house at age fifteen, I twisted around to look for Caleb. I hadn't seen him when I'd rushed in. He stood in the back of the room along with Richard Messerly. Lauren, in her assigned seat, wiggled her fingers at me.

"And so I started the Interpersonal Connections Event," the woman in the flowered dress said, "believing my father didn't deserve to have me in his life. And ended by calling him to tell him I'd been living in Past, stuck in this narrative where he threw me out of the house. When really he helped me grow up and move on to the next phase of life. That was a year ago. And guess what? He's here today, at his very first Event. Dad, stand up!"

I gripped my green placard, thinking I must have misheard the woman's age at the time her dad threw her out. I'd only been a year older, sixteen, when my parents moved back to Edwardsville to be nearer the original Q.C.'s grave. That had felt awful enough. But I moved one apartment over to live with my Gram, who'd more or less raised me anyway. This woman, from what I caught of her story, needed to trek across the country on her own to an older sister who got her involved in the sex trade.

A man in the front row, using a cane, struggled to his feet. He turned to face the crowd. His narrow frame and sunken cheeks suggested he might be ill. A smile spread across his face and his whole body swayed as he waved at us.

Everyone applauded him, and he waved again and smiled.

My hands stayed still. Given her father's age, if the woman wanted to reconnect I supposed it was good she'd done it before it was too late. And if she was willing to pretend it had somehow been her fault, it must be worth it to her. But in no universe would I clap for a man who'd thrown his fifteen-year-old daughter's belongings out of the house and changed the locks.

TUESDAY, MAY 20, 7:25 P.M.

For what I guessed was about an hour, Caleb and Richard led volunteers through exercises where they free associated and, with some strong hints that reminded me of leading questions in cross-examination, linked current problems to childhood memories. Frank announced we'd break into small groups for the rest of the night and directed us to leave the auditorium.

I flattened myself against the auditorium wall to let the crowd pass and waited for Caleb. In a quiet voice, I asked him about Attending and Spending. When he said he didn't know what it was, I explained it the way Angela had to me.

Caleb's shoulders stiffened and he slowed his steps so we dropped farther behind everyone. "Is this more Gina Lenzi?"

"No," I said.

"Or Zipporah?"

We were the only ones left in the auditorium. "I haven't been able to reach her. It doesn't matter who. Are you telling me that's not one of Scott Gary's policies?"

"Look, we hope people will take more than one Event or we wouldn't offer a whole series of them. But no one at Seminar wants anyone to go bankrupt. People come back because Seminar exponentially enhances their lives. Makes them more effective."

"But if someone spends hundreds of thousands on Events, that's great for Seminar's bottom line," I said.

"Sure, just like it's great for yours if someone spends that in legal fees. But it doesn't mean you want your clients to go bankrupt."

"I didn't say you wanted them to," I said.

We reached the hallway. Lauren waited near the sign in

table. Caleb thanked her for sending him the name of her client who rediscovered Seminar through her.

The three of us stepped onto the up escalator. The nearest group of participants had already exited the building.

"So Seminar doesn't follow up with people who stop taking Events?" I said.

"That's different than what you said before. We follow up. We want to see why they weren't satisfied. Try to improve. You must do that when a client drops you."

"I've never hung out in a lobby to ambush a former client," I said as we reached street level and stepped outside. "Or called repeatedly."

The black and white sculpture that stood near the northwest corner loomed over us.

"I'm sure that's an exaggeration," Caleb said.

We crossed Randolph first, then Clark, and headed south, skirting Daley Plaza. The rest of the group had already reached the Temple Building across the street, where Seminar had its offices.

I told Caleb what I'd heard about the young man who disappeared in New York.

"That's an old rumor Scott's ex-wife started," Caleb said. "During their divorce. There's nothing to it but people keep repeating it."

"Does she live here? His ex?"

"New York."

We'd reached the Temple Building. When the twenty-three-story skyscraper was built in the 1920s it was the tallest building in Chicago. Now newer buildings dwarf it, but its spire and ornate gothic exterior make it a landmark. I'd often studied its features through the Daley Center's plate glass windows while waiting for clients or for court to start.

It houses a Methodist church on the ground floor and a chapel on the top directly below the steeple. The church's pastor lives in an apartment on one of the top floors. The rest is mainly law offices and businesses. I'd looked at two different offices for rent there before I started my firm. I loved the hallways with their marble floors and glass office doors with frosted panes. Like I was in an old-time law movie. It was too pricey for me, though, being downtown and directly across from the state courthouses.

"We should meet and go over things," I said. "I don't like catching you in minutes here and there."

In the marble lobby some Seminar participants were signing in at the security desk.

Caleb and I compared schedules, with me relying on memory because Seminar still had my phone. We agreed on ten a.m. Thursday morning.

"How about the Rock 'n Roll McDonald's?" Caleb said.

He meant the McDonald's that comprised an entire block of River North across from the Hard Rock Café and the Rainforest Café. It had once had oversized Golden Arches outside, double-decker seating inside, and tons of rock music memorabilia. That building, though, had been torn down.

"You remain singularly unobservant," I said.

Caleb had always been good at noticing people, but not so good with his surroundings. Following his blocking — his designated physical movements on stage — had truly challenged him as an actor.

"What are you talking about? The McDonald's is still there. I walked by the other day."

"Did you look at it? It's McDonald's but it's not rock 'n' roll. It's a giant glass building with plants across the entire second level."

He grinned as he signed in. "All the more reason to meet there so I can check it out. I'll buy you a vanilla shake."

"You're on."

It was the one thing where I preferred vanilla to chocolate. It was nice that he'd remembered.

The Seminar office suite upstairs looked far less glamorous inside than the building common areas. Light gray carpet covered the floors. The center of the space was empty, with armless padded folding chairs set in a large circle around it. Beyond the layer of chairs were cubicles made of gray plastic. Beyond those, offices lined the back wall.

It struck me as a surprisingly uninspired space for a company dedicated to enhancing people's lives.

Frank Hernandez motioned to me. "Quille, over here." He ushered me into an office that the nameplate next to it said was his.

Caleb took Lauren in a different direction.

20

A guy with stringy long hair who smelled like stale sweat sat in a tall leather chair next to me. He asked to speak first. The chairs were arranged in a circle, and the back of his rested against the front of Frank's desk.

Despite the unpleasant scent, I'd taken the chair next to the man because it was angled in a way that allowed me a view of the desktop, the credenza along the side wall, and the corkboard on the side wall.

"This is my third Event," the man said. "I came to Seminar originally because I struggled with chronic back pain. My chiropractor thought it was a mindset issue. It got better after my first two Events. But last week I moved wrong, and it's like I'm right back to Square One. It's a constant battle. That's why I called Frank to see if he could squeeze me in for a refresher."

A guy with an owl tattoo on his shoulder slapped his knees in drum riffs. "What were you thinking about when it happened?"

The man's face scrunched. "I bent down to get my keys

after I dropped them. Wham, sharp pain in my low back, left side. Like always."

"Like always." Frank paused between the two words and after, letting them hang in the air. "Chronic. Constant. And you wonder why your back pain returns? It's good you came back. Remember, words have meaning, and words have effects. Listen to your words."

The man's shoulders relaxed. "You're right. I'm so glad I came back."

"Is that something you think is important?" I said to Frank. "People returning to Event after Event?"

He smiled. "The heart of education is repetition."

It was certainly a sentiment a lot of teachers agreed with. As a kid I'd spent the first couple months of each grade school year running lines for my latest play in my head or drawing endless doodles or both as we went over what we'd already learned the year before. I'd felt like a prisoner on parole when I was able to home school and learn at my own pace during my high school years.

"Do you think anyone ever masters Seminar concepts and doesn't need to return?"

Frank sat forward, his chair tilting. "We're all always evolving. Something in one Event might not speak to you because of where you are in life, but a month or a year later, it enhances your life exponentially. For example, I noticed you didn't applaud our first speaker tonight."

I sat straighter. Out of nearly a hundred people in a crowded auditorium, Frank had watched what I was doing. But perhaps he'd watched everyone he knew would be in his small group.

"It was the woman's father who was being applauded, not the speaker," I said. "I didn't see why we ought to cheer him for being a terrible parent."

"Ah, see, you got drawn in by the narrative the woman

constructed when she was only fifteen and carried around with her."

"But her father did throw her out."

"No, he put her things on the lawn and changed the locks. She called it throwing her out."

"I don't see any other thing to call it," I said.

"You heard her. Those actions helped her become the successful woman she is today. She chooses to focus on that now, and it enhances her life to do that and include her father in it. Is there a similar challenge you experienced?"

I gripped the sides of my chair seat. I didn't need Seminar techniques to understand that I identified with the woman's fifteen-year-old self. And that I still felt angry at my mom for being mostly absent from my life and my dad for doing little to fill the gap. But I couldn't let any of that distract me from why I was here.

The key was to get information from Frank while still playing the part of Caleb's friend who'd paid a small fortune because she thought Seminar would help her.

"I grew up hearing about how my middle sister, who died before I was born, sang and acted and modeled and would have been a star." With the door shut, the office felt warm and stuffy. My neck sweated under the weight of my hair. "Nothing I did could ever match that. Have you experienced something similar?"

I purposely adopted his phrasing to show I'd been listening and absorbing his points.

"We're not here to talk about me," he said, "but about how to enhance your life."

"Yes, but maybe I could learn from your experience coming to Seminar through your cousin Vincent. And now he's gone. Did you ever feel he overshadowed you?"

Frank blinked, and his smile faltered. The rest of the

group members sat forward in their chairs, suggesting the family relationship might be new information.

"That wasn't my experience, but I'm interested in why that idea resonated with you specifically. You and I can talk after tonight's session." Frank shifted in his chair, spreading his arms wider as if to encompass the group. "Who else wants to share a childhood narrative?"

The drummer guy waved his green placard. As he and the other group members spoke, I studied the corkboard behind Frank. Yellow cards with Seminar phrases printed in black marker were pinned all over it, like an analog word cloud. When we'd walked in, I'd asked about it, and Frank said he'd written them out to inspire himself throughout the day.

I doubted they held any hidden meaning that would give clues to Vincent's death or Caleb's future in Seminar. The terms might help me find more information on Seminar, though, so I did my best to memorize them. I grouped them in my mind by first letter. Starting with the As, I recited the words silently to memorize them.

I was on the Ts when it hit me that everyone was standing to file out of the room. It must be ten o'clock, and we were being released at last.

Frank rested his hand on my shoulder. "Caleb shouldn't have told you about the family connection. We want participants to focus on Seminar concepts, not on the personal lives of the Coordinators."

"Good point," I said. "I'm sorry I mentioned it in the group. Is it something that you ever felt, though? That Vincent overshadowed you?"

He rested his crossed arms on his belly and studied me. "I can't say I did. He invested in my business early on, and what I learned in Seminar helped me grow it exponentially. Seminar has been there through every challenge since then."

"Is it the same without Vincent?"

"Nothing's ever the same," he said. "Another reason to live in Now and leave Past behind."

———

WEDNESDAY, MAY 21, 7:25 A.M.

"Is this business or personal?"

It took me a second to answer. I'd gotten into the office early and called Zipporah's line, figuring she might be more likely to answer if in her business, like mine, things tended to be quiet before eight a.m. That someone else answered her direct line this early surprised me. In most companies, it's rare to have an assistant or receptionist in before eight-thirty. Or, these days, to have one at all.

"Both in a way," I said. "I met her husband recently. I'm also an attorney, but this isn't about a legal issue."

I sipped my extra-large Earl Grey tea from the café downstairs.

The woman asked my name. After I told her, the line went quiet.

Once I became an attorney, I discovered that despite how many people hold negative views about lawyers, being one gets me taken more seriously than being an actor. Or an accountant, for that matter. With an accountant people tend to assume you know numbers and nothing else. As a lawyer, people think you can fix almost everything. I can't, but it doesn't matter.

It was hard to say if my lawyer card worked this time because the same woman got back on the line.

"You called before," she said. "Mentioning Seminar. Zipporah's not the person to ask about Seminar."

Her words sounded clipped. The way I sound when I'm about to hang up on a salesperson.

"In this case maybe she is." I stood and walked to my office windows. I was wearing the headset for my landline, so she'd still be able to hear me. "A friend got me involved. He's worried about what people there think of him. I'm hoping for her thoughts as someone who left."

"Why? Is your friend thinking about leaving?"

"No, but I've heard disturbing things about how Seminar treats people who do. I want to make sure nothing happens to him if I end up rejecting Seminar."

It wasn't exactly true, but it was close enough. It shouldn't get Caleb in trouble, I hoped, if everything I said got back to someone like Frank Hernandez or Karla Lenzi.

I heard a sigh. "This is Zipporah's sister, Jacinda."

"Oh." I sat in my chair again. I supposed the two sisters might both work at the agency, but that didn't explain Jacinda answering Zipporah's phone.

"Your friend, he didn't tell you why Zipporah left Seminar?" Jacinda said.

"He doesn't know," I said.

"What's his name? When did he join?"

I noticed she referred to it as joining, contrary to Seminar's party line.

"Caleb Jackson. He got involved about three years ago."

"After my sister left. So how did you hear about her?"

I heard keys clicking in the background. Maybe she had access to some sort of database where she could check on Seminar people. Or she was taking notes on the conversation to relay to Zipporah.

"I went to a party — what they call a Celebration. I met Frank. Another person I talked to, someone critical of Seminar, said Zipporah used to belong. Or, not belong, I guess that's the wrong word. Used to take part in Events."

"Oh, they're big on wrong words, that's certain," Jacinda said.

"I got that impression," I said.

"Someone critical of Seminar. Gina Lenzi?"

"I don't want to say any names. All I can tell you is I've talked to a number of people."

"If it was Gina, she should know why Zipporah left."

I rocked my chair back and forth. "I don't think anyone knows."

"Frank does. So did Vincent."

"You know Vincent's dead?" I said.

"We heard."

"I don't think he or Frank told anyone why Zipporah left."

"Figures."

I scribbled a few notes on a pad of paper. "Why do you say that?"

After another few seconds, she sighed again. "My sister was diagnosed with breast cancer."

"Oh, no. I'm so sorry," I said.

"In Seminar, you know what happens when you get a diagnosis like that?" Jacinda said.

I straightened in my chair, mind racing through last night's session and Gina's critiques of Seminar. "They tell you it's your fault?"

"So you've been to an Event."

"Only part of one. But I didn't really think that was the point of all of it."

"Oh, it is," Jacinda said.

"How long ago was she diagnosed?"

"Five years ago. She left Seminar two years after."

That timeframe almost overlapped with Caleb's. Or maybe it had. Yet no one told Caleb or Gina about it. These people really didn't talk about anything in the past or people who left.

"Is she — what's her prognosis?"

I heard myself resorting to medical-type language. That way of distancing ourselves from pain and death. Jacinda didn't do the same.

"Dying. She's dying. And it's Seminar's fault."

21

WEDNESDAY, MAY 21, 7:33 A.M.

Jacinda told me she was at the office to clean out Zipporah's things, as she couldn't work anymore. Hadn't been able to for the last month.

I shut my eyes. I'd never met Zipporah, but in my mind I saw the vital woman in the photo in a hospital bed.

"How? What did the Seminar people do?"

"Did you get to the See It, Speak It, Say It concept?"

"No."

The idea reminded me of something else, though. I'd played a preacher's daughter in a play when I was thirteen. Part of it was about the prosperity gospel, a running theme of which was speaking what you wanted in life into being. The idea was that God delivers blessings and prosperity to those with enough faith. So the wealthier you were in the world of the play, the more God had smiled on you. More money meant you were a better person.

But nothing about Seminar so far suggested it had a religious nature.

"No, I suppose you wouldn't," Jacinda said. "It's all a big

secret. You need to go up the steps or however they say it to hear about it. Zipporah never told me about it until she began having so many problems."

"Is it like affirmations or vision boards?"

I'd heard of both as an actor. A lot of my friends wrote out their goals as if they'd already achieved them or added photos of what they wanted to real or electronic bulletin boards. I've always been more of a facts and figures person, but it inspired some people.

Others seemed to get lost in a world of hope and aspiration and forget to work for what they wanted.

Jacinda snorted. "Vision boards on steroids if it worked the way they say. You see what you want in your mind. Like a vacation home in Aruba or a perfect body or a bigger balance in your checking account. Then you speak it in your mind in detail. Then you say it to other people as if it's already real."

"That was supposed to cure cancer?" I said.

"They dress it up some way or other, but yes. People in Seminar said that to her more or less. Frank said that to her in those words."

"He mentioned something about imagining things, but he didn't say anything like that. No wonder she left Seminar."

"Any sane person would. Though it took her a while."

"What tipped her over?"

"Me. That's what Seminar says and for once it's right. Because at first she believed it. She deferred any treatment, saying she didn't need chemo or radiation or surgery. She just needed to do a better job seeing and speaking and saying. That's what those people told her. With Frank's support. She went to Events constantly. Every penny she made, and Frank made, went right into Seminar's coffers."

"And it didn't help."

"When she went back for a follow up mammogram the

tumor had grown. Faster than expected. And do you know what Frank did? Insisted she go to more Events."

"And did she?"

"Yes. But she had a mastectomy too. After I sat her down and told her she needed medical treatment before it was too late. She didn't tell anyone in Seminar except Frank. They both pretended she got very busy at work or something and couldn't get to Events."

My tea had grown cold. I drank a little more anyway. "Was Frank supportive of her treatment?"

"If you call insisting she be cheerful all the time supportive. Any time she felt afraid or low, he said we needed to 'jolly her out of it.' He'd tell jokes or insist we see a funny movie or talk about happy things. At first I went along. It's not like feeling sad or anxious was going to help her get better. But she finally told me it was exhausting. All her energy went into putting on a happy face. Not for herself but for me, for him. For the other Seminar people when she did see them."

The line between feeling your feelings and wallowing in them is one I've always struggled to walk. After Marco's death I felt myself sinking. I fought it by staying busy, working, and constantly watching old TV shows or playing audio so I never had to think. I was afraid of ending up like my mom, who cycled through mild to severe depression regularly and struggled with anxiety.

But I didn't start feeling better until I finally let myself feel bad.

"Are they still together?" I said.

"On paper. Zipporah moved in with me. But she agreed to stay married so Frank wouldn't need to redo all the relationship events."

I tapped the paper with my pen. "Why would he need to do that?"

"When you get to the advanced levels if you have a

setback, like an illness or divorce, they make you take certain Events over."

"Make you?"

"All right. They don't literally make anyone do anything. But people move up to levels, they call them Steps with a capital S. It's a status thing. Maybe a money thing, too. Show you're doing so well you can afford it. All good for Seminar's bottom line."

"Attending and Spending."

"You heard of that too."

"Yes. But I got the impression it was an insider thing. Not something all the people who come to the Seminar Events hear."

"You're right. And they don't call it that anymore. Frank told Zipporah by mistake once. It sort of slipped out, and he made her promise not to repeat it, though he said it's a joke. That nothing in Seminar is about making money."

"Sure," I said. "That's why it's organized as a private, for-profit corporation. And why they're so good at sales techniques."

I'd been able to discover that much about Seminar through the databases I subscribe to. But because it was a private corporation, the only other information I learned was that Scott Gary was the founder and president.

"You got it," Jacinda said. "So if Seminar knew Frank and Zipporah had split, he'd lose Steps. And he'd need to start over with a Basic Event. They'd already spent a fortune on extra Events for Zipporah. At first I told her who cares, let Frank spend, but it didn't help her for him to be broke. There's a lot not covered by insurance, and he at least keeps chipping in."

My mom and dad struggled with similar insurance issues. She didn't do well on a lot of the traditional anti-anxiety medications or anti-depressants. The ones that worked best were out of my dad's insurance plan even when he had a regular job. And now that he was self-employed again, like me, his deductibles were massive.

"At least he does that," I said.

"Don't give him a medal. He's doing fine. It's less the money for someone like him and more that it's embarrassing to redo Events. Everyone in Seminar who knew him would know. And he'd be banned from being a leader or whatever they call it while he was doing it."

"So even if he redid Events he might not be considered to be on the Expert step?"

"Right. That's a quality judgment."

"Who makes it?"

"I don't know who does now. Scott Gary, I suppose. But before he died, it would have been Vincent."

22

———

I got into the courtroom just as my case was being called. I'd been lucky and caught the Number 22 bus a minute after I stepped out of my office building. It drops me right across from the Daley Center.

"Your Honor, I apologize for the delay," I said when it was my turn. "My clients travel quite a bit and have only a one-person office staff. They've been doing their best to search the last ten years of records for everything plaintiff asked for. I've been sending documents on a rolling basis, and we've provided everything save for what's on one last old laptop of a secretary who left four years ago. It was in a storage room, and my clients only realized yesterday that it was there."

As I spoke, pain needles jabbed the back of my head. I gripped the ledge in front of me where attorneys can rest their notes when talking to the judge. Sometimes my migraines start gradually, giving me time to take three Advil to try to head them off. Other times, like today, they hit out of nowhere. When I'd been acting, I'd been able to hold them off by sheer force of will for an hour or two. On breaks I'd breathe deep and imagine the air in my lungs expanding into my head and cushioning my brain. But at some point the pain always took over.

"Judge, counsel has gotten two extensions already, and now we learn there's yet another laptop her clients 'forgot' about. This is exactly the kind of shady behavior that led to this lawsuit."

The lawyer continued in that vein. Each time his voice rose it felt like he was driving a stake through my forehead. I struggled not to clench my jaw, which would worsen the pain.

When he finished, fighting a wave of nausea, I answered as to the only part I'd really retained: "I object to the 'yet another' characterization, Your Honor. As I said, I've been sending data and documents on a rolling basis."

The judge gave me two weeks, which was better than nothing.

The second I got out of the courtroom I hurried toward the Women's Room. Each click of my heels on the floor sounded like a gunshot in my head. Cupping my hands under the faucet for water, I swallowed three Advil. A second later I was in the stall, vomiting my breakfast and the Advil.

I leaned against the metal wall, head pounding, until I felt sure I wouldn't throw up again. I'd try again later with my prescription medication, but right now clearly nothing was going to stay in my system.

The sunlight felt like needles stabbing my forehead. I flagged a cab and went straight to my condo. An excruciating fifteen minutes later I lay fully dressed on my bed, an ice pack under my neck. I'd closed the blinds. I told the voice assistant on my phone to play classical music, but the strings sounded like they were wailing, and I turned it off.

Before court I'd texted Caleb that I had some questions

about Zipporah. If he answered, though, I didn't know it. Looking at my phone screen caused stabbing pain behind my eyes, so I abandoned it.

I practiced deep breathing and focused on the ice, imagining it drawing the pain down from my head and out my neck. Eventually I crawled to the refrigerator, drank some milk, and took my prescription medication. It made me slightly loopy and only dulled my migraine rather than getting rid of it. But it was better than nothing.

After lying down for another half hour I told my phone to text Caleb that I couldn't make it that night to Seminar but I'd see him in the morning. I was lucky compared to a lot of migraine sufferers I'd met in online forums. My worst ones rarely lasted more than eighteen hours. After texting Lauren as well, I finally drifted to sleep. In my dreams my head still throbbed and I heard multiple texts coming into my phone, but eventually everything went black.

―――――

THURSDAY, MAY 22, 7:08 A.M.

My head, neck, and shoulders felt achy in the morning, but after a long shower with the water extra hot I felt almost normal again.

My phone showed Caleb texted me eight times as I lay flattened. One said he'd found something he really wanted my input on. The other six urged me to attend the Event despite my migraine, saying people would be suspicious if I didn't and that I'd made a commitment. I shoved the phone aside and poured myself some orange juice. Caleb knew what migraines did to me.

At my office, after I caught up on the email I'd missed, I searched Karla Lenzi's social media, especially anything with photos showing where she usually went. She hadn't called me. Other than Scott Gary, of the five people in the office the night Vincent died, I'd spent the least time with her. I still didn't plan to question her as if she were a witness in court. But if I could run into her, maybe I'd be able to draw her out without upsetting her.

Before Vincent's death, almost every day Karla posted lattes with swirled designs in the foam. The talented baristas worked at a LaVazza coffee shop near her condo. She hadn't posted from there since Vincent's death, but I hoped that meant only her social media routine changed, not her coffee habit. I noted the times, as well as the places she went most often for lunch and dinner.

It was already 9:20 and I was meeting Caleb at ten, so finding her drinking her coffee wouldn't work. She usually posted closer to eight anyway. But she often ate lunch at one of three restaurants near her condo. If I veered a bit out of my way to Wabash I could pass by all three on my walk home.

I grabbed my shoulder bag and phone and hurried out the door. It had stormed while I was in my migraine haze, but the sun shone now, and it was a perfect seventy-three degrees outside. Traffic was a little lighter now that rush hour was over, so a cab would be quicker than walking the two miles to the McDonald's. But after being shut inside all day yesterday I wanted the exercise. Especially on one of the few beautiful days we'd had this May.

THURSDAY, MAY 22, 9:49 A.M.

The Walk sign at Dearborn and Kinzie lit. Before I could react, an SUV blew through the red light and screeched around the corner, nearly jumping the curb. I leapt back. My shoulder bag slipped from my shoulder and hit the curb with a thunk. Half its contents spilled into the gutter. The gray-haired man next to me shouted curses after the driver.

"Unbelievable." He crouched to help me gather my things. He wore a suit and a baseball cap, an incongruous combination I've seen a lot of older men adopt. Maybe to hide balding spots on the top of their heads. "You see that banged up front end? Guy probably runs lights all the time."

"I didn't."

My phone lay in a puddle from last night's rain. Three years old already, the dunk in muddy water wasn't going to do its battery any good. I was waiting for the release of new, flashier models in the fall so I could get the current model at a lower price.

The man wiped my phone on a handkerchief he drew from his suit jacket pocket and handed it to me. "Smashed headlight and dented grille. People drive worse all the time. I gotta get out of this city."

"But people like you make it a nice place," I said. "Thank you."

"Well, thank you young lady. You be careful."

I glanced at my phone as we waited again for the Walk sign. Caleb had texted at 9:42.

On the way.

If he was coming from home, he'd be early. Sirens sounded as I headed farther north, but I was used to hearing them in River North. I'd passed a fire station on the way, and Northwestern Hospital was a mile or two east, so ambulances and firetrucks were common.

A few blocks later I turned left and headed for Clark Street and the former Rock 'n Roll McDonald's.

Flashing lights bathed the corner of Ontario and Clark. Police cars blocked the intersection. An ambulance sat in the driveway in front of the northeast entrance to the restaurant. The one Caleb almost certainly would have entered. Paramedics surrounded someone on the ground near the intersection. A bright green backpack lay on the sidewalk behind them. The same shade of green as the Seminar T-shirts.

I broke into a run.

23

Thursday, May 22, 10:02 a.m.

"Tell me more about this SUV you saw," the officer said. She sat next to me on a bench on the edge of the McDonald's gated parking lot.

I'd started to tell her about Seminar and Vincent's death. It seemed like too many coincidences. A planned meeting to talk about what I'd learned so far about Vincent's death, Caleb texting me that he'd found something he wanted input on, and a hit-and-run right as we were about to connect.

The paramedics had loaded Caleb, unconscious but alive, into the ambulance. His green Seminar backpack and phone went with him, sealed in a plastic bag. I'd already provided information about Caleb's parents so the police could contact them.

The officer had told me witnesses saw a dark SUV blow through a yellow light and hit Caleb, and I'd mentioned the SUV I'd seen.

I twisted long strands of hair around my fingers, struggling to set aside the image of Caleb on a stretcher. "I didn't see a license plate."

"That's all right. How about the model?"

I shook my head and explained that I'd never owned a car and never paid much attention to brands. When an Uber or Lyft picks me up, I look for the vehicle color and check the license plate. The model means zero to me.

"You're doing fine," the officer said. "How about size of the vehicle? Was it a compact one?"

I've always found the idea of a compact SUV an oxymoron, but I knew what she meant. "No. Large. Even for an SUV, it was huge."

"Good. That helps. You said a headlight was shattered. Did you notice the grille below it?"

"I didn't see the headlight. The man next to me told me it was shattered and the grille was dented." I rubbed my hands over the thighs of my jeans. "I should have noticed. Because it was such a new vehicle. Must have cost a lot of money. If he didn't care about anything else, you'd think the driver would at least be careful after spending so much."

"He? Did you see the driver?"

I shook my head. "No. Just a guess." Unfair, but I associated reckless driving more with men than women.

"What makes you think the vehicle was new?" the officer said. "The style of it?"

"No. Let me think." I shut my eyes and took a couple deep breaths. Imagined the street sounds, including horns and sirens. Remembered the smell of meat grilling from one of the nearby restaurants, the feel of the humid yet cool breeze on my skin. After a few seconds I felt as if I were standing on the curb again. It was a trick I'd used as an actor before going on stage. "Shiny. The paint. Very clean and shiny. And the windows were tinted dark and also looked clean. No spots or marks like you get from rain or bird droppings. No gravel dings or streaks on the doors from mud."

She typed notes into her phone. "All of that helps. It may

mean it's been kept in a garage. And we might find somewhere nearby that caught the SUV on camera. Or the man who stood next to you so we can question him."

The latter sounded like a stretch. I'd described him, but there must be hundreds of men like him all over the city.

"Are they taking Caleb to Northwestern?" I said.

"Yes. You know how to get there?"

I nodded, though at the moment the street, the cars, and the surrounding restaurants felt like a giant blur. Nothing looked familiar, and I had no idea which way was east.

I asked if I could call Caleb's mom myself. I didn't know her cell phone number, but she still lived in the same house, and I remembered the number from childhood. I didn't want her to get a call from the police.

The officer said she couldn't stop me from phoning anyone but that there would be an official call as well.

———

THURSDAY, MAY 22, 11:15 A.M.

I checked the round clock on the wall for the third time. Its thick, black hands had barely moved. I sat in a small, square, private waiting room on the hospital's ground floor near the Emergency Room, which is in one of the hospital's older buildings. Its walls were painted shiny off-white, but the brown vinyl chairs looked like they hadn't been replaced since the 90s.

Caleb had been rushed into emergency surgery. I didn't know why. Not being family, the hospital staff couldn't tell me anything more, though a chaplain had brought me to this room and gotten me a bottle of water. I couldn't stop shaking.

That a chaplain was involved seemed like a bad sign.

I stood and circled the small room, then peered out the door to see if I could spot Caleb's mom coming down the hall.

I'd called her from the bench outside McDonald's. Call Waiting buzzed while we were talking. She came back on briefly to tell me it had been the police and she'd see me at the emergency room.

Plastic wall bins held magazines. I took one about fishing. The words blurred.

A knock, and the door swung open. It was Ty.

I jumped to my feet. "You must have sped."

He'd been at a meeting in Oak Brook. That was farther away than LaGrange, where Caleb's mom lived and where I'd grown up, but he'd gotten here first.

He hugged me close. "How are you holding up?"

"I think I saw the SUV that hit him."

We sat side-by-side on the brown chairs, and I told him about it. He handed me a chewy chocolate power bar. "You probably never ate last night."

"Not since yesterday morning."

I bit into the power bar. A chewy piece stuck in my throat. I finally washed it down with some water.

I showed Ty the texts from Caleb that I'd missed the day before. "Caleb might have been right. My not being there last night made someone suspicious."

"Of what? Worst anyone would think is you didn't like Seminar. Not that you're investigating it for Caleb."

"Unless they knew about whatever it is Caleb found. And yesterday and the day before I talked with people who left Seminar and had terrible experiences. One wouldn't give me her real name or talk on a cell she was so afraid they'd go after her or her son."

He held my hand, his fingers warm over my icy palm. "But if those two people are afraid of Seminar, they wouldn't have told anyone about your calls. So that can't relate to what happened to Caleb."

"So you don't think any of this is related? Even though

Caleb asked me to look into Vincent's death, and he had something important to tell me, and now he's been run over?"

"Did he say it was important? Or about Vincent?"

"You sound like me questioning a witness." I ate a little more of the power bar. "But you're right, he didn't say that. But that's why we were meeting. To talk about Vincent's death and what I've learned."

"I'm not telling you none of it's related. And believe me, I want you to be careful." Ty moved his chair so he sat facing me and held both my hands. "If I thought you'd go I'd take you out of town with me. But hit-and-runs happen. And Chicago — I heard there were more pedestrian deaths than ever last year. Drivers on cell phones. Pedestrians wearing earbuds, texting."

"Caleb is bad at paying attention," I said. "But I should've told the cop more about Vincent's death. I don't think I did."

I tried to remember exactly what I'd told the officer. Though it had been less than half an hour before, my memory was fuzzy, as if gauze were wrapped around it. I'd mentioned our plan to meet for breakfast. And that Caleb and I had known each other as kids and reconnected recently. When the cop asked about his employer, I said Seminar. Then I remembered the SUV I'd seen.

"I'm sure you can call the station. Make a follow up statement."

The door opened again and Caleb's mom came in. A plump, gray-haired woman, she looked nearly the same as when I'd last seen her, which had been at my college graduation.

We hugged.

"I'm so glad you're here," she said. "Thank you so much for calling me yourself."

She stayed standing as I filled her in on what little I knew and introduced her to Ty as Mrs. Jackson.

"Call me Maureen," she said. "You too, Q.C. You're a grown up now."

I nodded, though I wasn't sure I'd be able to make the shift. Calling her by her first name felt almost as odd as if my Gram asked me to do the same. Plus her using Q.C. took me straight back to childhood. Not in bad way, though. She'd never known the original Q.C., so I knew she liked me for me, not as a substitute.

Caleb's dad was different. He'd insisted I call him Jack from the first, saying Mr. Jackson made him feel old. And everyone, even Caleb's mom, called him Jack. I wasn't sure I'd ever known his first name.

Jack had swept in every few months and taken Caleb and me downtown to brand new restaurants and R-rated movies. Mrs. Jackson was the one who reminded us to do homework, made us cookies, and insisted Caleb get home by ten.

Ty set off to find coffee for Maureen and look for a doctor or nurse to talk with her.

"I can't believe that driver took off." Maureen shook her head. "How could anyone do that? Not stop to help or see how he is?"

"It's awful," I said.

Maureen and I rearranged the chairs so they were angled toward one another, not face-to-face, and sat.

"The police told me Caleb had the Walk sign," she said. "But this couple who saw the accident said he stepped into the crosswalk without looking when it changed. He was staring at his phone. The girl said the SUV came from the north on LaSalle Street. The light turned yellow and the SUV sped up. She thought the driver did it on purpose, but the man with her thought the driver tried to hit the brakes and stepped on the accelerator instead."

"Did either one see the driver's face?" I couldn't imagine how they could guess at his motives otherwise.

"No. She thought the SUV veered toward Caleb when it accelerated. But he thought it was already in Caleb's lane. They both said the SUV leapt forward and that the driver never hit the brakes after hitting Caleb, though."

"I'm so sorry, Maureen."

She put her hand on my arm. "It makes me feel a little better that you're here."

I told her I'd last seen Caleb at Seminar's office Tuesday night.

"That organization's been so good to him. The founder, I forgot his name, but he's like a father to Caleb."

"The founder? Not Vincent, the man who died?"

"I thought he said the founder, but maybe I mixed up who was whom. Was it Vincent who hired him?"

"I think so," I said.

Maureen took a plastic bag of individually-wrapped Lifesavers from her quilted purse, pulled it open, and held it out to me. I took a pineapple one. It had always been my favorite.

She unwrapped a cherry candy and popped it in her mouth. "I should've pushed Jack harder to come around more when Caleb was little. But he berated Caleb so much when he did. I thought distance might be just as well."

We stared at the carpet with its zigzag pattern in silence. I took out my phone and texted Lauren what had happened, then Mensa Sam, asking if he could beg his friend for a number to reach her at. I wanted to know if she thought Seminar would do something like this and, if so, who in particular she might suspect.

"He tells me you're taking one of the courses now, too," Maureen said.

"I started Monday." That day seemed impossibly far away. "Thank you for paying for it. I really wanted to help Caleb, but that kind of self-improvement workshop isn't in my budget."

A knock at the door interrupted us. I sprang to my feet. It was Ty with the chaplain.

A thin man with a long face, he told us that Caleb was still in surgery. A woman came in at the same time with a stack of forms for Maureen to sign. She told us the surgeon was struggling to save Caleb's leg, which was broken in multiple places. His diaphragm was also torn, but that would be fixed later. From her cautious words, I took it that there was a good chance Caleb would survive, being as young and healthy as he was, but he'd need future surgeries.

We rode with the chaplain in a large elevator with silver walls. It smelled of rubbing alcohol and chemicals I couldn't identify. After a trek down a long hall, the chaplain ushered us to the far corner of a large ICU waiting room. On the other side of it a TV played what looked like a daytime cut-rate version of American Idol. A woman with long hair wailed a dirge into a microphone as bored judges looked on.

Someone switched the channel as Caleb's dad arrived. Jack looked a little older than the last time I'd seen him, but his silver hair waved back away from his face the same way, and he still favored a collared shirt with a sport jacket and no tie.

He hugged me and shook hands with Ty.

Jack sat against the shorter wall, so the four of us formed an L with him at the base. As Maureen told him everything we'd just heard, he typed notes about it into his phone. I rifled through my shoulder bag for the police officer's card.

Maureen paused. I asked Jack whether he thought we ought to call Caleb's lawyer. I figured he would know which detective was investigating Vincent's death. Also, the lawyer might have more credibility with the police in suggesting a connection between the two cases.

Jack looked up from the phone. "What lawyer?"

24

───────

"Whoever you hired when the police questioned him about Vincent's death," I said.

"The police questioned him? When? Why?" Jack's voice boomed. The people in the opposite corner, a couple with disheveled hair and wrinkled clothes, looked startled and pulled the thin blue blanket around their shoulders tighter.

Mrs. Jackson shushed him. I gave him a quick rundown of what Caleb had told me.

It turned out Jack knew that Vincent died, but he hadn't learned it from Caleb. A mutual friend told him.

Maureen frowned. "And it didn't occur to you to call Caleb, see how he's doing with it?"

"The boy calls when he wants to talk," Jack said. "Which is when he wants something. And it's by text. How hard is it to pick up a phone and speak into it?" He swiveled his head toward me and Ty. "Is it your generation, or just Caleb?"

"I text a lot," I said. While he'd been talking I'd flipped through the contacts on my phone for the name of the lawyer Caleb said he'd hired. "Do you know Al Silver?"

Maybe Al was a friend of Jack's, and Caleb chose him and blamed it on his dad.

Jack shook his head. "Been lucky. Only lawyers I've used are for the divorces and the one who handles my corporate matters."

"But you helped Caleb find a lawyer when he was in Los Angeles." Unless that story Caleb told me also wasn't true.

"Didn't know he told you about that." Jack shifted in his chair and crossed one leg over the other. "I helped by paying the bill. Some actor friend of his recommended the attorney."

"Probably the same young man who got him into trouble in the first place," Maureen said.

"For God's sake, Maureen, he was twenty-nine. Old enough to make his own choices."

"I think I'll see if I can reach his lawyer," I said. I motioned to Ty to step out into the corridor with me. If seeing Caleb's parents argue wasn't fun for me, it couldn't be for him either.

"It's normal," he said. "It's a scary time. People fight."

"This is pretty mild for them from what I remember," I said.

I got no answer at Al Silver's office, so I left a voicemail.

In his photo Al appeared to be an older white male lawyer. In law, people equate age with experience, which is often true. It makes it a good profession as you age, but tough when you're young and new. Many clients also still tend to feel safer or feel greater confidence about white men, seeing them as more a part of the overall system and thinking judges or juries will respect them the most. All of which makes it harder for women and anyone who doesn't appear white to get clients. I didn't want to believe Caleb thought that way, but when people are scared they do a lot of uncharacteristic things.

I hoped I'd get the chance to yell at him about it.

A text came in from Mensa Sam asking me to call him. I did, and I filled him in on Caleb and my investigation so far. For once he listened without interrupting. He said he'd try to get his friend, whom I knew as Angela, to contact me.

Ty and I stood in the stairwell. I ate a little more of the power bar and ran through with Ty everyone I'd talked to and all I'd learned so far. He held my water bottle while I made a list of what to do next on my phone.

"I need to talk to people at Seminar," I said. "But I don't know anyone's private phone numbers."

"Won't people be at the office?" he said.

"Right. That's right." Between shock and the migraine hangover, I felt like I was mentally trudging through molasses.

I dialed and got voicemail at Seminar, too. It was twelve-thirty, maybe everyone was at lunch. I considered leaving a message but decided it was better to go there in person. I couldn't do anything for Caleb sitting here. But if I saw the faces of people at Seminar when I told them the news, there was an off chance I'd be able to tell if any of them had been involved.

My phone rang as I hung up. It was Al Silver.

He had a deep voice with a slight Southern drawl.

"I'm not sure who you're talking about, but you sounded so upset I thought I'd call before I dive into my afternoon appointments," he said.

I rested my low back against the wall. "You're not Caleb Jackson's attorney?"

"Don't have a client now by that name. Can't promise I didn't represent him sometime in the past."

"But not recently?"

"How recently? My mind's like a sieve. I keep telling my partner it's time to retire."

"In the last month."

"That far I can remember. Definitely not. Did he tell you I did?"

I explained what Caleb had told me. Al had never heard of Seminar or Caleb. He did remember that someone was found dead in offices in the Temple Building a week or so ago but no one hired him because of it.

311 is the general information number for the Chicago police. I called it. After being transferred around, I finally got to speak to the partner of the officer who'd interviewed me. I did my best to fill in the blanks in my original statement about Vincent's death and Seminar. He listened, but his follow-up questions focused on the SUV I'd seen.

Back in the waiting room, Jack and Maureen sat three chairs apart. The TV still blared in one corner, and the air had that flat, sterile hospital smell. Ty and I positioned two chairs to create a rough circle and sat facing Maureen and Jack. I asked when Jack last heard from Caleb.

"Early January. When he got the key for the row house."

That fit with when Caleb said he had moved to Chicago, so at least that much of what he'd told me was true.

I looked at Maureen. "You've talked to him recently?"

"Every weekend. I call him. I don't wait and hope he'll call me, then get angry if he doesn't." She shot a look at her ex-husband.

Jack rolled his eyes and angled his body away from us and toward the TV across the room.

"And when did he tell you about wanting me to go to an Event to try to figure out what happened to Vincent?" I said.

Maureen rubbed her hands along the wooden arms of her chair. "Event? What event? And why would he ask you? Aren't the police investigating?"

"An Event," Jack said, stretching the second word into two distinct syllables as if talking to someone whose first language wasn't English. "What Seminar calls their week-long course."

"Have you ever gone to one?" Ty asked.

"A decade ago," Jack said. "Vincent convinced me it would help my business."

"Did it?" Ty said.

"Not hundreds of dollars' worth. Mix of psycho babble and woo-woo if you ask me."

"But you sent Caleb to Vincent," I said.

I folded one of my fingers down, a trick I use when I don't want to derail a conversation but need to remember to ask a particular question. This time it was why Maureen agreed to pay for my Event if she didn't know Caleb wanted me to investigate.

"Hoping he'd get him a job. Get him off my payroll and onto someone else's. Didn't know he'd get him into Seminar too. But there must be something to it. The boy's stuck with it for three years now, which is some kind of record."

"He stuck with college," Maureen said.

"Seven full-priced years of it. I bet Quille finished in four, didn't you?"

Caleb had told me six. I wondered if Jack was exaggerating or Caleb had been embarrassed and shortened the time.

Maureen swatted his arm with a rolled up magazine. "You know she did. You went to her graduation ceremony."

"Which Caleb didn't show for," Jack said.

I felt surprised he remembered that. Maureen was different. She'd always been a sort of mom to me. Jack never expressed a lot of interest in my life except where he could tell Caleb he ought to be more like me. Which would have been uncomfortable except that my mom told me to be more like Caleb, more outgoing and social, so it balanced off.

"He was in the middle of finals week," Maureen said.

Caleb attended Columbia College in Chicago's South Loop. Its school year started and finished a month later than all the other area universities, including the University of Illinois at Chicago where I'd gone.

Jack snorted. "I'm sure he needed to study on a Tuesday night."

Maureen patted my hand. "I know it must have hurt your feelings that he begged off at the last minute. But I wish you'd stayed in touch with him. You were such a steadying influence on him."

"You wish — he told you I was the one who stopped talking to him?"

"It's understandable. It was a big event and he missed it. But a little flexibility is a good thing in life, especially when it comes to people." She glared at Jack. "No one's perfect."

I stood and walked to the window. It overlooked an alley. A garbage truck below shuddered to a stop in front of a dented, overflowing garbage bin. With Caleb undergoing surgery, the last thing I wanted was to say anything bad about him. But there was a chance, however small, that unraveling his lies might shed light on what was going on now. Also, I hated Maureen thinking I'd abandoned Caleb.

I turned around.

"I think there's been a misunderstanding. I didn't stop talking to Caleb. He gradually stopped returning my calls and text messages. By the time I got to my senior year, I hadn't seen him in almost a year. I invited him to graduation anyway, but I was more surprised that he RSVP'd yes than when he didn't come."

"Makes more sense," Jack said. "Never thought you'd be one to hold a grudge."

"Oh, honey, I'm sorry," Maureen said. "He must have been embarrassed to tell me that." She frowned at Jack. "All that comparing him to Q.C. You broke up their friendship."

"I don't know if that had anything to do with it," I said.

"Doesn't matter," Jack said. "Maureen'll believe it did until the day I die."

"If Caleb didn't tell you he wanted me to investigate, why did he say he wanted you to pay for the Event?"

"He worried people at Seminar would think he had something to do with the death because of his past incident," Maureen said. "He wanted a friend with him, someone who'd known him forever and knew he wasn't violent. But he didn't feel right asking you out of the blue to spend all that money. I only said yes because it was you, Q.C. — Quille. I thought the two of you might work through some of your issues and become friends again."

I felt my face flushing. I felt awful that Maureen thought I'd abandoned Caleb, and that she'd spent her own money to reconnect us. My best guess was that Caleb didn't tell her he hoped I'd uncover the truth about Vincent's murder because he didn't want to worry her. Or because she might believe the whole thing was better left to the police.

As I explained that Caleb thought I might be able to help figure out what happened to Vincent and why, Maureen's brow furrowed. Jack's cheeks grew redder and redder.

He pounded his fists on his thighs. "This is so like him. Telling Maureen one thing and you something else. And now he's gotten himself run over. He'll kill both of us with worry."

"Jack, please. I'm sure Caleb didn't mean any harm. Maybe he didn't want to worry us about the police."

"He's asking for money, he at least ought to be honest about what it's for," Jack said.

"Maybe he would be if you didn't berate him all the time," Maureen said.

Jack's chin jutted forward, and he opened his mouth, then slumped in the chair. "Maybe. But, Jesus, Maureen, when are you going to learn? He got you to pay his way into that sales scam and you've still got cans of protein powder in the garage."

"When was that?" I said.

"College. His last year. He got mad when I suggested he get a job and chip in a little. So he conned Maureen into paying a thousand dollars to get him into some multi-level marketing crap."

Maureen's hands rose to her hips. "I wasn't conned. I thought he at least was showing some initiative. And you always said sales would be a good place for him."

"I need to let the Seminar people know he's in the hospital," I said. "The office isn't that far, so I want to tell them in person. See what sort of reaction I get. I'll be back soon."

Ty and I slipped out. When we reached street level I sucked in the outside air. Despite a tinge of car exhaust, it tasted fresh after the hospital.

25

———

Thursday, May 22, 2:03 p.m.

Though it was mid-day, the security guard made us sign in at the security desk and show our driver's licenses. He told us the Temple Building put the extra security procedures in place a month ago after bombings of churches in another part of the country.

I told him I needed to see someone about a Seminar employee, Caleb Jackson. We weren't on the visitor list, so the guard called ahead, then directed us to a narrow elevator.

"Security certainly seems diligent," Ty said. "If it's like this during the week it's hard to imagine a stranger getting in on a weekend night."

I agreed, though my own office had been broken into once during off hours. Someone determined can get in almost anywhere.

Karla stood in the hallway waiting for us when the elevator doors slid open. Her red-gold hair hung loose, and she wore a sleeveless dress with swirls of green and blue, a belt that highlighted her narrow waist, and heels. The bags under her eyes and her sagging shoulders made her look older than when I'd seen her last.

I extended my hand. "Quille Davis. We met at the Celebration at your home?"

"Oh, yes, Quille. You were very kind that night."

After introducing her and Ty, I asked how she was. It's a question with no good answer in the face of recent loss, but you can't not ask. Unless you're a Seminar person, I suppose.

Her eyes filled with tears. "Surviving. Barely. But what's happening with Caleb?"

I told her what I knew.

Her eyes widened and she pressed her hand against the wall to steady herself. "This is, this is awful. So awful. Poor Caleb. People are unbelievable. To drive off like that. His parents know? Do we need to call them?"

"They're at the hospital," I said. "I was on my way to meet him for breakfast. He must have been early, and he got hit."

"Oh, Quille, it's like a curse on Seminar. I know I'm not supposed to believe things like that. We all create our own lives. But first Vincent, now Caleb, it's hard not to feel that way."

She led us down the hall. Her ankles wobbled in her nude, three inch spike heel sandals.

A long hall to one side of a plain door led us in the back way to an office kitchen I hadn't seen Tuesday night. At Karla's request, Ty made coffee in the office coffee maker. She and I sat at the small square table.

"I can't believe any of this," she said. "Vincent, Caleb, they both did all the work. They were both Whole. I don't know what sorts of fractures happened for all this tragedy."

"You think they did something to cause what happened?" I said. If I'd wondered about the truth of what Jacinda claimed Seminar people told Zipporah, I didn't need much more confirmation.

Ty, behind Karla, held up a mug and teabag. I nodded. He filled the mug with water and put it in the microwave while waiting for the coffee to brew.

"Not purposely," Karla said. "But illness, injury, violence, we draw it to us when we're fractured. Once you're Whole, your life becomes smoother."

I clutched my leather shoulder bag on my lap and took a breath to stay calm. I didn't want to yell at Karla, who'd lost her husband so recently. But this sort of belief struck me as nearly as horrific as the religious people who'd told my parents God must be punishing them for something when the original Q.C. was abducted and murdered.

It also sounded like a great way to let an abuser off the hook. Make the person he abused at fault. I remembered Gina Lenzi's comments about knock down drag out fights between her parents and her suspicions that Vincent verbally abused Karla.

Ty must've been thinking along similar lines. He placed a full mug of coffee in front of Karla and said, "So if a serial killer goes after eight victims, or a car crash kills four people, each one of them was fractured in some way and that's why they died?"

"Well, there's some reason one person gets targeted over another." Karla spooned sugar into her coffee. "Or that those people were in the car."

Ty set a glass on the table a little too hard. Water sloshed. He wiped it up with tiny napkins from the dispenser on the counter. "How about happenstance? Or bad luck?"

"There's no such thing as bad or good luck," Karla said. "We all create our own universe."

"But how do you know if you're Whole?" I said.

"You'll know because your life will be smooth. And if it's not, you can repeat whatever Events you need to until it is."

I dropped my shoulder bag on the floor. I felt too tired

and concerned about Caleb to challenge her circular reasoning. It was a brilliant sales strategy. Seminar will make your life go well, and if it's still not going well, you need more Seminar.

"Was Caleb here early this morning?" I said. "He told me he had Seminar work to do."

That wasn't true, but her answer might tell me if Karla was in the office when Caleb was hit and if she knew where any of the other Seminar people had been at the time.

"I got in around noon. We all tend to gather after Events, so no one's ever in before eleven or eleven thirty."

That didn't help me with alibis, but it did tell me that if Caleb wanted to snoop around Seminar office space mornings would've been a great time to do it.

Karla told me she'd last seen Caleb at the Celebration I attended with him. She wasn't involved in this week's Event.

"So you don't know if Caleb ran last night's session or if he came to the office or went out afterward?"

Lauren had texted me that Caleb ran the previous night's session, all of it held at the Thompson Center. But I wanted to see what Karla would say.

She shook her head. Her earrings flashed in the light. "But Richard or Frank might know. I'm pretty sure they ran two of the small groups last night. Or Scott might know. He came in late last night."

"Scott Gary, the founder?"

The microwave dinged. I got up and retrieved my mug of hot water and dropped the teabag into it. The steam smelled of cardamom.

"Yes," Karla said. "He wasn't supposed to be in until Friday, but with Vincent gone he thought he needed to be on hand sooner."

So Scott had come into town unexpectedly, and Caleb

had been run over. The two things might be related in time only, but I wanted to talk with the legendary founder.

"Where is he now?"

"Right here," a voice behind me said.

26

<hr>

THURSDAY, MAY 22, 2:15 P.M.

I twisted around in my chair. A tall man filled the doorway behind me. His eyes were an unremarkable bluish-gray, but his dark eyebrows slanted down toward his nose in perfect symmetry. His sharp cheekbones and strong jaw, with its shadow of dark stubble, gave him a look that crossed between businessman and musician. The online profile I'd read said he was fifty-five, but I would have guessed him in his early forties.

His clothes added to the slightly off-beat business guy vibe. He wore a tan sport jacket over a maroon shirt with an open collar and dusky gray jeans that were almost but not quite too tight. A dark maroon stripe, barely noticeable but enough to add texture, crossed the top of his low-heeled gray boots.

It felt like I looked into his eyes for a long time, but Scott Gary held out his hand right away and introduced himself. His grip was warm and firm. I said something about being pleased to meet him, though I wasn't sure what words I used.

I hadn't heard him approach despite the tiled floor in the

hallway that led to the kitchen. He could easily have been listening to our entire conversation.

"Thank you for letting us know right away about Caleb," he said. "I put two rooms on hold under Seminar's name at the Warwick Allerton hotel. It's right by the hospital. Please tell Caleb's parents they're welcome to stay there at our expense."

"Thank you. That was quick."

So he had been listening to our conversation.

"I was coming here for coffee and overheard. I immediately asked myself how Seminar could help." He took a green plastic card from his pocket and handed it to me. "This is for any Lettuce Entertain You restaurant. If you don't mind, please order something for them — and you as well — for dinner tonight. It's hard to remember to eat at times like this, but it will help all of you get through this. If you can persuade them to go out that might be better, but I imagine they'll want to stay at the hospital."

"Thank you," I said again. "They probably will. But how did you — do you keep gift cards at the office?"

"We use them as a way to recognize Coordinators or Facilitators who go above and beyond," Karla said. "Well, more above and beyond than usual."

I noticed her use of "we," though from my research I knew Scott was the sole member of the corporation.

Scott drew a chair out and sat. "Sounds like you have some questions."

"I do."

In answer to my questions, he told me he'd flown into O'Hare the night before from San Francisco. He usually flew in late Thursday night for an Event, but he decided to come in a day early with this one being Caleb's first and Vincent being gone. He came straight to the office in an Uber and arrived around ten-thirty p.m. The small group sessions were finished, and no one else was in. He'd texted with Caleb earlier in the day and the two agreed to meet in the office today at noon.

Ty glanced at me, probably thinking, as I was, that it sounded like Caleb had planned to see Scott right after me.

"You must have been worried when he didn't show," I said.

"We tried calling him, texting, emailing." Karla refilled her coffee mug and Scott's.

"When we didn't hear back, I called Frank Hernandez to let him know to be ready to Coordinate tonight just in case," Scott said.

"Aren't you Coordinating?" I said.

"Oh, Scott doesn't Coordinate," Karla said. "He makes special appearances."

"And what do you do in Seminar?" I said.

Karla straightened her shoulders. "I help with overall marketing strategy."

"Especially branding," Scott said. "The bright green T-shirts and messenger bags are one of the things Karla thought of last year."

Ty finished the last of his tea. "So you were worried Caleb might not get here?"

"Worrying is a waste of emotional energy," Scott said. "I hoped Caleb was merely delayed, but it's important to be prepared, so I made sure we were ready."

"Did Frank say when he'd last seen Caleb?" I said.

Ty nodded to me and took out his phone as if he were checking email or texting someone. I hoped his nod meant he was taking notes. I didn't want to spook Karla or Scott by taking out my notepad.

"I didn't ask. He'll be at tonight's Event, but tomorrow is a better time to talk to him. He's got quite a bit to prepare since he's filling in at the last minute." Scott rocked the chair back. "Why all the questions?"

"I'm wondering if it's more than coincidence that Vincent was killed and Caleb's so badly injured," I said.

I moved beyond the wondering stage while still at the scene of the hit-and-run, but I didn't want Karla and Scott to suspect Caleb had asked me to look into Vincent's death.

Scott rested his hand on his knee. His fingers looked strong yet flexible, like a piano player's. "You think someone is targeting Seminar personnel?"

"Isn't it possible?" I said.

"I can't think of anyone who'd have reason to do that." Though Scott didn't smile, I noticed that his teeth were blinding white, much like Caleb's. I thought again of Maureen's comment about the founder of Seminar being like a father to Caleb. Maybe she hadn't been mistaken about which man Caleb felt closer to. "Do the police think that's a concern?"

"I don't know," I said. "But I got the impression they don't understand much about Seminar."

"That might be true," Scott said. "No Chicago police have taken part in Events so far."

"That's why I think it's worth exploring it ourselves," I said, using "we" in the hope of making them feel we were all on the same side. "Could a non-Seminar person have gotten into the suite the night Vincent died?"

"Unlikely," Scott said. "It would have been like today, plus on weekends you need a key fob to make the elevator work. Only Seminar employees have them."

"Stairwells?" I said.

"Locked from the outside, though they open from the inside so no one gets trapped. I understand that was an issue with a building near here some time back."

I shuddered. I'd still been in college when six people died

after getting trapped in the locked stairwell of a thirty-five story office building in the Loop. During fire drills at every Chicago building I'd worked or gone to school in since then the fire department personnel stressed the importance of security systems automatically unlocking stairwell doors during emergencies.

"You weren't here the night Vincent died, were you?" I said.

"Yes, I was. I flew in for the day and left the next morning."

I set my mug down. Caleb hadn't told me Scott was there. I wondered if he didn't mention it because he felt sure the founder would never hurt anyone.

"Caleb didn't mention you were here."

Karla looked at me. "Why was he talking to you about it?"

"He was pretty shaken up about it." At this point I didn't care if that was how a good Seminar person should feel.

"He might not have known I was in. When I'm in a zone I shut my office door and leave the lights off. A lot of us do that. It hones focus," Scott said. "But I'm still at a loss as to why you're asking all these questions."

I held his gaze. "I want to help Caleb, but I'm not a doctor. I can't help with his medical issues. But asking questions, figuring things out, that I can do. It might protect him if someone's targeting him."

Scott tilted his head. "That's a big if."

"What does it hurt to humor me?" I said.

Scott and Karla exchanged glances.

"All right," he said. "I can see a small chance the hit-and-run relates to Seminar. What do you want to know?"

"Where's your office compared to Vincent's?"

"We're next door to each other. Caleb is across the suite."

"And were you here the night Vincent died?" I asked Karla.

"Only until eight. Vincent was fine when I left. He told me not to wait up."

I looked at Scott. "What time did you leave?"

"Around eleven p.m. As far as I know, Vincent was still in his office."

"Did either of you hear anyone arguing with Vincent?" I said.

Karla shook her head no.

"No, but I wouldn't have," Scott said. "I wear noise canceling headphones. Cutting off as many senses as possible heightens concentration."

"Did you say goodnight to Vincent when you left?" I asked Scott.

"I did not. We generally don't disturb one another when we're working."

I turned to Karla. "And you didn't think anything of it when Vincent didn't come home that night?"

Scott patted Karla's shoulder. "Quille, I understand you're upset. But Vincent's death is Past. There's nothing to be gained by focusing on what we can't change."

"Except it might relate to my friend being run over."

"If it does, the police will figure it out. It's their job," Scott said. "Ours is to enhance our own lives."

"And we're Caleb's friends, too," Karla said.

Friends he didn't trust, but I didn't think it'd be helpful to reveal that.

"Then why not answer me?" I glanced at Karla. "If you're comfortable with it."

She looked at Scott, who lifted his shoulders a centimeter.

"If I'd been awake, I would have," Karla said. "But I have trouble sleeping sometimes. I took an Ambien that night around ten-thirty and fell dead asleep."

"Was it unusual for him to work that late?"

"Not the night before an Event. He sometimes didn't come

home until two in the morning. That's why I didn't stay up waiting for him."

I remembered Gina saying that Vincent had an affair the year before. "Did he ever not come home at all?"

Karla wound her fingers together in her lap. "That's none of your business."

"Do either of you have thoughts about who might've been angry with both Vincent and Caleb or had something against them?"

"No," Karla said.

"I can't think of two people less likely to have anyone that angry at them," Scott said.

"Did the autopsy report come back for Vincent?" I said.

I'd asked Karla, but Scott answered. "Not yet. All we know is he had a head wound. There was a lot of blood."

"Could he have slipped? Or passed out?" I said. Maybe it had been accidental.

Karla rubbed her hands together and looked at Scott again.

"It's not clear," Scott said. "We're told he might have slipped, or had a heart attack and fallen, and hit the back of his head on the desk on the way down. Or someone might have attacked him. There are a lot of unknowns until the report comes back."

"Did the medical examiner say when that might be?"

Karla shook her head, staring at the floor.

"Let's give Karla a break," Scott said. "If you have questions about something else, I'll answer them, but no more on Vincent's death."

27

───

Thursday, May 22, 2:28 p.m.

Scott held my gaze as he shook my hand to say goodbye. His eyelashes were so dark it almost looked like he wore eyeliner. They set off his pale irises.

"Thank you again for coming in person to tell us about Caleb," he said. "Oh, and I understand you missed last night's session. I assume you won't be returning given Caleb's situation."

"I was thinking of going," I said. I harbored no great desire to sit through more pseudotherapy, but it was my best shot at connecting the dots between Vincent's death, Seminar, and the hit-and-run.

"Each Event night builds on the last. That's why we ask participants to commit to every night. So we can't allow you to return. It's not our usual practice, but I'll make sure you get your tuition refunded."

He left Karla to walk us out.

"You shouldn't have been so confrontational with Scott." Karla fiddled with her necklace as we waited for the elevator.

"Why not?" Ty said.

"I didn't think I was confrontational," I said.

"He gets so much criticism from the outside world," Karla said. "Seminar is the one place he can be at peace."

"Is that why he doesn't want me to come back to the Event?" I said.

"Oh, no. That's standard. You have to attend every night."

The doors opened. I pressed my hand against one of them to keep it from closing. "Who criticizes Scott?"

She twisted her wedding ring around her finger. "People who don't understand. Like my stepdaughter Gina."

"I saw her blog. She didn't say that much about Scott personally."

"Attacking Seminar is the same as attacking Scott."

I found it interesting that Karla equated the blog with an attack on Scott rather than on Vincent. But right now I was more interested in other possible critics.

"And Zipporah Hernandez?" I said.

It was a guess, but it seemed the most likely reason no one talked about Frank Hernandez's wife anymore.

"Zipporah? She no longer found Seminar helpful, but she never said a bad word about it."

"Would you hear if she did?" I said.

Karla frowned. "Maybe not. I don't go searching for things that are negative about Seminar. I focus on what enhances my life."

The elevator buzzed insistently. I let it go, and it closed. "Do you know why Zipporah left? She was ill."

"I'm sure that's not true," Karla said. "She was Whole."

I didn't want to go into detail about Zipporah's cancer. Jacinda hadn't said I could talk about it. "Does Caleb know her?"

"I doubt it. I'm pretty sure she stopped taking part in Events before Vincent invited him to his first Celebration. So they wouldn't have met."

I hit the Down button again. "Anyone else who criticizes Seminar? Or Scott?"

She glanced at the closed door to the Seminar office. "No, no, no one. Gina's who I was thinking of."

"You seem very protective of Scott," Ty said.

"He's a good man. Doing good things in the world. Like Vincent was."

The doors opened again. I said good-bye and stepped inside with Ty.

Maybe Karla simply admired Scott. And associated him with her husband. But I couldn't help but wonder if there was more to the relationship than that, and if that was why Karla dressed up to come to the office on a Thursday morning.

"That was unnerving," Ty said once the elevator started down. "The way she kept looking at Scott before she said anything."

"You noticed it too."

"Oh yeah."

"It fits with how Gina said she acted with Vincent."

The doors slid open and we stepped out onto the marble floor. "So she just defers to men?" Ty said.

"Maybe. Or to other people generally. Lets them take the lead. But it could be something more. Something Scott doesn't want me to know."

Our shoes clicked on the marble floor as we exited the building.

"If there is, I wish you'd leave it alone," Ty said. "Though I don't suppose you will."

"I won't," I said.

THURSDAY, MAY 22, 2:58 P.M.

An electronic board listed patients by assigned numbers

with their status after each one. When we got back to the ICU waiting room, Caleb was still listed as in surgery.

Maureen and Jack weren't willing to leave the hospital to go to a restaurant. But around four, after I promised to watch the board and text Maureen with any change, they took the elevator down to get something at the Au Bon Pain off the lobby. At my urging, Ty had left to catch a flight. He'd already missed a business dinner. I didn't want him late for his morning's meetings as well. And a little time alone would help me think.

I decided on a strategy for this evening's Event session. Keeping an eye on the board, I called Lauren to ask her to help me with part of it.

After that, I found a seat near an outlet, plugged in my phone, and started searching. Social media didn't reveal photos of anyone in Seminar with a dark gray or black SUV. But that didn't mean very much. Lots of people never post photos that include their cars.

Vincent appeared to be a car lover, though. His posts featured three different vehicles. One was a pretty basic Toyota, another a late model BMW, and the third a red Mazda Miata convertible. Gina Lenzi's feed included a photo from a few months ago with Vincent and a brand new mini-Cooper. I guessed he might have bought it for her.

A different photo the night of Vincent's death showed Gina's location as Germantown, Wisconsin. All her photos for that weekend showed her being there along with a chubby, fortyish man. I supposed GPS and other location data could be hacked, but I tentatively crossed her off the list for his death. Other postings showed her at work this morning around the time Caleb had been hit.

Because Mensa Sam's friend had said the missing young man had lived in Queens, I checked out the New York Attorney General's office, which was in charge of consumer protection complaints. Unable to find a portal to search for company names, I flipped through complaints and attorney general opinions from different years, but it was like hunting for a needle in an endless row of haystacks. The New York Attorney General's office often takes the lead in high-profile investigations. One of my clients at my old law firm ran afoul of it, and it created years of work for those of us on the team. It ended with the corporation selling off the company in question to a competitor that engaged in all the same practices but that hadn't caught the Attorney General's eye.

A general Google search for Seminar and consumer complaints also got me nowhere. The generic name made it next to impossible to get targeted results. Scott Gary's name, other than the short profile I'd already found, likewise listed only unrelated webpages and articles.

Finally, I contacted my paralegal. I asked her to spend two hours manually checking New York and Austin attorney general opinions and complaints for five to ten years ago for anything involving Seminar. Also to use my PACER subscription to search federal court filings for anything about Scott Gary.

She asked me what case this was for. The long day and worry caught up with me and my voice broke as I told her it was personal but I'd rather not relive it by sharing it.

"Whatever it is, I'm sorry," she said. "I'll get this back to you as soon as I can."

———

THURSDAY, MAY 22, 5:54 P.M.

Richard Messerly was one of two people checking people in at a table in front of the auditorium. "Quille. Didn't Caleb explain? You missed last night — "

"I know. I can't stay. I'm just meeting my friend Lauren

here for a few minutes before you start. You know, you should get to know her. She's a real estate agent."

I said it as if I'd just thought of it. Lauren's good at drawing people out, and real estate attorneys and agents often develop relationships and refer clients to one another. If Richard thought that was a possibility, he might drop his guard and share something with her that he wouldn't with me. I told him about the neighborhoods she focused on and how she was looking for more attorneys to connect with.

Lauren texted that she was upstairs.

"She's almost here," I said. "Before I forget — when's the last time you saw Caleb?"

"Uh, last night. At the Event. Why?" Richard said.

"You didn't get together with him this morning? He said he was going to meet you about preparing for the rest of the Event."

It was complete fiction, but with Caleb fighting for his life, I didn't care.

Richard frowned as he rearranged some brochures about the Hunger Cure on the table. "No. I don't know why he'd say that. My only active role for the rest of the Event is checking people in and minding the door."

"Minding the door?"

I vaguely remembered Lauren saying something about trying to leave to use the restroom during last night's session and Richard trying to talk her out of it. A useless move. Talking Lauren out of anything is pretty much impossible.

"In case people need anything after the session starts," Richard said. "But why are you asking about Caleb?"

"You didn't know? He's in the hospital," I said. "Someone ran him over."

His eyes widened and he stood very still. "That's why Frank's taking over tonight?"

I nodded and told him about the hit-and-run as he

mechanically handed badges to a group of about twenty people who'd streamed over from the escalators. If Richard was telling the truth about not knowing, Seminar definitely wasn't a place where news traveled.

"Karla didn't mention it?" I said. "I told her and Scott Gary this afternoon."

"I haven't seen her since the Celebration. She's staying pretty isolated these days."

That didn't quite fit with my impression that Karla spent a lot of time at the Seminar offices, but maybe Richard wasn't there very often.

Lauren appeared, and I introduced her. As she asked Richard about his practice, I entered the auditorium to look for Frank. Richard, immersed in conversation, didn't try to stop me.

Tonight Frank wore a navy blue suit with a light blue shirt and red tie. He broke off his conversation with a boy holding a Columbia College water bottle to hug me.

"Quille, I'm so sorry about Caleb. Karla told me. Can I do anything?"

So she had filled Frank in on what happened. I didn't know if that meant anything or not. He'd been in Seminar much longer, so she most likely knew him much better than Richard.

"I don't think so. He was still in surgery when I left the hospital. I'm going back in a few minutes."

"Thank you for letting us know this afternoon," he said.

"Last time I saw him was Tuesday night. How about you?" I said.

"Why?"

People here really didn't like questions. Even if I weren't trying to learn about the hit-and-run, it felt normal to ask people close to Caleb when they'd last seen him. Everyone at

Marco's wake talked about their last contact with him. Caleb wasn't dead, but he was severely injured.

But one advantage of quiet time in the waiting room was that I'd planned how to answer the questions I might get.

I let my shoulders droop and shrink toward the floor. "I'm feeling a bit guilty. He was coming to meet me when he got hit. I keep thinking if I'd gotten there a few minutes earlier...."

Frank folded his arms over his chest. "Guilt is an unproductive emotion. If you come back to another Event, you can work on that. Or I offer one-on-one Seminar coaching."

"That's part of Seminar, too?" I said.

I wondered if he'd adopted his view of guilt as unproductive before or after Zipporah's illness.

"At the advanced levels. Some people find it helpful. You might. Since you don't seem comfortable talking to a group."

"You're right, I'm not." I twisted a long section of my hair into a spiral curl. "So did you see Caleb this morning? He told me he was meeting someone from Seminar."

"It wasn't me. I was home on Skype with the manager of my vitamin business."

I glanced around the auditorium, which was now almost filled. "I thought Karla might be here tonight. Though it must be hard for her without Vincent."

I didn't expect her to be at the Event, but I wanted to open the topic of spouses and Seminar to see what I could prompt.

He straightened his tie. "She'll be fine His death is Past. She needs to focus on Now."

"Did I hear that your wife used to be in Seminar?"

He'd been watching the Green T-shirt helpers seating people, but now he glanced at me. "She did. But she felt she'd gained enough from it, reached the highest level she could, so she finished."

That was one way to rewrite the narrative.

"Karla mentioned being upset about all the people critiquing Seminar lately."

He frowned. "All what people? There's only that one ebook as far as I know."

I kept my expression the same as my thoughts raced. "I think she meant Gina Lenzi's blog, too."

Frank waved a hand. "Who reads blogs?"

28

The electronic board in the ICU surgical waiting room listed Caleb, by number, as being in recovery. I'd memorized Caleb's patient number, but I doublechecked. When I compared it to what I'd noted in my phone and it matched, I sagged against the wall in relief. I found Maureen and Jack at a round table in a long, wide hallway with windows on either side. It served as a bridge connecting two of Northwestern's massive buildings.

Maureen told me his status had updated to recovery only ten minutes before. Someone from the surgical team had called the designated waiting area phone and told them Caleb wasn't yet awake but he was considered stable. They hoped to transfer him to a room in the ICU in two or three hours.

As Jack paced between the table and the TV in the waiting area at the far end of the hall, Maureen took out her knitting. I texted Gina Lenzi and Zipporah's sister Jacinda. I wanted to know from both whether they thought Karla, Richard, Frank, or Scott had it in them to try to run over

Caleb. Also if they had ideas about what Caleb might have uncovered that could prompt an attack on him.

Neither answered.

Ignoring the search engines I'd tried before, this time I searched only for books. I found one called *Give Me All Your Money: Seminar, Self-Help, and Scott Gary*. Published two months ago, it was available in digital format for five different types of e-readers for $2.99. Author: Anonymous. As best I could tell, it wasn't a huge seller, but each platform where it was for sale included a handful of reviews. I couldn't find any associated website.

I downloaded it to read on my phone. The letters blurred after a couple paragraphs, and I was too tired to retain much. I scanned the table of contents. The chapter titles showed good organization. I clicked to the section on retaking Events.

Give Me All Your Money didn't use the words Attending and Spending, but it described a practice of urging people to take more and more Events no matter their financial circumstances. The theory was that it was an investment that would pay off down the road for everyone. Confirming Angela's stories, the book claimed retaking of Events led some people into bankruptcy to get out from under the credit card debt. Not only that, but people who went bankrupt often then started taking the Finance Events. An anonymous Seminar participant claimed in a review that if he'd taken the Finance Events sooner, he could have avoided the bankruptcy.

Outside, dusk had morphed into night. I started a list in the Note section on my phone of possible authors, putting Angela at the top, then Gina Lenzi, then Zipporah and Jacinda.

In another chapter, *Give Me All Your Money* said that Scott Gary opposed on-line learning and coaching. According to the author, it was because both competed with Seminar. Also, unnamed Coordinators believed one-on-one coaching could never be as effective as the group dynamic Seminar created.

I couldn't find anything saying the policy ever changed. Yet Frank offered the coaching to me without hesitating, making me think it must be all right with Scott. If Frank won the day on the issue, it didn't seem like a motive for murder. Unless the change came only after Vincent's death or the hit-and-run, but it seemed unlikely it would happen that fast. Still, I needed to be sure. It was the first hint of conflict among the top Seminar people.

The book also told me that Scott's ex-wife ran her own self-help company. It focused on in-person empowerment workshops for women. Her website said she also offered one-on-one business coaching.

Caleb was moved to a room in the ICU around eight-thirty. Maureen and Jack went in first, then let me have a few minutes.

The nurse warned us all that he was retaining fluid from the surgery and that he would look much better tomorrow. I barely recognized him. His eyes and forehead looked double their normal size and his face was black and blue everywhere that it wasn't yellow. His shoulders and neck looked puffy and banged up. One leg, in a partially open cast from toes to hip due to multiple breaks, appeared giant under the blankets.

A machine near his bed wheezed and hissed, breathing for him.

I bent close to speak into his ear. "Listen, Tiny Boy. What's the deal with telling your mom I stopped talking to you? You need to wake up. We have a lot of talking to do." I gripped his hand. It, too, felt puffy. "And no way am I letting you disappear on me again. Not when I just got you back."

He lay still.

———

Thursday, May 22, 8:47 p.m.

Maureen wanted to stay in the waiting room overnight, insisting she could sleep on two chairs set face-to-face. The chair arms made it impossible to sleep lying across them. She didn't want to stay in the row house because it was over two miles away. Or the hotel Scott reserved, though it was only a block away.

"I know it makes no sense, Jack," she said. "It's a five-minute walk. But I want to be near my boy. I feel he'll know I'm close by."

Her face had a gray tinge that worried me. Between us, Jack and I convinced her to go to the hotel.

Jack, a night owl, said he'd stay until one a.m. and then go to the row house. He promised to call Maureen and text me if there were any significant changes. He also gave me Caleb's key to the row house in case there was a time Caleb needed something from it and neither of them could get there.

I doubted that would happen, but I appreciated that they still trusted me after all these years apart.

At home I struggled to sleep despite the long day. I turned on the lights and dug through my closet until I found a University of Chicago sweatshirt of Marco's. I wore it a lot the week after he died and had finally washed it and stored it away late last summer. Now I pulled it over my head, put on sweat pants, and climbed back into bed.

A shrill ringing jolted me awake what felt like only moments later. Once again it was my phone. At midnight.

29

Friday, May 23, 12:02 a.m.

"Guess what I'm doing," Lauren said. She's one of a handful of people other than family whose numbers ring on the phone's Do Not Disturb setting.

I huddled against the brick wall behind my bed, heart pounding. "Scaring the hell out of me?"

Despite the phone display telling me it was Lauren, my immediate thought had been that the call would be someone saying Caleb died.

"Sorry. Really, truly sorry. I didn't think. How is Caleb?"

"Stable when I left. But unconscious. So where are you? Home?"

I'd texted her regular updates about his condition all evening, but now I realized she would only have gotten them all at one time when her phone was returned to her. It didn't matter, though. Texting had helped me feel as if she were with me.

"No, still at the Event. In the Thompson Center. At the edge of the now very creepy deserted food court."

"At midnight?"

"Yeah, they kept us this late. Long session. Tell you more about it later, but it was all getting us in touch with what they call child narratives. Trauma, bad relationships, blah blah. It was hard to come up with something to talk about."

"Must be tough," I said.

Lauren leads a charmed life as far as that goes. Her mom and dad love her and shower her with presents, money, and help with her business. If she weren't such a great friend there are times it would truly make me sick. In a weird way, though, it puts a sort of pressure on her I've never felt. Her mom in particular wants to know every aspect of Lauren's life and shares advice on all of it. Much as I liked her mom and sometimes envied Lauren, it made me grateful for my independence. Gram was always there to offer guidance, but she had so much else on her plate that she never tried to micromanage me or my career.

"I dredged up a few stories about mom trying to convince me she should sneak in and write my exams for me. Massively overprotective and all that, I'm so scarred. But mostly I listened and watched and here's the unbelievably coincidental thing — not. Culmination of all of this was lots of people in tears in front of an auditorium full of people, pushed into supposed insights by Frank. No surprise everyone's having breakdowns after six hours with nothing to eat, no water, and one ridiculously short bathroom break. And then we're given back our phones and told to find a private space to call one of the people we've been so upset about all night. We're supposed to share everything we've learned, especially these new narratives we've created, and invite that person to our Celebration."

"Probably what happened to that woman who reconnected with her dad." I rubbed my eyes. They felt dry and hot.

"Yes, and?"

"And what?"

"We were practically ordered to call people. On a Thursday night. At midnight."

"The same time Caleb called me last Thursday." I swung my legs over the side of the bed. "No, wait. That was Wednesday."

"Still. I bet he totally called from an Event. Why else would he call at midnight?"

"But he didn't invite me to a Celebration. Or tell me about an emotional journey or what have you." The hardwood felt cold beneath my bare feet. I didn't have my air conditioner on, but the neighbors below probably did. "At least, not that night."

But he had done both the next day.

"See what I'm saying," Lauren said.

I walked into the open living area to the sliding glass door. With the lights on inside, I saw my own reflection in the glass rather than the darkened deck.

"So Vincent's dead, and Caleb's worried about it," I said. "And he calls me from the Event. To make it seem real that he brought his long-lost friend in? Or did he make up the whole thing as an excuse to get me into Seminar?"

"Oh," Lauren said. "I totally assumed the first. It'd be a weird thing for your friend to do, come up with a ruse about a murder investigation just to get you to a Seminar Event. Seriously manipulative and kind of whacked."

"More than kind of." I rattled the door, double checking the lock. It had been sticking lately and not closing all the way, but it was fine. "But I could almost see it."

After all, he'd come up with a whole story for Maureen about why we weren't friends anymore, and another to get her to pay for my Event. Why not one to get me into the Seminar orbit? I rested my forehead against the glass for a moment. If it were all a ruse, it would mean Caleb was in no further danger from anyone at Seminar. Except to his emotional well-being.

"Really? What's the plus if he got his mom to pay?"

"The upsell." I thought about Attending and Spending and Gina's long list of Events. "At the end of the Event, get me to buy another. And don't forget it got you to come. He might not get a commission, but bringing people in seems like something Seminar pushes everyone to do."

"Huh. That's genuinely twisted if that's what's happening."

I turned away and sank onto my couch. "But when I saw Karla today she seemed so afraid to talk about it. Kept looking at Scott Gary — the founder — like she needed permission to talk."

"That might just be a Seminar thing. Those green T-shirt volunteers? They've been very involved tonight, but I swear they can't make a decision alone to save their lives. Totally undercuts the whole empowerment vibe Seminar's trying to sell when their own people need the leader to decide whether to pass out papers left to right or right to left."

"How much of an exaggeration is that?"

Though she's great at assessing people and situations, Lauren occasionally heightens the facts to make her point.

"I am so very serious. This one girl almost had a meltdown when I insisted I needed to leave to use the restroom and Frank Hernandez was busy on stage and couldn't tell her what to do."

I ran my free hand through my hair. "But it was my specific questions about the autopsy and the night Vincent died that Karla didn't want to answer. And it's a pretty hard coincidence to swallow that Vincent's dead, Caleb asks me to investigate — then says he found out something — and gets run over."

"What if he asked you at first just to get you into Seminar and one of you stumbled onto something real?"

"That could be too."

After I hung up the phone, I ran through my interactions with Karla. She'd been nervous talking with me the first time I met her at Vincent's Celebration, and I'd barely talked to anyone yet. So far as I knew, Caleb didn't ask any questions about Vincent's death. He just wanted to be sure the police didn't hone in on him. Yet Karla lied to Richard about why she took my card. So she hadn't felt nervous about me, she'd been worried about what Richard would think of her talking to me. Almost as if she weren't allowed to have friends outside Seminar.

After texting Jack and learning there was no change in Caleb's condition, I poured myself a glass of water and wrote out a plan for tomorrow.

———

Friday, May 23, 6:58 a.m.

I left the lights off in my office and set my extra large Earl Grey and chocolate chip scone next to my laptop. I'd awakened to a text Mensa Sam had sent at 3 a.m. His friend, the one I knew as Angela, was willing to call me in the morning on my office landline between seven and eight a.m.

She called at 7:02 and apologized for making it hard to reach her. "But Sam told me your friend is in the hospital. You see why I worry. These people are dangerous."

"Who in particular?"

"Anyone at the top."

"I need names."

"All I can tell you is Sam convinced me to call my son. He never met your friend Caleb. Also never met the founder of Seminar. Two different Seminar people tag teamed him —

calling him and coming to his work. One was the friend who got him involved in the first place. That friend finally left Seminar three months ago. And he still lives in Austin. My son saw him yesterday, so he didn't commit the hit-and-run. The other was someone who ran one of the groups in his advanced class. They've lost touch."

She still wouldn't give me any names for fear of anything being traced back to her son. But she confirmed that neither person who hounded him was Richard, Karla, or Frank. The only name she was at all familiar with was Frank's.

"He ran a lot of the courses my son took. And the two I took. He and his wife. Her name started with a Z, I think."

"Zipporah?"

"That's it. Black lady, but very nice."

I refrained from commenting on the "but." Suggesting she was biased wasn't likely to make her open up to me. "But Frank and Zipporah weren't pressuring him?"

"No. It wasn't any Seminar leader. It was these two people who took a lot of courses, like my son did."

"But you said people at the top are dangerous."

"I just think that's who's behind it all. Luring people in. Pressuring. Hounding people who leave."

"Have you ever written about your concerns about Seminar?" I said.

"Like a letter to the editor? I'd never do that."

I sipped more tea and rested my elbows on my desk. "There's a book out there about Seminar. An ebook."

"Like one you read on your computer?"

"More likely on a phone. Or ereader."

"I don't like online things."

Last night I'd compared the sales pages for three books: *Give Me All Your Money*, a guide an actor friend wrote and self-published about stage acting, and an autobiography by a former U.S. vice president that a major publisher released. Based on the way the three pages listed the publishers, I was pretty sure the author of *Give Me All Your Money* had self-published it.

Angela sounded far too unclear about ebooks to have published one herself.

"So you didn't write *Give Me All Your Money*?" I said.

"That's the title? It's a good title. But no."

"What about the man from Queens. The one who disappeared? Can you give me his name?"

"Sam suggested that. Since he already disappeared, I guess Seminar can't hurt him. I asked my son. He thinks the last name was Stroger or Stoger. Or Stauber. Something like that."

That the son had heard a name for the supposedly missing man made it more likely there was truth behind the story. Most urban legends are about a nameless friend of a friend. I emailed the possible names to my paralegal.

"I shouldn't have told you any of this," Angela said.

Exhaustion and stress had me on edge. "Angela, I don't know your real name, I don't know your number. I don't know where you live. I get that you're worried, but I've never so much as hinted to Caleb or anyone that you exist."

"I don't mean because of me. Because of you. And your friend. You know how they say don't poke the bear? That's what you're doing. You should stop before it's too late."

"If that's true, it's too late," I said. "If someone did this to Caleb, they'll keep trying. And he was right. The police can't understand Seminar well enough to do anything about it."

FRIDAY, MAY 23, 10:12 A.M.

"If Scott Gary asked them to run someone over, I don't doubt there are Seminar participants who would do it,"

Jacinda said after telling me how sorry she was to hear about Caleb.

I sat in the office kitchen drinking another of Sam's root beers. I'd probably consumed too much sugar already this morning, but it helped me stay awake. I'd called Jacinda after dealing with the most pressing emails in my queue and thanking Sam for his help.

"But which Seminar participants?" I said.

"The people who go back time after time."

That didn't narrow it down. I also didn't buy that, enthusiastic as they were, people like the artist or designer of men's business clothes I'd met the night of the Celebration would commit murder for Seminar.

"How many times?" I said.

"I can't say there's any set number. But there are people who go back year after year. They're like addicts. They see Scott Gary as the ultimate authority. They retake every Event on the roster just to get to talk to him for a few minutes on the last night."

I sipped some more soda. "Was Zipporah like that?"

"Not the part about needing those few minutes with Scott. But she used all the buzzwords. She believed he served a greater purpose."

"But would she kill for him?" I didn't suspect Zipporah. I wanted Jacinda to distinguish between people who might be a little too into Seminar with ones she believed might commit crimes.

"She's practically killed herself. But no. She wouldn't hurt anyone else."

"And Frank? Could he be violent?" The back of my chair pressed against the kitchen wall near the doorway. I rested my head on the wall and shut my eyes. My whole body felt heavy.

"Pains me to say it, but at heart Frank's a decent guy. I can't see him hurting anyone."

"He's devoted to Scott. More loyal to him than to his wife," I said.

"I'm no fan of Frank's. But if it weren't about my sister, I'd almost get his loyalty. Scott Gary gave him the tools to take his business to a new level. Before that, Frank was the man who worked his butt off but never rose to the top. Without Scott and Seminar, that's still who he'd be. Owner of a midling online business that pays the bills but barely."

"Frank mentioned doing personal coaching. Is that a Seminar thing?"

"Personal coaching? Frank? That's new. Maybe he started it after he and Zipporah split."

I asked about *Give Me All Your Money*. Jacinda denied that she'd heard of it or that she or Zipporah had written it. "Neither of us has time or energy for that. And Zipporah, she already spent too much of her life on Seminar. Believe me, she's got no interest in filling her last days with it."

She didn't think Gina was the author, her theory being that Gina wrote her blog as a cry for Vincent's attention. And had tried to fit into Seminar as a way to connect. An anonymous book wouldn't serve either purpose.

When I pressed, the only person she said she could see possibly hurting someone on Scott's behalf was Karla. "She followed Vincent everywhere. With no Vincent to tell her what to think and where to go, she'd turn to Scott. It's what everyone in Seminar does."

"That's a long way from being willing to hurt someone else," I said.

"Maybe. But she's been in Seminar since she was nineteen. It's her everything."

Jacinda hadn't heard anything about someone in New

York disappearing, and the last names Angela had given me didn't ring a bell.

Before we said good-bye I asked if I could tell people that I'd spoken to her.

"Why not? Seminar people already hate me."

I rinsed my root beer bottle and dropped it in the glass recycling bin. "You're not worried about violence against you?"

"I already watch my back. Upped all the security at my condo. And they can't do worse to Zipporah than they've already done."

I hung up, uncertain. If Jacinda truly believed someone in Seminar could have run over Caleb on Scott Gary's say so, she'd be worried for her own safety and Zipporah's, and she wasn't. Angela, on the other hand, worried enough for both of them.

30

I called Maureen before working on a motion I needed to write and reviewing electronic documents my difficult clients had finally sent me. She was in Caleb's hospital room. He still hadn't awakened post-surgery, something that worried the doctors. She said he looked much better, though, and while his brain still showed swelling, there was no bleeding, so that was good.

By three-thirty, I'd finished and e-filed a motion to continue. In it, I asked for more time to file a reply to the other side's brief opposing my motion trying to dismiss a case. I needed to add an affidavit about my friend being in the hospital, something judges now require because so many attorneys took to lying about reasons they needed extensions.

I didn't know if the judge would give me the extra fifteen days I asked for, but she'd at least give me a few days after the motion was heard, which would be next Friday. Maybe I'd be able to get it done by then.

I texted Gina Lenzi again. She'd never gotten back to me, and she still didn't. I wished I could text Karla, but I didn't have her cell phone number. After checking every website and paid database I subscribed to, I concluded she didn't have a landline here or in New York. No one answered at Seminar's office. I left a voicemail with an update on Caleb's condition, not wanting to reveal that I was looking for Karla.

My best hope was to camp out at Seminar's offices or find her at one of the places social media told me she frequented. I knew what I'd be doing for the next twenty-four hours.

———

FRIDAY, MAY 23, 4:01 P.M.

I keep a styling wand and a suit in my office for surprise trips to court. At four I changed into the suit, straightened my hair, and pulled it back in a clip. At the Temple Building, the security guard told me Seminar's offices were closed for the day. He knew Karla and said he hadn't seen her today. Next I tried four different coffee shops and restaurants I'd seen on Karla's social media. Lauren texted at 5:57 that she'd seen no sign of Karla at that night's Event. At Karla's condo the doorman told me he didn't think she was home, but he'd try her line.

"Sorry, no answer. Want me to leave a message?" he said.

I shook my head. "I'll text her. Must have gotten the night mixed up. But I'll wait a few minutes."

Hoping the way I looked would make him see me as trustworthy enough to chat with, I commented on how shocked I'd been to hear about Vincent's death.

He agreed, and we talked about how difficult it is to lose someone suddenly, how relatively young Vincent was, and how sad it was for Karla to be widowed. As we talked, I kept an eye on everyone coming and going. They swiped in with cards that opened the double glass doors. But if a group went in, rarely did every person swipe separately.

The guard watched, but it didn't look to me like he knew everyone.

He paused once to call someone about a package. After the messenger signed in, he was allowed into the residential area.

"My Gram always says when someone young dies there's such an outpouring," I said. "Cards, flowers, donations. Long lines at the wake."

The doorman nodded. "You're absolutely right. Mrs. Lenzi still gets flowers every other day."

I glanced at my phone as if checking the time. "I better run. It's been so nice talking with you. Karla always says what a wonderful building this is."

"That's good to hear. You have a good evening, Miss."

I walked to State Street so I could flag a cab heading north. Maureen had texted that Caleb showed some improvement.

———

FRIDAY, MAY 23, 9:25 P.M.

Caleb remained unconscious in the ICU, but he'd been extubated. That he could breathe on his own seemed like a good sign. And he was no longer swollen with fluid, so he looked a little better. But he periodically grimaced and shifted as if in pain. The nurse assured us he wasn't with the amount of morphine in his IV drip, but I wondered how anyone could know for sure.

Around nine-thirty an orderly asked Jack and me to leave so she could change Caleb's bedding. Maureen had gone downstairs to get coffee from one of the shops.

Fifteen minutes later Lauren appeared and dropped onto the narrow couch across from me in the Intensive Care waiting room. Jack slumped in a green armchair in the corner.

"You weren't kidding about the upsell." Lauren put her Marc Jacobs shoulder bag, the one I loved, next to her. "I'm a seriously good salesperson and these people ran rings around me. Talk about overcoming objections to purchasing."

"Like what?"

"They brought in more people to tell heartfelt stories, empathized with my concerns before I said them — I'm pretty sure someone takes notes through all those small group sessions so they can do that — emphasized the unique selling proposition that you can only get the full Seminar experience in this group, not online or in one-on-one therapy. Even offered a compromise. If I wasn't ready for the Intermediate Event, I could prepay a quarter now and take it any time in the next year. Non-refundable deposit of course."

"You didn't, did you?" I said.

"Of course not. But I did promise to convey that compromise offer to you if you want to try again with the basic Event. Which I have now done."

"Was Scott Gary there?"

"He was the closer. Any time someone seemed ready to leave, he was called over. I've got to say, he's totally gorgeous."

"He is," I said. "Though more your type than mine."

Lauren tended to prefer men at least twelve or thirteen years older than her. I didn't have a set cut off, but someone in his fifties or sixties, no matter how good looking, didn't appeal to me.

"It's those eyes," Lauren said. "The way he looks right at you. Like you're the only person in the world. And he makes everything sound so logical. But I flipped it around on him. Started asking him if he has a home here, if he wants to upgrade to a penthouse, whether I could show him some properties. So totally the best way to deal with people like that, by the way. I insisted he take my card. And he texted my info to someone he knows who is looking."

Jack, roused from his exhaustion by Lauren's brightness, laughed. "You ever want a job, come see me."

"When everything in real estate shifts to online, I may take you up on that."

"Any insights on anybody else there?" I said.

"Frank wasn't part of it tonight. But that Richard Messerly guy? I don't think his practice is doing well. He seemed desperate to meet with me for coffee next week. I agreed, so let me know what you want me to find out from him. What about you. Any luck?"

"No, but I've got a plan for tomorrow."

SATURDAY, MAY 24, 9:10 A.M.

I doubted the doorman from the night before would be on duty Saturday morning. But just in case, in the morning I washed my hair and scrunched it with my hands as I dried it. That left me with crinkly waves that looked very different from yesterday's smooth, slicked back hair. I dressed differently, too, in faded jeans, a plain white tank top, and gym shoes. A cross body canvas bag completed my outfit.

The Printers Row Farmers Market is on Saturdays in the park near the neighborhood bookstore. I brought over a large green glass vase from flowers Ty gave me on Valentine's Day and bought two bunches of flowers. The florist at the market helped me arrange them and added a dark blue ribbon. He also was happy to give me two business cards for his shop. During a quick stop at my office I wrote Karla's name on the front of one, stapled it to the ribbon, and put the whole arrangement in a cardboard box with white tissue paper around it.

Twenty minutes later I strode into the marble lobby. It was a different doorman.

"Delivery for Karla Lenzi, unit 3202." With my free hand I gave him the extra business card. "Do I need to sign in?"

The doorman pushed the sign in book toward me. I scrawled an illegible J. Jones for my name and printed the West Loop florist's name for the company. He called and told Karla she had a floral delivery. A minute later, I rode up the elevator.

———

SATURDAY, MAY 24, 10:45 A.M.

I held the floral arrangement so it partially obscured my face in case Karla looked through the eyehole when I knocked.

"I don't know what to do with them anymore," she said when she opened the door.

I stepped partway in and lowered the flowers.

"Quille." Lines formed on Karla's forehead as she stared me. "Are you? You don't — what are you doing here?"

I handed her the bouquet. "These really are for you. From me. I need to talk to you about Caleb."

31

She looked down, her nose buried in the yellow and pink tulips. "Why me?"

"A lot of reasons. Could we sit down? Please?"

"I guess so." She led me into the kitchen. It smelled of warm milk. "I just started to make hot cocoa. I can't seem to eat lately. Scott suggested it would be filling and easy to drink."

A brown bag of Burdick cocoa sat on the counter. A small pan of milk was heating on the stove.

"I lost five pounds after Marco's death," I said.

Karla poured cocoa shavings into the pot and stirred with a tablespoon. "Maybe I should retake the Life Planning Event."

"You've taken it before?"

"At all three levels. But as your life changes, Events become relevant in new ways."

That sounded like a Seminar slogan, though I hadn't seen it in the book. I'd skimmed most of it last night as I sat in Caleb's hospital room while Maureen and Jack got dinner.

Cocoa shavings floated on top of the milk.

"My Gram uses a whisk," I said. "Blends the cocoa better."

"Good idea." Karla rummaged in a drawer and found one.

"I read a critique of Seminar saying it pressures people to take events over and over. In a book called *Give Me All Your Money: Seminar, Self-Help, and Scott Gary.*"

Karla whisked the cocoa. "Sounds like a terrible book."

"I went looking for it after you said people criticize Scott. I want to find people who are angry at Seminar."

The cocoa had dissolved. Karla set the whisk on a ceramic spoon holder. "And you think whoever the author is fits the bill?"

I found it interesting that she'd acted as if she didn't know anything about the book, yet the way she phrased her question made it clear she knew the author was unknown.

"It's published anonymously," I said. "Have you read it?"

"No. I heard of it, but I'd never read something against Scott. It shouldn't be allowed to be published as far as I'm concerned. It's slander. Or libel. Whichever the written one is."

"Any idea who'd write something like that?"

Without asking if I wanted any, she took out two bone white mugs and poured cocoa into each. She did it expertly, with none of it dripping on the counter or the sides of the mugs. "Gina. She always wants to prove Vincent wrong."

"I got that impression, too," I said, "when I read her blog. But she put her name on that, why not on a book?"

Karla carried her mug to the couch in the family room area. I followed her and sat on the armchair across from her.

"True. She loves to embarrass Vincent."

The cocoa tasted wonderful, dark and rich. "Is that how he saw her?"

"He said she'd always been like that."

That sounded like one of those forbidden narratives

Seminar liked to challenge people about. But I supposed self-help gurus might be no better than some doctors at healing themselves.

"But do you think she's violent?" I said.

"She's Hostile. Scott says those people can do anything. They hate themselves so much that they can't do what they need to do to heal, so they take it out on everyone else."

"But to kill your own father?"

Karla set her mug on the round Art Deco coffee table and stared at it. "I thought you were asking about Caleb."

"You don't think the two are related?"

"I know you do. I don't know what to think."

Maybe because Scott wasn't in the room to tell her, but no good would come from suggesting that. "Okay, Caleb then. You believe Gina would run him over? They've never met so far as I know."

"You're asking the wrong questions. You want to know who did something to Vincent or Caleb. But the issue is what Vincent and Caleb needed to do to become Whole."

I gripped the mug handle. I wanted to ask if she believed that about Zipporah Hernandez dying of cancer. But that would draw more canned Seminar responses, not help me sort anything out.

"You and Scott seem very close," I said.

She raised her eyes. "He's a lifeline. Without him keeping me on track, guiding me back to Seminar principles, I'd be lost."

"Have you always been close?"

"Are you asking if I'm having an affair with him? Because I know Gina tells everyone Vincent cheated on me."

"Did he?"

Her eyes shifted sideways and she studied the blank television screen. "Things happen sometimes when people work together. You can create a narrative where it's a betrayal, but that serves no purpose."

"So that's a yes?" I said.

"Yes. But we worked through it."

"And you and Scott?"

"That's none of your business. There's no way anything about Scott and me relates to Caleb."

That sounded like a yes as well, though she was right. I didn't see a connection. "You're right. I'm sorry. I'm only asking questions because I'm worried for Caleb. And the police don't understand that he could still be in danger."

"I understand," Karla said.

We both drank more cocoa. As odd as it was to have it on a warm spring day, the hot milk and dark chocolate taste made me feel calmer than I had since the hit-and-run.

"You know what my neighbor told me?" Karla said. "She's fifty-five, and she said men her age and up are all looking for a nurse or a purse. She doesn't want to be either. So she's just alone."

"You're much younger than that," I said, though I hate the idea that women need to market themselves to men based on age. "And my Gram was widowed in her fifties. She told me it was really hard losing my grandfather. At first she felt so alone, and she had some financial struggles. But all the time I've known her, she's been happy."

"But did she remarry?"

"No. She says once was enough. But she doesn't feel alone. She has a lot of friends."

"And she has children. And at least one grandchild. Neither of Vincent's daughters want much to do with me. Tina and I are about the same age. She didn't much like that. And Gina is, well, Gina."

I felt worse for Gina Lenzi than I had before. A father

who viewed her as a disappointment, a mother who died early, and a stepmother who accepted the husband's view wholeheartedly.

I set my empty mug on the table. "Still, you really think she could kill someone?"

Karla frowned. "As I said, she's Hostile."

"Do you mind telling me where you were Thursday morning?" I said.

"Me?"

"You're willing to accuse her. Suppose I talk to her and she points a finger at you?"

She shrugged. "Fine. That's the day you came to the office, isn't it? Scott and I met at 9:30 for breakfast at the Corner Bakery, the one in the Goodman Theater building, before going there."

The Corner Bakery that's in the same building as the Goodman Theater is a block and a half from the Temple Building. According to Karla's social media posts she and Vincent had occasionally stopped there for quick meals before Events.

I intended to ask Scott where he'd been. But whether they'd been together or not, I felt sure they'd back one another up. There was probably some Seminar rule about supporting other people's narratives in these circumstances.

"Caleb had something he needed to talk to me about the morning of the hit-and-run. Something he found out. I think it was about Vincent or Seminar. Any idea what?"

"Nothing about Vincent. But Scott told me he had Caleb working on a project."

"I guess it wasn't a secret since you're telling me about it."

"It's a sign of gaining Steps to be asked to do a project for Scott. But what it is, that's always confidential."

"I'll talk to Scott then."

"If you have any questions about taking part in another

Event, please call me," Karla said as she walked me to the door. "I really won't mind talking about it. It'll give me something positive to do."

Sales above all. It ought to be Seminar's slogan.

"I will," I said.

32

———

Saturday, May 24, 2:22 p.m.

When I got into my office, before turning to the stack of files on my credenza I sent Jacinda a text:

Has Zipporah ever contacted Gina since leaving seminar? Seems like Gina could use family around after her dad's death & no way will she spout seminar slogans

I also texted Scott Gary that I needed to talk to him. To my surprise, he answered right away.

He was working in the morning at Seminar preparing for the following week's Event, but he could make time around ten. He proposed that I meet him at Seminar. It occurred to me that since I kept poking the bear, being alone with him might not be the best idea. I had no idea if I could count on anyone else being in Seminar's office suite on a Sunday morning. I suggested we meet for breakfast at a restaurant a block away from the Temple Building instead.

———

SATURDAY, MAY 24, 6:30 P.M.

Ty and I ate dinner at the Italian restaurant in his neighborhood after I finished work. But he needed to get up at four a.m. for a flight, and I was exhausted, so I took a Lyft home around nine-thirty. The weather had turned cool, and the air through the half-open car windows and my racing thoughts left me wide awake when I got home.

I made some herbal strawberry and cocoa tea and checked the 10-day weather forecast. Nothing below forty predicted. Something that when I'd been a kid would have been a given for May, but now couldn't be taken for granted. I decided it was safe to move my large potted plants onto my deck for the season.

I put on a worn denim jacket, one I saved just for things like this, and started hauling the plants from the narrow area between my small dining table and the sliding glass doors out to my deck. I arranged the plants among the wooden benches near my building's brick wall. It was the best spot. They got some sunlight but were shielded from the worst of the wind.

Using my shiny metal watering can, I drenched each plant. I'd paid a premium for a condo with outdoor space. When I struggled to make mortgage payments I kicked myself for it. But as I sat breathing in the smells of wet mud and berry and chocolate tea I felt it was worth it. Much as I love Chicago, the noise and crowds of the city make me feel hemmed in. The deck saved me from that.

It reminded me of the cherry tree I'd climbed in my aunt's yard on visits to Edwardsville, Illinois. I'd loved the feeling of hiding in the trees way up high, feeling the breeze, and letting the world go by without me below.

The phone buzzed with a text from Gina Lenzi. She thanked me for reconnecting her and Zipporah. After she got over the shock of hearing how sick Zipporah was, the two had a long talk. Gina also apologized for not getting back to me sooner. Her work week had been busy, but she had time to talk now.

To my surprise, she wanted to come over. At first I said no. She shouldn't have to come out and go home again at a time when the streets would be deserted. But she insisted. It was a ten-minute cab ride from River North to my place this late, and she preferred to talk in person so long as I had wine, which I did.

Finally, it occurred to me that she wanted company. In those days and weeks after Marco's death I'd been lucky enough to have friends around me who were there whenever I needed them. Maybe Gina didn't have that.

So I said yes, come on over, if she didn't mind hanging out on the deck while I tended to my plants.

33

———

SATURDAY, MAY 24, 9:55 P.M.

I decided the best approach with Gina was honesty. After we talked about Zipporah's illness and Caleb's condition, which hadn't changed since yesterday, I told her Caleb had asked me to look into Vincent's death.

She paused directly in the beam from one of the uplights beneath a large Norfolk Island Pine. It cast jagged shadows across her face. "I — wow, that's weird. Who knew Cool Cal cared that much about my dad."

"He said he did." I retrieved a pale green leaf that had fallen off my neighbors' ficus and turned it over and over between my fingers. "Since I'm sharing, though, I need to tell you he also cared about what other people in Seminar thought about him. Worried they'd think he had something to do with the death. I wasn't sure which was more important to him. It's awful to say, but I haven't seen him in so long that I didn't know how to tell."

She returned to the table for a drink of wine. I'd brought out two glasses of water for us and two glasses of Pinot Noir, leaving the bottle inside.

"That's Seminar," she said. "Everyone there is paranoid about moving up the steps or whatever."

I sank onto the bench across from her. "It doesn't bother you that Caleb might have been more concerned about Seminar than your dad?"

"My dad was more concerned about Seminar than about me. Why should Caleb be any different?"

I nodded. "But in that circumstance, it doesn't seem human to be more worried about your job than someone's death."

"Seminar humans might talk about relationships and careers and saving the world, but Seminar matters more than any of those things." She jiggled the water glass back and forth, making the ice clink, but not drinking any. "It's like a dark version of that old thing where you add 'in bed' to every fortune cookie saying, you know?"

"How do you mean?"

"End world hunger — by recruiting more people for Seminar. Improve your relationships — by attending more Seminar events and bringing your friends and family. Become more successful — by spending more time and money on Seminar."

She took another long drink of wine.

"So no matter what you want or care about, you get there through Seminar," I said.

"Yep. And Scott Gary gets your money."

The comment made me think of *Give Me All Your Money*. I asked if she'd read it, but she said no.

"I remember D.O.D. saying Scott was upset about it, though."

I wished we were inside in the light so I could see her face.

"It crossed my mind you might have written it."

She laughed. It sounded strained. "I can see why you'd think that. I didn't really hate my dad."

"I didn't think you did."

"Anyway, I'd put my name on it." She finished her glass of wine.

"Any idea who did write it? It includes a lot of concepts only people who are advanced in Seminar would know. Attending and Spending. See It, Speak It, Say It. Personal things about Scott."

"You got me. But hey, maybe whoever wrote it is making a lot of money on it. Which'd be ironic."

"I finally met Scott. On Thursday." I retrieved my watering can from near the door and began watering again as I told Gina about Karla's protectiveness toward Scott.

She trailed a few steps behind me, as if supervising my plant care skills. "Everyone in Seminar's like that about Scott. It's like he's a god. Better, maybe, because he never threatens people with hell. Only excommunication."

I poured water into a large potted plant. It probably would be smarter to sit and take in everything Gina said, but I couldn't sit still, and obviously she also couldn't. Plus the chill in the air combined with fatigue was making me shiver. Moving helped.

"Excommunication?" I said.

"Oh, no one outright says it. But D.O.D. said you know that if you fail to do every last thing Scott wants, in exactly the way he directs you to do it, he'll shut you out. Plus no one from Seminar will talk to you anymore. Ever. Nice, huh?"

She rubbed her hands over her arms.

"Have you had dinner?" I said.

She held up the empty wine glass. "Just drank it."

I wasn't hungry, but when friends cooked for me after Marco's death it had helped me feel cared for. Right now, Gina could probably use that, and so could I.

"Could you eat? I'm thinking of pasta. And it'll be warmer inside."

As I got out a package of fresh three-cheese tortellini, Gina refilled her wine glass and took a seat at one of the bar stools at my kitchen island.

"You ever hear about someone feuding with Seminar and disappearing? Someone in New York?" I said.

"Disappearing? Like a mafia hit or something?"

I crushed a fresh garlic clove after putting on a pot of water over high heat. "Yes."

My paralegal hadn't found anything so far, but she still needed to search three more years. She's freelance and works for five attorneys besides me, so she couldn't put all her time into the project.

"Nope. But my dad wasn't one to pass on negative things about Seminar."

I poured the tortellini in the boiling water and started slicing cherry tomatoes in half. "Let's forget about Seminar for a while. How have you been?"

She shared her job frustrations as I chopped green pepper and sautéed it with the tomatoes and garlic. By the time we ate, she'd moved on to her years growing up in her sister's shadow. It was almost midnight by the time I loaded my dishwasher.

"Hey, sorry, I've been talking this whole time." She handed me her empty wine glass.

I fitted it onto the top rack. "That's all right. You needed it."

"I really hope Caleb gets better. If there's any way I can help, let me know."

She put on her cardigan and tied it at the waist.

"Could you tell me when the autopsy report on your dad comes back?" I said.

"Karla didn't tell you? I figured you knew since you said

you saw her at the Seminar offices. The tox screens all came back negative early last week. Final verdict was he had a heart attack and fell, hit his head on the corner of the desk on the way down."

I stared at her. "The police don't think anyone else was involved?"

"Nope."

"Why wouldn't Karla tell me that?"

"Ask Scott. She'll never explain herself unless he says it's okay."

"I will. I'm seeing him tomorrow."

The outside air and talking with Gina and cooking had helped me wind down. I was in bed ten minutes after she left. I fell right asleep.

I awoke to the sound of shattering glass.

34

Sunday, May 25, 3:08 a.m.

I'd been dreaming someone was walking around on the deck outside my condo. As I drifted to wakefulness I thought how ridiculous that was. Only four condos, including mine, open onto that deck. I'd never heard or seen any of my neighbors out there after midnight.

Yet I still heard footsteps. I opened my eyes just as something shattered the sliding doors.

I sat up.

My bedroom area is below a loft and bordered on one side by my walk-in closet and the other by the bathroom. But the front is open to the rest of the condo, and I felt exposed and vulnerable, though at least I was shrouded in darkness. The motion lights on the deck silhouetted a figure with its arm cocked backwards. It pistoned forward and something flew through the second of the glass doors.

I grabbed for my phone.

I'd plugged it in the night before, so it was right next to my lamp. Pressing the button, I held it to my mouth and told it to call 911. I heard ringing on the other end as I yanked the phone from the cord, jumped out of bed, and ran for the door to the common area hallway.

All at the same time, I yanked the door open, the emergency operator answered, and the intruder shouted something I couldn't understand in a hoarse voice. In the hallway, I started for the stairwell but remembered it had a door onto the deck, the only way to access it other than through one of the condos. I darted in the opposite direction and hit the elevator button, banging on a neighbor's door on the way as I told the operator what happened.

The elevator came before my neighbor answered. I took it down to Lauren's condo.

———

SUNDAY, MAY 25, 3:24 A.M.

Police arrived in less than eight minutes. I waited at Lauren's while they checked my home and dusted for fingerprints. They didn't find anyone inside. Based on the glass on the floor, which didn't look like it had been stepped on, they guessed that the intruder had stayed outside. Two rocks from my neighbors' landscaping had been thrown through the glass.

Lauren and I cleaned up while the police interviewed neighbors and the night doorman.

My shoulder bag sat on the counter stool where I'd left it. My wallet inside appeared to have all my credit cards and money. I checked the shoebox where I keep my jewelry and my hiding place for spare cash — I keep it in my coffee canister in a small plastic baggie — and nothing appeared to be missing.

"It looks like this was meant to frighten you," the lead officer said. He had dark hair and a nice build, and I guessed him about my age.

With help from Lauren, I explained what must've sounded like a convoluted story about Vincent's death, Caleb, and Seminar. He wrote all of it down.

"It must've been someone who knows I have sliding glass doors that open onto a private deck. You can't see it from the street," I said.

From Plymouth Court or State Street on either side of my building you see only the walls surrounding the deck.

Though I had to think this attack related to my investigations, no one from Seminar had been to my home, not even Caleb. The only person connected to all of it was Gina. I didn't want to think that she would do anything like this, and I couldn't see any motive.

"No, but you can see it from the sky. Anyone who knows your address could check Google Earth," the officer said.

Our building doesn't have an onsite manager. The overnight doorman said no one came in after Gina Lenzi signed out.

There are six cameras in the building. But like so many of the warehouses and factories turned to condos in Printers Row, our budget was always straining with old building problems. Over the last six months we'd finally replaced deteriorated, failing pipes. But our camera system was old, too, and while it transmitted video it no longer recorded. It was next on the list to be fixed, but that wouldn't do me any good. Unless the security guard had seen something in the moment on the monitor, and he hadn't, there was nothing to help identify the intruder.

––––––––

SUNDAY, MAY 25, 8:32 A.M.

My insurance company was surprisingly helpful, putting me in touch with a glass company that came out early

Sunday morning. The price was high, and I'd be paying most of it, but it was worth it to be able to shut the doors again immediately. I also researched security systems. I hadn't thought I needed one because so few people have access to the deck.

Staying home to guard the doors and meet the service people meant pushing my meeting with Scott to the afternoon. He had multiple conference calls and a lot of work to do, so his time was limited. I declined again to meet him at Seminar, but agreed to his suggested compromise that we meet across the street in Daley Plaza around two p.m. With all the theater matinees and the Block 37 shopping center across the street it seemed public enough.

I decided not to tell Scott about the intruder. If he did have something to do with it, he might say something to give himself away.

———

Sunday, May 25, 1:57 p.m.

He was waiting for me on a concrete bench along the Washington side of Daley Plaza. On warm weekend days residents often sit near the plaza's bubbling fountain, surrounded by flowers and plants, reading or talking. But today the temperature was in the mid-fifties, too cool for that. All the same, little kids climbed up and slid down the slanted metal base of the Picasso. City workers set up chairs for tomorrow's Memorial Day celebrations.

The wind off the lake today felt chilly, but the sun shone through gaps in the clouds. Scott wore a lightweight distressed lambskin jacket over expensive looking jeans. His off-white cashmere turtleneck made his skin look very tan, tanner than when I'd seen him a few days before. I saw no hint of orange or white spaces around his eyes from salon glasses. Maybe he'd jetted off to Aruba Friday night and returned this morning. According to the book, he owned a vacation condominium there.

I'd pulled on a navy blazer over jeans and a tank top, adding my long gray leather jacket. I wanted to look somewhat professional despite my exhaustion.

"Karla tells me you were fishing for more information about Vincent and Seminar," he said before I sat down.

I sat a foot or so from him on the bench. "That's what I want to talk to you about. Caleb asked me to look into Vincent's death. But maybe you already knew that."

As I'd watched the work on my sliding doors this morning I'd thought about my interactions with Scott and Karla. Although he'd put the brakes on Karla telling me what I wanted to know that day in the Seminar office kitchen, he expressed less surprise than I expected at my questions. In fact, both of them answered a little too easily. That Caleb had hidden from me Scott's presence the night of Vincent's death made me think that Scott might be behind the request. Maybe for some reason of his own he wanted to learn about Vincent, Richard, Frank, and Karla while keeping his life private.

"Didn't know." He sighed, his shoulders heaving. "But I was afraid he'd done that."

"Because?"

"He'd been looking for a way to introduce you to Seminar."

"And you thought he might come up with an imaginary murder?"

"Originally we did think there might be something suspicious about Vincent's death. That's when Caleb mentioned you were good at these kinds of things, but I told him the police would handle it."

A gust of wind blew my hair into my face. I gathered it

and tucked it under my coat collar. "If that's true, why wouldn't he listen to you?"

"I don't think you understand how much he wanted to share Seminar with you, Quille. But he kept telling me there would need to be something special to get you to consider it. That you go your own way and always have. You aren't a joiner."

I studied the skateboarders careening across the open areas of the gray and white concrete plaza. I had preferred to be homeschooled, yes, because it allowed me to arrange my school projects around my acting and because I liked racing through books and lessons at my own pace. But I'd learned, partly through Caleb's help, that being isolated meant I needed to make more effort to meet people. Part of what I loved about having done so many different things — acting, music, accounting, law — had been meeting people in each area. But Caleb didn't know that because he hadn't stayed in touch. He still saw me as the awkward girl he'd known who was only really comfortable playing a part on stage.

"He doesn't know me," I said.

"I'm glad to hear that," Scott said, "because I'm hoping you'll work with me."

"I'm not interested in wearing a green T-shirt and paying you to work for your business."

One of the longest chapters in the book covered the vast amount of unpaid labor the author claimed devoted Seminar participants did. Seminar compared the green T-shirt people to ushers at concerts who volunteered but then got to see the concert free. And it called people who ran small groups for it at the intermediate levels interns. But the green T-shirts paid to retake the Event in addition to working at it. Likewise, those who ran the small groups were paying tuition to be allowed the privilege of doing so. I knew people in law school who paid tuition while doing externships, but that was because the school gave them credit for the work towards their degrees. Seminar offered no similar benefit.

Scott made a sideways cutting gesture with his right hand. "That's really not what happens in Seminar. But we can talk about that another time because that's not what I'm asking you to do."

Above us clouds drifted together to block the sun. "So what are you asking?" I said.

"Caleb might not have understood, but I do. You're a sharp, determined investigator. Which is why I want to hire you to find out who tried to kill him."

35

SUNDAY, MAY 25, 2:25 P.M.

"Vincent died of natural causes, but you think someone purposely ran into Caleb?"

Scott nodded. "Exactly."

"Why?"

A few raindrops spattered down, but we both stayed on the bench.

"There was an issue I asked him to look into. The last time I talked to him, he said he had an answer for me. And proof." He shifted on the concrete bench and crossed his legs. "We planned to meet Wednesday afternoon and he never made it. And I understand he had something he wanted to talk to you about right before he was meeting me."

"What was the issue?"

"I'm only willing to tell you if you agree to investigate for me."

I zipped my jacket higher. Shouts and laughter came from the kids on the Picasso. "I'm a lawyer, not a licensed private investigator. And I'm not your lawyer."

"Do you need a license?"

"No." It was something I'd made sure of when I was trying to find out what happened to Marco. "But I don't charge people for investigating. It's something I've had some luck with, but I've only done it for people close to me."

"Like Caleb." He put his hand on the side of my upper arm and looked me right in the eyes. The light gray of his irises matched the sky. "Don't you want to know who did this to him? And make sure he's safe in the future?"

I inched away from him. "Yes. But it doesn't mean I want to work for you. Especially when I suspect you told Caleb to lie to me to get me into Seminar."

"I never told him to do that."

"But you weren't surprised that he had."

"Because I knew how anxious he was about the move here. He'd been away from Chicago so long that he feared not doing as well here as he did in Austin. Other than his parents, you're who he knows best here. The person with the most contacts with all different kinds of people. Actors, artists, lawyers, finance people. In his zeal to bring Seminar to you and to as many people as possible, it occurred to me he might step over the line. But I never encouraged him to do that."

A group of tourists, colorful umbrellas in hand, gathered on the corner nearest us and turned to look at the Picasso.

"And what exactly is that line?"

"If Caleb truly believed Vincent was murdered, it would be fine to reach out to you and ask for your help. If, in the process, you found Seminar enhanced your life, that would be a wonderful bonus. But if Caleb did not in his heart believe Vincent had been murdered, telling you that to draw you in would be stepping over the line."

"So it's all about subjective beliefs," I said. "Not objective truth?"

Scott smiled. "I forgot you didn't finish your Event. If you had, you would have learned that there is no objective truth."

"Vincent died. Caleb was run over by an SUV. Those are objective truths."

"You choose to say he died. Perhaps Vincent moved to another plane of existence."

His comments reminded me of why I'd never gone beyond Philosophy 101. The different ways people see the world intrigues me. It's part of why I found both acting and law so fascinating. But I have no patience for theorizing about whether anyone can ever know anything for certain.

"Sure," I said, "and maybe you and I aren't really having a conversation, it's all an imagined universe in my head. If that's the road you want to go down, there's no point to my looking into anything."

Scott waved his hand. "Facts differ depending on who's telling them. You must know that, as a lawyer."

In true Chicago fashion, despite the drizzle, the sun appeared, making me squint and shift position. "As a lawyer, I present the facts in the best light possible for my clients. I tell their stories using the facts. That's my job. But the facts are what they are."

"That's your limited view."

"And your more expansive view, and Caleb's, is fine with you as long as it brings Seminar more money."

"It's not primarily about earning Seminar money."

"Really?"

His lambskin jacket said otherwise. It looked like one I'd seen in the window of Overland Sheepskin with a price tag over twelve hundred dollars. Between it, his tailored jeans, loafers, and cashmere turtleneck, I guessed the clothing he wore exceeded my monthly mortgage payment plus my office rent combined.

Scott shrugged. "I'm sure you charge a significant amount for your time. So does Seminar. But like you, we can't force anyone to buy, and we're not right for everyone."

I stood. "You're right about that."

Scott stood too. "Quille, please. I know you must feel betrayed. I would too if I were you. It must feel like Caleb was manipulating you."

"Because he was. And he's not the only one."

Sunday, May 25, 2:25 p.m.

Without thinking I headed north toward the river. I shouldered past slow-walking tourists outside the Goodman Theater and darted around construction saw horses and under scaffolding in the next block, barely noticing which streets I crossed. The rain had stopped, but the pavement remained damp and slippery.

On the north side of the river, I paused near the concrete steps to the upper river front walkway and dialed my mom's number. She answered after three rings.

"Q? What's going on? You didn't call this morning."

I call my mom most Sunday mornings but today I hadn't had a chance.

"There's some bad news," I said. "About Caleb. There's hope that he'll recover, but he's in the hospital."

As traffic rumbled over the bridge and past me, I explained what happened.

"Why didn't you tell me Thursday?"

"I was hoping he'd be in a better condition today." That was only partly true. I hadn't wanted to worry her, but my mom's also the last person I think to call when I'm upset.

"It's all so horrible," my mom said. "Maureen must be so worried. This is why I hate you living in the city. It's dangerous. The traffic, the crime. I can't sleep at night I'm so worried about you all the time."

I took a breath and switched the phone to my other ear.

Pointing out that the original Q.C. was abducted from a pizza place in small town Edwardsville wouldn't help anything. My mom was already afraid enough of going out of the house.

"There's something I need to know. What did you tell Caleb about me?"

"About you? When?"

"Last week when he called. Or the first time, whenever he let you know he was moving back to Chicago."

A CTA bus pulled up, disgorging a large group of passengers laughing and chatting in a language I didn't recognize. They headed for the restaurant near the House of Blues. I put one hand over my ear so I could hear my mom better.

"Why does it matter? You know my memory's not good with this new medication, and the doctor refuses to let me go back to the old one."

"It's important, Mom. Did you talk about me at all?" I said. "Besides that he couldn't get through to me?"

Another call buzzed my line. I ignored it.

"I suppose we must have. Though he did ask a lot about how I've been doing. And told me about the company he's working for. Some sort of education company for businesspeople?"

Caleb had to have found out about my investigating Marco's death somehow, but it wasn't as if my role had been in the news. Only people close to me knew about it.

"Seminar," I said.

"I don't remember the name. Oh, when he called last summer, I think he did ask about you. He was worried you were unhappy not acting. Also that you might have trouble making friends outside the theater world."

"Ten years later and he was worried about me making friends without him? You didn't think that strange?"

"Well, you were a sort of odd child. Oh, and he saw online that you'd started your own firm. He thought maybe it was so you'd have more time to act, but I said no, you gave up on it a long time ago."

I started walking again. "Did you say anything about Marco? Or me investigating?" I was still too upset about Caleb deceiving me to express exasperation at her "gave up" comment.

"Investigating? When did you — oh, you know, I probably talked about you getting mixed up in the police investigation when Marco died and getting yourself hurt. Because he called in the summer when you were still recovering, so it would have been on my mind."

So much for Caleb's claim that she'd sounded proud of me.

"What's all this about investigating?" she said.

Probably because I was sleep deprived and still shaken from the intruder, against my better judgment I gave my mom the short version of what had been happening.

"Why would Caleb ask you to investigate a murder? You should've known that was just pretend. It's like that game you two used to play, what was it?"

"Clue," I said.

"Yes. He tells you there are just four people who might have done it and the police won't be able to figure it out?"

"I — never mind. It doesn't matter."

Caleb had played me so very well. He might not have seen me for a decade, but he'd still known how to push my buttons.

After I hung up, I saw that Scott Gary had left a voicemail. I tucked my phone into my shoulder bag without listening and headed east, aiming for the lake. Staring at its rolling waves for a while might help me calm down.

Instead, in a few blocks I turned north again and was at Northwestern Memorial Hospital.

I found Maureen in Caleb's room. He was still unconscious. The doctors had told her that with the extent of the trauma and the surgery, his brain might simply need quiet time to heal. But the longer he stayed unconscious the worse his prognosis became. I wanted to strangle him and cry at the same time.

Maureen asked if I'd eaten. I remembered the Lettuce Entertain You gift card from Seminar. I'd forgotten all about it. I showed it to Maureen and suggested she and Jack go out when he arrived.

"Oh, no, no. More of that man and I'll throw him across the room. And I'm sure he feels the same about me. Let's you and I go once he gets here. Have a girls' evening."

I dozed in one of the visitor chairs in Caleb's room while we waited for Jack.

SUNDAY, MAY 25, 6:25 P.M.

Over spaghetti and red wine at Maggiano's Maureen told me the police so far had no luck in finding video footage from any of the red light cameras or retail establishments in the area that showed a dark SUV with a damaged front end.

I told her about my meeting with Scott Gary.

Maureen's features froze. "Someone did this to Caleb? On purpose?"

"That's what Scott suspects. Or says he does. I don't know if I believe him."

"Why would he make that up?"

"Why would Caleb lie to me and you?"

She squeezed my hand. "Oh, honey, I understand why you'd feel that way. I'm sorry Caleb lied. But do you think the police will figure it out if someone did try to hurt him?"

My wine had a flat aftertaste and I set it aside. "Seminar is insular. That's one thing Caleb told me that I believe. I've seen it, and it makes me think the police won't understand anyone in it or their motivations. But finding the driver of the SUV has more to do with tracking the vehicle."

"Did this Scott person say why he thought someone tried to kill Caleb?"

I looked away. "We didn't get to that. But he left a voicemail."

She urged me to listen. I held the phone so we could both hear.

"Quille, I handled our talk badly, and I take full responsibility for that. I should have been more specific. Caleb called me the day before he was hit to arrange our meeting. He said he'd learned something through you that he thought I needed to know, which I'm guessing is why he wanted to talk to you first. I assumed it related to the project I'd given him, but it may not have. Please call me back. If once we talk further you still don't want to work for me, I promise I'll leave you be."

"He sounds worried for Caleb," Maureen said.

I set the phone on the table between us. I wasn't sure I believed Scott about anything Caleb had said. It all seemed perfectly designed to make me feel partly responsible for what happened and guilt me into doing Scott's bidding.

Guilt might be considered an unproductive emotion in the Seminar world, but it was also a useful one.

"Or he knows exactly what to say to give that impression," I said.

"But you were looking into things for Caleb. Is there a chance you uncovered something somebody wanted hidden?"

36

———

Sunday, May 25, 7:17 p.m.

I tapped my fingers on the table. "I've been trying to figure that out, but I can't think what it would be. I learned things not many others in Seminar know, but nothing criminal. Nothing you'd use to blackmail anyone. And I didn't pass it all on to Caleb."

"That narrows it down then. Figure out what you did pass on, and maybe Scott can give you context. That could pin down what might have made someone go after Caleb."

"The problem is, I don't trust Scott." I twirled spaghetti around my fork, but I didn't eat any of it.

"Do you have to trust him to work for him?"

"Yes. I'd be reporting what I learned to him."

"Isn't it worth it if he can help?"

"I'm not sure cooperating with Scott would make Caleb safer. He could have already told Scott whatever it was, and Scott's the one who went after him. Or got someone else to do it."

"Then why would he ask for your help?"

"To find out what I know."

"I didn't think of that." Maureen cut a meatball in half. "Then I want to hire you. You trust me. And I need to know what happened to my son."

"I'll do whatever I can to figure this out, but no one's hiring me. I could never charge you, even if investigating were my job, and it's not."

"You're underestimating yourself. I asked your friend Ty, and he said you know what you're doing."

"Ty's a little biased," I said, but I felt pleased. I'd been getting the impression Ty wished I would stay out of all of this. "If I can get Scott to cooperate with me I will. I just need to be sure I don't cause more trouble by digging into things."

Talking about Ty reminded me that I hadn't called or texted him all day. When we got back to the hospital, I reached him in between drinks and dinner with a potential client. He was upset I hadn't contacted him sooner, though there was nothing he could've done.

After that I joined Maureen in Caleb's room and we took turns reading to him from *The Call of the Wild*, one of his favorite books in high school. Other than his casted leg, he looked small in the bed. A few days of hydration and nutrition gotten only through tubes and his wiry body had already become gaunt. He somehow looked shorter, too, as if he'd become again that tiny boy I'd met. His eyelids fluttered when we spoke, but he showed no other signs of improving.

I wished he'd wake up. For so many reasons.

———

Tuesday, May 27, 11:09 a.m.

I should have contacted him sooner, but I don't exactly have an easy relationship with Detective Beckwell of the Chicago Police Department. He'd interviewed me about Marco's death. We crossed paths again when my search for a missing woman turned into a murder investigation. While he could hardly blame me for what the criminals I helped uncover did, I somehow felt he did. He probably thought I should stay out of police business. Or he thought I was bad luck.

When I was ushered into his office the day after Memorial Day, he confirmed it. He opened his mouth, then closed it and waved to one of the wooden visitor chairs in front of his desk. "This can't be good."

His tan suit jacket hung over the back of his chair. He wore a crisp white shirt with gray vertical stripes and darker gray suspenders. With that and his silver hair he looked to me more like an old-time private investigator than a modern-day police detective. I half-expected him to pull out a cigar and light it up.

I gave him a ten-minute rundown of Vincent's death, Caleb asking me to look into it, the hit-and-run, and the rocks thrown through my sliding doors. Plus a short description of Seminar and critics' claims that it was a money grab that drove some people into bankruptcy. He listened, forearms on his desk, hands folded.

"Starting at the simplest point, murder by SUV's unlikely unless the driver was so lucky he ought to play the lottery."

"It'd be hard to plan," I said.

"Traffic the way it is, finding an opportunity to run him down with a clear path to drive away wouldn't be easy. The driver would have to had to follow your friend around a lot to find the perfect moment. He ever mention seeing a black SUV following him?"

"No, but I'm pretty sure he's glued to his phone when he's walking alone."

"That also weighs in favor of it being an accident. Lots of distracted drivers and pedestrians these days."

"I thought of that."

"But you think it relates to this other death?"

"I did think that. Until I heard the autopsy of Vincent Lenzi showed he died of a heart attack. Is it possible you can verify that's what the autopsy says?"

I'd sent a request to the Medical Examiner's Office, but it could take weeks or months to get a response.

His eyebrows, which were darker gray than his hair, rose. "You think the investigating officer lied to the family?"

"I think people could be lying to me."

It didn't seem likely Gina, Karla, and Scott conspired together to lie. But Gina had been angry at her dad and jealous of Caleb. And someone threw rocks through my glass doors a few hours after she left my place. Nothing about her suggested she was homicidal, but that didn't mean as much to me as it once might have. I'd uncovered a killer just before Christmas who'd seemed like a completely normal person.

"I'd say you're paranoid but you've proven me wrong before. All the same, you understand I can't give you information just because you ask." The detective raised a hand before I could interrupt. "But I don't see any harm in confirming something you've already heard."

He put on his reading glasses and tilted his monitor so it faced him directly, making it impossible for me to see the screen.

As he clicked away at the keys, I scrolled through my work email. I'd slept late this morning and come straight to the precinct after calling to be sure Detective Beckwell was in. My assistant had sent my revisions to the brief I planned to file Friday if the judge gave me permission. I opened the document and read the redlined sections to review my changes.

She still hadn't found any complaint in New York about Seminar or the supposed disappearance of the young man connected to it.

"The autopsy finding is what you said," Beckwell said. "Natural causes. Heart attack. I'm not sharing all of what's in the police reports, but I can tell you what's not there. Anything about anyone arguing with Vincent Lenzi the night he died."

"Caleb told me he reported that to the police. They interviewed him the longest of anyone."

He clicked through more keys and studied the screens. "They did spend the most time with him."

"So?"

"Looks like your friend spent that time telling the reporting officer about Seminar."

I rubbed my finger along the edge of the metal desk. "He told me he wanted to make sure they understood who the people were and how it worked."

"No, I meant trying to sell them on Seminar. Pitching for the whole department to come for some kind of specialized training."

My shoulders sagged. So Caleb had never had any reason to think the police suspected him other than his felony record, if he really had one. I supposed I ought to be glad my former friend hadn't really been in trouble, but at the moment only the fact that he was currently struggling for his life kept me from stalking out of the detective's office.

It was no wonder the police didn't take seriously my fear that Seminar related to the hit-and-run. I asked Detective Beckwell if he could update me on that investigation.

There was at least some news there. Police had located video footage showing a dark SUV that matched the description of the one that hit Caleb. The license plates were from Indiana, but the angle of the camera didn't catch the plate number. He told me at this point Chicago police would coordinate with the Indiana state police. Chicago area and nearby Indiana body shops would be canvassed for repairs to a matching vehicle. But if the driver garaged the vehicle or took it to another state without being spotted, that wouldn't lead anywhere.

Fingerprints from my condo, deck, and the rocks probably wouldn't come back for another week. Unless the prints matched someone with a record, there wasn't much hope of finding the intruder.

"Does the driver taking off make it more likely Caleb was run over on purpose?"

Beckwell's chair creaked as he rocked back and took off his glasses. "More likely than if the driver stopped? Sure. But it doesn't mean that's what happened. Often a driver takes off if drugs or alcohol are involved. They don't want to be charged criminally. Death or serious bodily injury — that's significant jail time, especially if the person has a prior DUI."

I thanked him and started to stand.

He put his hand flat on his desk. "Ms. Davis, before you leave."

I settled into the chair again. "Yes."

"I'd try telling you to leave this to the police, but why waste my breath. But if you insist on helping out friends with these kinds of issues —"

"You make it sound like I'm out there looking to investigate murders."

"Maybe not. But you're not saying No when people ask you."

"Would you?"

"No, but it's my job. And it's part of why I went into this line of work. Which is why I'm telling you, if you plan to make a habit of it, you need to be more cautious. Get that security system installed. Think about getting a concealed carry permit. You need a lot of training to get it, but that would be good for you."

"I don't want a gun."

My depression during my college years hadn't been severe, but with my mom's history I felt I had a greater risk than most people. If I ever became suicidal, the last thing I wanted was a gun in easy reach.

"At least self-defense classes then. You've been lucky so far. But in my experience, nobody's luck lasts."

37

"Any chance Gina and Scott are colluding with each other? Telling you Vincent died of a heart attack and he didn't?" Lauren said.

We sat outside at one of our favorite Printers Row restaurants. I'd gotten drenched walking from the police station to the bus and the bus to my office. But late in the afternoon the sun had broken through and an unexpected warm front swept the city.

"Only if either Detective Beckwell or the medical examiner is in on it. Which seems like too big a stretch," I said.

Lauren topped off our water glasses. Our waiter seemed to be covering all the tables along Polk Street and half a dozen inside the restaurant. We hadn't seen him in what felt like ages. "Got it. No conspiracy. And no idea if Caleb told you the truth about anything."

"Right. But one thing I know for sure is I don't trust Scott. If Caleb would lie to me to serve Seminar's purposes, no question its founder would." I carved into the Burrata cheese and transferred a mound of it to my plate along with red and yellow beet slices. "What about Richard? How was your coffee with him?"

They'd met this morning, around when I'd been visiting Detective Beckwell.

"He seriously makes me question how Seminar helps anyone with business," Lauren said. "The guy has never done a residential real estate closing in his life. He did some sort of real estate law in New York, but it was commercial."

"But he could learn."

"Sure, but will he? I doubt it. He spent twenty minutes trying to talk me into another Seminar Event instead of pitching me on how he'd get up to speed on residential. I only set aside twenty minutes to meet with him, so too bad, very sad for him."

"Did he say anything about Vincent? Or Caleb?"

"Only in the context of how exceptional Seminar is. How Vincent invested in Frank Hernandez's online nutritional supplement business, and it launched into the stratosphere because of Scott's concepts, which later became Seminar, blah blah. Nothing about Caleb."

I hadn't realized Scott as well as Vincent had been involved in Frank's company. I wondered if Frank felt being left alone to run it was a good thing or a bad one.

———

TUESDAY, MAY 27, 7:25 P.M.

Jack had moved out of the row house over the weekend. He lived and worked in Woodstock, which is close to the Wisconsin border. He decided that since he needed to make a long drive twice a day to see Caleb regardless where he stayed, it made more sense for Maureen to move into the row house. She looked through Caleb's things and brought me his laptop. She said the desk and file cabinets in the row house's home office were half empty. What was there related to three different businesses Jack ran years ago.

Caleb's laptop was heavy and black, with scuffed sides and a name brand I didn't recognize. The battery no longer worked.

Neither Maureen nor Jack knew the password.

For many years I'd created passwords based on Caleb's background rather than my own, drawing on his favorite books, plays, or family members' names. I knew as much about him as myself, and I doubted anyone else would guess that I used his info. My first password at the accounting firm where I'd worked was Percy?6, which incorporated his cat's name and the cat's age when I first met Caleb. My security question for my investment accounts was based on his high school's mascot.

After I got home from meeting Lauren, I set the laptop on my kitchen island, plugged it in, and tried different combinations based on Caleb's life and mine, ever in fear of being locked out. The password turned out to be fairly simple. It had nothing to do with me. It was Jackson1.

I saw right away why it had been so easy. The hard drive mainly included documents from Caleb's acting career before moving to Austin and his sales job there. All were dated over three years ago, before he'd gotten involved in Seminar.

But once I connected the laptop to my wireless, his email started populating into the laptop's old Outlook folder. He must have set it up a long time ago and forgotten it. As what looked like thousands of emails loaded, I got myself another glass of ice water.

The account appeared to be a junk email address. The kind you give out in stores when they want to send you promotional emails in exchange for giving you a loyalty rewards discount. He must have a separate one for Seminar.

My guess was that he hadn't used this laptop in forever. Maureen had found it in a case on the dresser in the master bedroom.

But just as I turn over every last stone for my clients, I did the same for Caleb. After opening a playlist of Guster, one of my favorite bands, on my phone I started scrolling. I started with the most recent.

The message was dated three days before the hit-and-run.

This is in response to your voicemail. Do not call my office again or email me at any address. I've had nothing to do with Seminar for nearly a decade, so I doubt I can tell you anything that could be useful to you. But because you say you were close with Vincent I'll try calling you tomorrow morning.

Do not tell anyone in Seminar that I responded to your inquiry.

The email came from greycat5389@Smail.com.

———

Tuesday, May 27, 8:22 p.m.

My attempts to research the email address led me to non-functioning websites or warning messages about suspect sites.

I went through the chapter on Seminar history in *Give Me All Your Money* and reviewed my own notes. Seminar a decade ago had revolved around two places: Austin and New York City. And everyone I met or learned about connected with one of those cities or the other.

Caleb met Vincent in Austin. Zipporah still lived there. Richard had worked at a large firm in New York, and the young man who supposedly disappeared had lived in Queens. Gina's older sister lived in and practiced medicine in Manhattan.

The book said that Scott's ex, Stacy Vance, ran a workshop called Empower Your Life. She held it every other weekend in Austin in fall and winter, and in New York City in spring and summer.

The empowerment website gave Stacy Vance's email contact information as her name at the site's address. But a photo showed her with a gray cat, making me think she might be greycat5389. The British spelling of grey suggested someone from the U.K. or who'd gone to school there, but no one's online biographies showed a U.K. connection. Maybe somebody just liked that spelling.

Over the next few days I researched and made phone calls. For all I knew, the email Caleb received led to the hit-and-run. For that reason, I hid my identity as much as possible without doing anything that would put me too far afoul of the Illinois ethics rules for lawyers.

I did my best not to lie, but I was as good as anyone at Seminar at telling stories.

38

———

On Wednesday afternoon I called Ty.

"Any real estate developers you need to visit in Manhattan?"

"Why do I get the feeling this isn't about you trying to help my business?"

"It's not. It's also not exactly a vacation."

I explained to him what I wanted to do. While I could swing the airfare to New York without too much trouble, hotels in Manhattan are pricey. If Ty had a business reason to go it would at least be a business expense for him and I could chip in for the room.

Happily, it turned out he could set up several meetings. He also was eager to be around when I investigated. Like Detective Beckwell, Ty was getting nervous about my safety.

Before I left, though, I needed to get back to Scott. I promised Ty I would meet him in a public place.

———

Thursday, May 29, 2:02 p.m.

I told Scott to meet me inside the Chase Tower, a sixty-story curving glass building that, along with its plaza, takes up an entire block in the heart of downtown. It houses Chase Bank's main branch and a huge food court on the lower level. Its wide street-level concourse includes a Starbucks, a gift shop, and multiple seating areas, all of which have a view of the sunken plaza below it. The plaza features a jet fountain on the lowest level surrounded by tables and chairs for lunchtime dining. Chagall's famous Four Seasons mosaic wall stands near street level on its east side.

The tower is three blocks from the Temple Building and about eight from my office, so it gave me a much-needed walk. I brought my refillable mug and got a Classic Chai tea latte at the Starbucks. Then I parked myself near a bronze sculpture that had armchairs, padded benches, and ottomans all around it. The sign on the sculpture's base said No Loitering.

Nothing like a little irony.

The city's brief flirtation with warmer weather had ended. The temperature was below fifty, but sun shone on the plaza and made the fountain sparkle.

I got right to the point as soon as Scott arrived.

"I intend to find out what happened to Caleb, and I need your help. But I'm not working for you," I said.

He sat on a black and chrome chair across from me. "You don't trust me."

"I don't, and you shouldn't want me to. Finding out what happened means questioning everything."

"That'll limit what I can share about Seminar. Unless you'll sign a non-disclosure agreement."

I sipped the latte and set my mug on the small marble table between us. "Send it and I'll look it over. For now, what do you think Caleb found?"

"He told me his proof involved someone high up in Seminar."

"Meaning who?"

"Besides me, now that Vincent's gone there's only Frank, Richard, and Karla."

"Is Zipporah's illness a problem for Frank in Seminar?"

I couldn't see how it related to the hit-and-run, unless Caleb learned about Zipporah from me and tried to use it against Frank, and Frank retaliated. That was a pretty quick escalation of a conflict though.

"In what way?"

"Did it hinder his standing in Seminar when Zipporah stopped participating? Or his pay?"

Scott settled into the chair and crossed one leg over the other. "Quille, there is no standing or status in Seminar. Only people living their Exponentially Exceptional lives. Frank's was no less Exponentially Exceptional because of his wife's choice. Hers was less so, but she's responsible for that, not Frank."

I had to give him credit for the tongue-twisting repetition of Exponentially Excellent. Also, referring to Zipporah as Frank's wife suggested he might not know about their separation. Though she was technically still his wife.

"Did Caleb know Zipporah?" I said.

"No, unless he met her outside Seminar. She stopped taking part about four years ago, and Vincent brought him to an Event only three years ago."

"What else could Caleb have learned about Frank?"

He shook his head. "I doubt anything. They don't work together very often. Caleb knew Vincent the best."

"Were Caleb and Richard competing with each other?"

I figured he'd dispute my word choice, but that in itself might tell me something.

"It's not a competition. If both did equally well it would

mean more new participants, so the number of Events and Celebrations to Coordinate would expand, too. There's room for everyone."

That fit with what Caleb told me when he first came to see me, and it only made sense in one scenario that I could imagine.

"Are these positions commission only?"

"There are no commissions. Commissions on what?"

I frowned. "If you really want to help Caleb, you need to stop quibbling about how I say things. Whatever you call it, bonuses, whatever, is everyone paid based on how many people they bring into Seminar?"

He drank some of his coffee, and answered before lowering the cup so it hid part of his face from me. "Seminar finances are confidential. But if Caleb told you that's how he was paid I wouldn't have a reason to dispute it."

"Did Caleb have the potential to earn more once he started leading Events?"

If he did, that could explain Olivia's comments about Caleb skyrocketing to the top of Seminar. And cause problems between Caleb and everyone else vying for the same work.

"No. Think of it this way. If you're busy arguing in court, you can't simultaneously be out wining and dining clients. Sure, someone might happen to see you arguing, be impressed, and want to hire you. But if that person is sitting in the courtroom, they probably already have a lawyer unless they can't afford one. If Seminar employees were compensated on a commission basis, and I'm not saying they are, they'd always be better off sharing one-on-one what they love about Seminar with people in their personal network. Not talking to participants already in the door."

"Does Caleb know Vincent's daughters?"

I deliberately switched topics to see if I'd throw Scott off balance. It's a technique I honed in depositions. Witnesses expect you to keep going down a certain path. When you diverge, they occasionally forget their prepared answers.

Scott, though, barely paused before answering. "Maybe. He and Vincent were close. But I don't think Vincent spent a lot of time with either daughter."

"What's your best guess on what Caleb wanted to tell you?"

Scott typed into his phone, then held it out to me. The screen showed a sales page for *Give Me All Your Money*. "A purported exposé about me was published late last year. It's been aggressively advertised and it's getting a lot of downloads."

"I read it."

"I asked Caleb two months ago if he could find out who wrote it, and he said he'd try."

"But he hadn't figured it out yet?"

"Not that he told me, but it's the only thing I can think of that he would've needed a special meeting with me about."

"Who do you think wrote it?"

"Someone jealous of my success. Someone who started Seminar but didn't persist."

The sound of a man swearing came from my left. I glanced over and saw a tall, skinny guy yelling at the middle ATM in a row of machines near the Dearborn Street exit.

"That doesn't narrow it down much," I said.

"No. That's why I asked for Caleb's help. People like him. I thought if he asked around someone might confide in him."

An eerie series of notes that sounded like the theme of a Sci Fi show blared, startling me. A woman a few chairs away dug through her purse and answered her phone, cutting it off.

"Can you get me into Caleb's work computer?" I said. "Or his home one for that matter?"

I saw no reason to let Scott know I'd already gotten into Caleb's personal email and laptop.

"Home, I've no idea what's there or how to get into it," Scott said. "But you shouldn't find anything Seminar-related. That's forbidden. Work I can do. If you sign a non-disclosure agreement. I did take the liberty of looking at Caleb's calendar and the hard drive on his computer. Nothing gave me a hint why Caleb wanted to see me."

"Does that surprise you?"

"It's what makes me think it was about the book. I told him not to let anyone know I asked him to look into it. I don't want people to think I'm worried about it."

"How does your ex-wife feel about you?"

"She's not my biggest fan. Or Seminar's. But she likes the alimony."

39

The non-disclosure agreement landed in my email In Box before I got back to my office. It included such broad language that I'd violate it by saying the word Seminar.

I doubted any reasonable judge would enforce it. Seminar probably used it less for legal protection and more to scare people into secrecy. Or make them feel they were getting something special and exclusive when they signed it. But I couldn't afford to spend my time fighting it if Seminar tried to enforce it. I also didn't have the spare funds to pay on the odd chance that I lost. You never know what a judge or jury will do, and the agreement included heavy penalties.

After lining out the broad language and writing in narrower terms, I emailed it to Seminar's attorney. The answer came back within a minute. It couldn't be modified for any reason. I called and left a voicemail explaining that these were not normal circumstances and asked that the lawyer go over the changes with Scott and reconsider. I also left a voicemail for Scott. He texted a response that, as he was sure I understood, he had to follow his attorney's advice.

He wouldn't be the first client to ask his lawyer to take a position and then hide behind that advice. It made me wonder if he was hiding something else.

———

Friday, May 30, 8:01 a.m.

On the plane I organized my notes about *Give Me All Your Money*, highlighting in green information not available in public records and bolding negative information. Then I handwrote a list of points that fit both.

- Scott's first sales work was at a distributor for a web-based business that sold healthcare products for men. He got fired for doing an end run around the company's proscribed sales channels.
- Scott and his ex-wife originally organized Seminar as a nonprofit but Scott changed it to a for-profit enterprise, saying he didn't want to suggest that money and prosperity were bad.
- Seminar lower-tier employees were paid low wages, supposedly to encourage them to focus on their own careers and businesses rather than solely on Seminar. The higher tier, like Caleb, were paid based solely on how many people they brought into Seminar each year, and on how many others their recruits convinced to take part in Events.
- With his Seminar profits, Scott bought multiple rental properties in different states under various names and corporate entities, which generated a lot of wealth. Despite that, he often claimed the bulk of his wealth came from an online nutritional

supplement business he and Frank Hernandez started.

- At least twenty percent of Seminar participants were in debt because of Seminar. Ten percent of Seminar participants declared bankruptcy within five years of taking their first Event.
- In the early days of Seminar, Scott demanded shares or an ownership interest of any company if he personally coached one of the owners.

The book didn't include anything about Scott's childhood, any relationship before his marriage to Stacy Vance, or any job during the four years between his supposed firing and starting the company with Frank Hernandez.

———

FRIDAY, MAY 30, 10:24 A.M.

"Good thing we like each other," I said as I edged around the side of the bed to set my laptop on the built-in counter that served as a desk.

It was my first trip to New York. The hotel rate was fairly inexpensive considering we were in a nice area near Midtown. But by Chicago standards the room was minuscule. At best, there was about a foot of floor space around the bed. The bathroom barely looked larger than the one on the airplane. The sink was nothing but a basin stuck to the wall and the shower was a triangular wedge in the corner.

"And that we're light packers." Ty tossed his nylon duffel bag on the ledge next to the flat screen TV. "Sure you don't want me to go with you? Second set of ears." He cupped his hands behind his ears.

"I think I can handle a law firm on my own," I said. "And a doctor."

I didn't mention that I'd noticed a man in the lobby of our hotel whom I felt sure I'd also seen on our plane. He was white, a little shorter than average with a round belly and narrow shoulders, a clean shave, and brownish hair sliding toward dull blond. His clothes were on the generic side — tan pants and a pale green golf shirt — but he carried a burgundy-colored messenger bag.

When I left our hotel in the late morning I saw two men who looked like him in the lobby. Neither carried a burgundy messenger bag. I wasn't sure I'd recognize my potential stalker without it. I strode past both men, pretending not to notice them and gritting my teeth against the blaring techno-pop music the hotel had apparently decided its guests would love.

Living in Chicago, I'm used to checking all around me, and behind me, as I walk. I decided I'd better do the same here, and step up my vigilance in whatever other way I could.

FRIDAY, MAY 30, 11:03 A.M.

Fewer people on the streets of Manhattan wore business attire than I expected. I'd imagined New York as more formal than Chicago, and so far it didn't seem to be, though people's clothes overall struck me as better-fitting and more stylish. I guessed the average body size a bit thinner, too, despite food trucks and carts everywhere and what seemed like triple the restaurant choices compared to Chicago.

Far more fast food wrappers with muddy footprints on them, squished fruit or gum, and paper scraps littered the streets and sidewalks than at home. Sometimes in the evening in downtown Chicago I walk past workers washing the sidewalks in front of retail establishments and offices with a hose. It was pretty clear no one was doing that here.

And the number of horns blaring throughout Manhattan made the busiest streets in Chicago seem like an oasis of calm.

In contrast to the noise and dirt, the waiting room of Tina Lenzi's clinic had a trickling fountain and brightly colored fresh fruit in bowls on side tables. The consultation room I was taken to fifteen minutes after arrival looked more like a reading room in an old-fashioned library.

It took me by surprise. I'd expected something gleaming and modern like the waiting area. Instead, I sat in a soft cream armchair across from a nurse surrounded by worn oak bookcases overflowing with books. Add a few interior brick walls and I could almost imagine myself at Café des Livres. If Tina had chosen the decor, it made me think we might get along.

I'd worn my best pantsuit and only pair of designer flat shoes, hoping to look as professional, non-threatening, and able to pay for lots of cosmetic procedures as possible.

"I came here desperate to squeeze in a few minutes with Dr. Lenzi. But I don't really want anything done to my face," I said.

The nurse, who wore dark purple scrubs, nodded and smiled. "Lots of people feel that way when they come here. And we don't want to do anything you don't want. If someone's pushing you —"

"No," I said. "I don't mean anyone is pressuring me. I mean that I really need to see Dr. Lenzi, but it's not about any sort of procedure."

"She's booked all day," the nurse said.

"Please. It's about her father. Related to his death. It's very important."

I'd thought about mentioning I knew Gina, but I couldn't put aside my doubts about her.

"Her father?" She looked at her watch. It had an old-fashioned clock face on a plain black band. "I don't know. She's with a patient."

"If you could just give her this note whenever there's a break and ask if she can spare me fifteen minutes. I'll wait all day if I have to."

Or at least until three-thirty, when I'd need to leave to visit Richard's old law firm.

Though the nurse took the sealed envelope I gave her, she didn't stand. Instead, she studied me for a few moments. I straightened my back and kept my hands resting lightly on my knees, pretending someone was taking my portrait.

The nurse picked up her clipboard. "It's a strange story. But I'll talk to her when I can."

————

Dear Dr. Lenzi,

You don't know me, but after your father died an old friend of mine, Caleb Jackson, came to me for help. He claimed he thought your father's death was suspicious, but the police would never figure it out because they'd never understand Seminar. He asked me to look into things for him. I'm a lawyer, not a private investigator, but I've had some luck figuring out similar questions before.

Less than two weeks later my friend was badly injured in a hit-and-run. He's in a coma.

He worked for Vincent, and they were very close. I'm afraid the hit-and-run relates to Seminar (though maybe not to your father), and Caleb might still be in danger.

I'm trying to find anyone who can give me background on

Seminar or Vincent. I know it's a huge intrusion, and I wouldn't ask except that I'm so worried for Caleb.

Friday, May 30, 2:08 P.M.

Two and half hours later, I still sat in the waiting room. I bill my non-tax work by the hour, so at least an hour and a half of that time I'd been earning money by reviewing documents and editing a motion.

I also looked at every page of the website where Lauren's client took online courses after attending Seminar. Scott might think the attack on Caleb related to the book, but I didn't want to ignore other possibilities. One piece of information I'd passed on to Caleb was that a website existed that people thought offered concepts like Seminar's.

This site, though, struck me as more of a take off on the book and film *The Secret* than Seminar. But maybe it copied something from more advanced Events I hadn't taken. Or it might look different on a laptop or tablet than a phone.

The payment tab for the courses didn't give me any clue to the site's origin. When I clicked through on Paypal as if I were buying in, the sender was a generic-sounding company name. As I exited out, the phone gave me a 20% power warning.

My three-year-old phone went quickly from twenty to ten to zero, so I shut it off. I was looking for an outlet when the receptionist beckoned me over. "The doctor can see you now."

40

———

Friday, May 30, 2:28 p.m.

Dr. Tina Lenzi's office was barely large enough for her modular desk, the leather armchair behind it, and the too-firm straight-back seat in front of it. Tina must use the book nook to meet patients. Her desk featured photos of herself with a man, two kids, and a Golden Retriever.

No cats.

I'd just sat down when a slimmer, older version of Gina Lenzi appeared in the doorway. She had the same dark hair, but hers was styled in a sleek bob that evoked the 1920s flapper era and highlighted high cheekbones. She wore a white coat over a topaz top and black dress pants. A white takeout bag was in her hands.

"This better not be some ruse to harangue me about joining Seminar."

I stood and turned to face her full on. "Does that happen a lot?"

"It used to. So what is it you want?"

I gave her the shortest version I could. She ate her lunch, a large salad, at her desk while I talked.

"Good choice not to work for Scott," she said. "But other than my father, my last contact with anyone at Seminar was over a decade ago."

"The email Caleb got was from someone who also hadn't been in Seminar for a long time."

"Well, it wasn't me."

"Your sister's blog said you call Seminar people Wanna-Bes. Is there someone in particular who fits that?"

"Oh, Gina. Still so angry about Seminar. No it wasn't anyone in particular."

"I figured it wasn't your dad. He sounded very successful."

She speared her fork through a few pieces of greens and anchored them with the cucumber slice. "He was and he wasn't. He liked to talk as if he were a self-made man, but he inherited a lot of properties from my grandfather and grandmother. The income pretty much let him do what he wanted, and what he wanted was to pour money into Seminar."

"Are you saying he lost money on it?"

"Not in the very long run. But my guess is that for the first ten years he spent more than he earned. Scott sold him Event after Event after Event. Though Seminar is all about taking personal responsibility, so in its terms it's more accurate to say my father bought Event after Event after Event."

"Who else in Seminar did you know well?"

Based on my research, I had a pretty good idea who it might be.

"I suppose there's no reason not to tell you. I just don't see how it will help. I was involved with Richard Messerly during college and for a while after. About three years total."

I'd guessed Richard based on his age and that he and Tina went to the same university, but I hadn't expected they'd dated.

"You were seeing Richard but you weren't in Seminar? I

got the impression that Seminar people stayed pretty much with their own."

"That was the problem. The first one."

"Did you meet through your father?"

"No. I avoided all things Seminar by that time. Richard and I both went to Columbia University for undergraduate. Met in a humanities class, one of my last general education requirements. He came up to me and said he wondered about my last name. He acted so excited to hear I was Vincent's daughter."

"Acted?" I said.

She nodded. "Yep. I found out much, much later that Scott put him up to all of it. My dad claimed he hadn't known, and maybe he didn't, but I never felt sure about that."

"With how you felt about Seminar, didn't Richard make you run the other direction?"

"I almost did. But he was really sweet back then, and his enthusiasm for Seminar helped me see a different side to the organization. It didn't make me want to join, but I could understand a little better why it meant so much to my dad. At least until I found out it was all a set up."

"What was it that impressed you? Before you knew Scott was behind it all?"

Tina poured some more dressing on her salad. "Richard had trouble making up his mind. Lots of people change their majors in college, but he couldn't pick one to begin with. He was so afraid of doing the wrong thing. During his second Event, though, he finally decided on a political science major and law school after. He said it finally hit him that no decision was absolutely right or wrong. That he'd get feedback and make adjustments, and that was okay."

"So he wasn't the WannaBe."

"No. But I started noticing how many people seemed to

return for the sake of returning. Like it was a drug or addiction."

Gina had said something similar.

"Or a support group?" I said.

"I suppose that's the closest analogy. If your support group was for-profit and charged you thousands of dollars a year."

"Scott Gary would say people are getting value for that."

"Maybe he believes that. But compare it to therapy. A good therapist's goal is to become unnecessary. To help you learn to go forth on your own. Seminar's goal is to keep people coming back forever."

"Some people might say the same about cosmetic procedures," I said.

"They might. But as long as people understand what they're getting and the limits of what it will do, there's no reason it shouldn't be available to them."

"When did you realize Scott put all this in motion?"

"It got to where Richard and I were fighting constantly. One time he got so angry that I wouldn't come to a Celebration and let something slip about all the work he'd put in. I got it out of him." Tina's landline buzzed. She glanced at the display, hit a button, and it stopped. "Scott had realized he went to the same university as me and convinced him that reeling me in would be the best thing anyone could ever do for Seminar. That's the night we broke up. I haven't seen him since."

"Do you know your sister calls him The Henchman?"

She laughed. "Perfect."

"She knew the story?"

"No. I never told her. We're not that close. But she obviously has a good eye for what's going on."

She remembered Frank Hernandez as being friendly and cheerful and not trying to pressure her about Seminar. She said she liked him the best of all her dad's friends, and she looked stricken to hear about Zipporah Hernandez's illness.

As far as anyone else in Seminar, she had nothing to say and no idea if any of them might be involved in creating a competing website or had written *Give Me All Your Money*.

She claimed she'd never heard of the book. Nothing about her manner or voice made me think she was lying. Not that I knew her well enough to feel sure, but it would be strange for someone who stayed so far from Seminar for so long to take the time to write about it at length.

She looked over my handwritten list of points from it.

"I couldn't have called any of these to mind before seeing your list. But none surprises me. I feel like they're things my dad knew and that I might have heard."

She handed the list back to me. I tucked it under the last page of my legal pad. "So Richard would have known them?"

"Not through me," Tina said. "I did my best not to talk about Seminar. And my dad was more of a contemporary of Scott's. So was Frank Hernandez. I think either of them would be more likely to know. But I can't see any of them writing a book critical of Scott or Seminar."

"If Frank knew, maybe Zipporah and her sister did, too."

"The Frank I knew would never have passed on anything at all negative about Seminar to anyone, not even to his spouse."

"How about Scott's ex-wife? Might she have written it?"

"They've been divorced for ten years. It'd seem odd to me if she suddenly wrote about Seminar. Plus she has her own positive-thinking type business. I think it'd make her look bad if she were attacking her ex."

"Do you know her well?"

"She came around once in a while to the house. But I avoided Seminar things, so I didn't see her a lot."

Like me, Tina didn't think it likely Gina wrote it. "She'd

put her name on it," Tina said. "No question. Also she was a lot younger, so she didn't know Scott very well or hear as much about him from Dad."

"I am a little surprised you and your sister aren't closer, only because you both seem to share a strong dislike of Seminar."

She sipped water from her plain white mug. "Things were tough for Gina. Our mom developed a serious drinking problem. But she didn't get really bad until after I went away to college. The more Mom drank, the more distant my dad became. For a while I was in an adult child of alcoholics group. Everyone there thought Seminar was my dad's way of trying to get control of his life. And my mom. He kept pushing her to join thinking that would solve her issues. She refused."

"Gina said they had some pretty awful fights."

"She told me that, too. I didn't see it. I feel like my parents both tried hard to pull things together when I came home to visit. Gina was left with their day-to-day behavior. I don't think she ever really forgave me for being older and getting away."

I kept writing notes without pause, but I clutched my pen. I'd never phrased it to myself that way, but her words were ones I could have said about my oldest sister.

Tina said she needed to get back to her patients. I thanked her, and she walked me to the reception area. "Did anything I told you help?"

"Maybe," I said, thinking about Richard and my next stop.

41

Friday, May 30, 3:15 p.m.

It was a good thing I had a long time between appointments. In Chicago, each one hundred in an address number equals a block. So a walk from 200 North Wabash to 800 North Wabash is six blocks.

In New York, a difference of six hundred turned out to be more than twice that long. Though it was cool out, by the time I reached my destination I'd unbuttoned my trench coat. Strands of my hair, which I'd straightened and carefully fashioned into a bun, began springing out in all directions. Before entering the glass and metal skyscraper that housed Richard's former firm, I checked my reflection in the silver panel next to the revolving doors. I fixed my hair and applied red lipstick, something I rarely wear other than to court.

My meeting was with a senior associate in the commercial real estate department. As when I'd made the appointment at Tina Lenzi's clinic, I'd used my middle name, calling myself Cathy Davis.

"So you're thinking of making some big changes," Alfredo

Hines said. He had a closely-trimmed beard and wore a crisp buttoned-down shirt and charcoal gray dress paints.

"Yes. My fiancé is a real estate developer in Chicago, but he has an offer with a firm in Manhattan. And I've been wanting to get out of litigation for a while. I thought commercial real estate might be a good place for me. I've heard it's intellectually challenging but not so contentious. Since everyone wants the deal to go through."

I wondered how Ty would feel about my upgrading him to fiancé. He'd given me a crash course on what the lawyers he often dealt with did, enough so that I was able to ask a number of questions about the work.

"Probably true compared to litigation. You do need to fight for your client's position at times but for the most part everyone wants to work things out."

Alfredo seemed very nice, something I'd noticed about most of the real estate attorneys at my old firm. He let me plug in my phone to an extension so that I could tuck it into my shoulder bag while it charged. That way I couldn't forget it.

I'd called him based on his online bio, asking if he could spare me twenty minutes for an informational interview. The name of my old firm had gotten me in the door. Over a hundred fifty attorneys worked there — enough that if he asked around it wouldn't be unusual for no one to specifically remember Cathy Davis. And I doubted he'd check. I learned when I was launching my own practice that a lot of lawyers are happy to help someone else out and talk about what they do.

"I met someone recently who used to be a partner here," I said after I felt I'd asked enough general questions to make my supposed purpose appear legitimate. "You might not have known him because it was a while ago. Richard Messerly?"

"What's he look like?"

I described Richard and added that he talked a lot about the self-help program he was involved with.

"Oh, Richard." Alfredo's voice got quieter. "He was here for about a year after I came on board. I think he moved on to start his own firm."

When researching Richard on the Illinois attorney registration website, I'd learned not only about his education and years of practice but that his law license was suspended for six months shortly before he left his old firm. I couldn't tell if Alfredo knew anything about the suspension. But it seemed likely the firm notified the other attorneys at the very least so no one would refer anything to him.

"He told me he had to stop practicing for a while," I said. "Some sort of mix up. But he's got a small firm now in Chicago."

His shoulders relaxed. "Oh, that's great to hear. Yeah, it was a tough thing. He'd brought in this huge piece of business. You know the 50th Street office tower?"

I didn't, but I nodded. I'd look it up later.

"He represented one of the parties. Created lots of work for the firm. Then suddenly he was gone. We still handled the deal, so no one could figure out what the problem was."

I exited ten minutes later, not having learned anything more that was helpful. Across the street a man in khakis and a golf shirt with a burgundy messenger bag over his shoulder stood near a news stand. Though he didn't look my direction, I felt sure he was aware of me. I descended the steps into a plaza on the building's east side and went into a Starbucks, hoping for a second exit. There was one along the side. I ordered an Uber to pick me up there, hanging back among people waiting for their drink orders until it arrived.

———

FRIDAY, MAY 30, 4:50 P.M.

No one questioned me as I headed past the reception desk at the Sheraton. I took the escalator up to the second floor where Stacy Vance's workshop was being held. As in Chicago, wearing business attire made me more or less invisible. People assumed I was either a hotel guest or attending one of the two conferences listed on the hotel's website.

On the second level I sat on a bench near the elevators and studied people's conference nametags, all on lanyards hung around their necks. Bright yellow belonged to a gas and oil conference. Larger bright orange nametags with curly letters advertised the Empowerment Conference. From the conference website, I knew Stacy Vance was speaking in the morning.

On the ride over I'd emailed my paralegal to ask her to see what she could find about the office building Alfredo mentioned. Now she texted to say she could spend a few hours tomorrow. I was particularly interested in plans filed with the city and documents showing the parties to the deal. Developers, investors, lawyers. I hoped that somewhere in there was the key to why Richard had been suspended. It might be as simple as him having forgotten to pay his bar dues. That and stealing a client's money are the two biggest reasons lawyers lose their licenses permanently or temporarily. But there was an off chance it related to Seminar or why he moved to Chicago.

The gas and oil attendees striding past me were mainly middle-aged men, mostly white, dressed in bland business casual. Many wore khakis and polo shirts. Minus the burgundy, if my stalker were here, he'd be hard to spot.

The Empowerment Conference participants appeared to be mostly women of all ages and ethnicities. They wore everything from shorts and T-shirts to long, flowing dresses, to pantsuits and skirt suits, though formal business attire was the least common. I expected tomorrow, being Saturday, would be more casual.

Multiple women carrying books and journals with rainbows and stars on them streamed past the check in table and down a hall that I assumed led to conference rooms.

I headed for registration. "Hi," I said to the woman at the table. She wore a long crystal pendant. "I'm staying at the hotel, but your conference looks fascinating. I might come next time it's held. Is there an information or book room?"

Every business conference I'd been to set aside a place for speakers, who were often unpaid, to sell products or give away promotional items. Typically you didn't need to show a pass or ticket to get in. The idea was the more people the better.

She smiled. "Across the hall. Go right in."

Two rows of folding tables held books, flyers, and brochures. At the back, people I guessed were today's speakers talked with attendees and signed books.

I bought one of Stacy Vance's books and a deck of cards featuring abstract images of animals meant to spark creative thought. Both would make excellent props.

42

———

"Ah, I know it's Manhattan, but business attire is not actually required for wine and cheese."

"Sorry." I slid into the chair opposite Ty at a tiny metal table. Five of the eight other tables were filled. "No time to change. I'm surprised they seated you without me."

A wrought iron railing separated the restaurant's narrow outdoor seating area from the sidewalk. We were half a block from a pile of garbage bags on the corner. There are almost no alleys in New York, so bagged garbage waits near curbs for pickup. I tried not to think how many rats that must attract. At least the restaurant was far enough from the corner that I couldn't smell the trash.

"I swore on my life you were only five minutes away, ordered, and promised to eat everything myself if necessary," Ty said. "Plus six is really early in New York even for appetizers."

A bottle of Pinot Noir already sat on the table, a glass in front of each of us. Ty's was full, and the waiter materialized a moment later and filled mine as well.

We clinked glasses. The wine tasted tart with a hint of raspberry.

"Productive day?" Ty said.

I'd just gotten to my conversation at the law firm when the waiter brought out a marble serving plate with five cheeses arranged in a circle on it. We started with a mild, firm goat cheese that had been cut into two perfect triangles. By the time we got to the last one, a creamy, runny sheep's milk cheese with a tangy odor, Ty had filled me in on his meetings. We moved on to talk about the Broadway plays that were popular now.

"We should come back one weekend just for fun," Ty said. "If we plan now I can get us great seats."

I scraped a last bit of cheese from the plate and spread it on a piece of multi-grain bread. "As soon as all this with Seminar is behind me. I want to be able to really enjoy the weekend."

Ty rested his knife on the edge of his plate. "I need to ask you something."

I'd been reaching for my wine, but I let my arm drop onto the table. "Okay."

"I know this weekend was about finding answers, and I'm good with that, so I don't want you to think that's what this is about. But I wonder if there will always be something in the way."

Ty and I had started seeing each other during tax season when I'm the busiest at work. We hadn't spent much time together, which was okay for both of us. Ty had been getting over a difficult breakup, and I still wasn't feeling ready for a new relationship after Marco.

In the second half of April and beginning of May I'd been catching up from tax time. And now everything with Caleb.

"My life is not always like this," I said. "Litigation is pretty quiet in the summer. Attorneys, judges, they go on vacation and it stretches things out."

"Maybe," he said. "But these types of investigations seem to find you. Like a second job you don't get paid for."

"This is only the second time anyone asked me to look into something like this."

As I heard my response, though, it sounded inadequate. Most people don't have anyone ask them to look into crimes ever in their entire lives, let alone twice in a six-month period.

"And you looked into Marco on your own."

I shifted my chair sideways as the waiter squeezed past with three new diners. The leg of my chair caught in a grate in the sidewalk and I struggled to free it.

"His son asked for my help."

Ty reached across the table and took my hand. "And I love that you want to help people. I also think you like using those acting skills, and I'd never ask you to stop. All I'm asking is that you think about whether our not spending more time together is just about how busy we both are. Or if it might be about you not being ready to be with somebody new."

"It's been over a year since Marco died."

The waiter set our check on the table.

"Time is not the only factor when you lose someone." Ty took his wallet from his pocket and pulled out his black and silver Visa card. "Just give it a little thought. Sometimes it feels like you're standing on the edge of the high dive, not sure you're ready to jump."

"I don't feel that way."

"Great." He slid his chair back. We were meeting two of his business colleagues for dinner at eight at Gramercy Tavern. "Let's head out."

———

SATURDAY, MAY 31, 9:25 A.M.

Ty tilted his head. "Looks like you're about to tell someone's fortune."

"Too much?" I said.

I'd styled my hair into tight, tiny long waves and fluffed them out. Rubbing my eyeliner had blurred it into soft lines. Glossy pale eyeshadow, pink-tinted lip balm over neutral liner, and rosy cream blush gave my face a softer, dewier look than usual. Tinted moisturizer rather than foundation completed the natural earthy look.

The costume jewelry I'd brought with me included pieces chosen for the empowerment conference. My earrings, bought at a craft fair, were made of antique gold buttons. The pendant I wore featured an opal at the center and worn gold edging.

He laughed. "I'm kidding. But you do look like you might be open to having your Tarot cards read or your chakras balanced or some such thing."

"So long as I look totally different from yesterday."

He kissed my forehead. "It's like I've got a new girlfriend. Not that I wasn't happy with the old one."

I hoped my new look would fool the man with the burgundy bag if he were still around. I still hadn't mentioned his presence to Ty. Happily, he had a breakfast meeting this morning. Saying I needed more caffeine, which I did, I hung back in the room under the guise of making myself another cup of tea.

Ten minutes after he left, I took the stairs down rather than the elevator. The exit was opposite the hotel restaurant. I cut through and walked outside around the corner from the hotel's main entrance, then walked a few blocks, taking several turns and doubling back once. When I finally felt sure no one was following me, I headed for my real destination, a Duane Read drugstore a few blocks away.

At the second store I tried I found orange construction paper. Folded and tucked into my book so that only the edges showed, I hoped it would convince conference attendees that I was carrying my name badge. I didn't need to get into the presentations, just walk through the halls without anyone thinking I didn't belong.

———

SATURDAY, MAY 31, 11:25 A.M.

At the Sheraton, a woman a few people ahead of me on the escalator caught my attention. She had blond hair pulled back into a sleek ponytail and wore turquoise rimmed glasses, but that wasn't what I noticed. It was her pantsuit. Plain navy blue, its sleeves reached a little too far past her wrists and the pants bunched slightly above her loafers. The poor fit and the fabric suggested it was inexpensive and purchased from somewhere that didn't offer alterations.

There was nothing wrong with that, but it didn't fit with the business people at the oil and gas conference. And any sort of business suit, especially on a Saturday, didn't fit the empowerment crowd.

Under the guise of checking my phone, I paused near the ATM and watched her head toward the elevator bank. I couldn't see what sort of nametag she wore, but she veered left and passed the empowerment conference registration tables.

A few minutes later I followed, holding Stacy Vance's book so that the orange paper could be seen. The pantsuit woman sat on a chair outside one of the conference rooms. It was almost noon, so I slipped into the book room.

Conference attendees began streaming in through its double doors soon after, bringing a cold blast of hallway air with them. At the promotional tables, I browsed the items I'd seen the day before, keeping an eye on the signing tables. A sign with the speaker's name sat in front of each chair. Though she hadn't arrived yet, Stacy's line was the longest, probably twenty deep.

When she entered, I recognized Stacy right away from her book jacket. Her silver-gray hair hung straight to her shoulders and her frame was angular under her flowing, flowery dress. The pantsuit woman came through the doors a few seconds later and paused at the opposite end of the book tables. She stood out as much as I'd expected in the crowd. She ignored me but frequently looked at Stacy.

When Stacy's line got down to seven or eight I made my way over. Two more women joined the line behind me, which made me happy. I didn't want to be the last one. It would make me too noticeable, especially because pantsuit woman seemed to be watching her.

I handed Stacy her book open to the title page, but with the bottom corner of it folded to hide what I'd written. "Could you make it out to a friend of mine? He's in the hospital after a serious accident. Hearing from you could really make a difference." I flipped down the page corner and pointed. "His name is right there."

I'd written: *Are you greycat5389? Have you had contact with Caleb Jackson of Seminar recently? If so, I need to talk with you. Please.*

It was the quickest way I could think of to get her attention and draw the connection to Seminar.

Her narrow black marker hung suspended over the page as she read the note.

She cleared her throat. "I'm not sure that anything I can write will help him. Are you in town long?"

"Through tomorrow afternoon."

Curving her left hand to block what she wrote from view,

she scribbled something, closed the book, and handed it to me. "Good luck to your friend."

I waited until I got downstairs to the lobby and found an isolated empty armchair to read what she'd written. It was an address and a time: 3:45 p.m.

43

I underestimated how bad traffic would be and arrived late. Despite the cool weather and my light coat, I was sweating for fear of missing Stacy. The Uber dropped me in the middle of a long block of office buildings and stores, none with the address I'd programmed in. The driver shrugged. "This is as close as it gets."

At least I didn't see the pantsuit woman or anyone carrying a burgundy messenger bag. I took out the book and checked the address again. I was in the right place. A young woman with spiky hair pushed past me, irritated no doubt that I stood in the middle of the sidewalk. I was about to inch toward the open doorway of a shoe store when someone grabbed my arm from behind.

I spun and came face-to-face with a short woman with dull brown hair, a few strands of which stuck out from under her floppy hat. She wore an unzipped old army jacket over jeans and a baggy gray T-shirt.

"You wanted to talk," she said. I realized she was Stacy Vance.

She gestured for me to follow her into a narrow passageway between two stores. We came out at the top of stone stairs that led down into a vast plaza that had been completely hidden from the street. A fountain cascaded down giant, jagged gray rocks into a landscaped pond. Metal chairs spread out randomly. People sat reading books, staring at their electronic devices, or talking on the phone or with companions.

It was the first place I'd truly loved in Manhattan.

I still hadn't told her my name, and she didn't ask, just led me to two chairs near enough to the fountain that I felt its spray. The sound of the rushing water, though, would keep anyone not right next to us from hearing our conversation.

"Anyone follow you?" Stacy said.

"Not that I noticed. And I watched." I glanced over everyone in the chairs. No one looked familiar. "Do you think someone would have?"

"I'm often followed. You must have noticed Ms. Obvious in blue."

"I did. Who is she?"

"In a minute." Stacy took out a pack of cinnamon gum and offered me a piece. I took one to be polite. "Tell me why you think the hit-and-run connects to me."

"I never said there was a hit-and-run."

I have a good memory for conversation from my years as an actor. It's not verbatim, but it's close, and I knew I hadn't used the words hit-and-run or referred to an automobile crash at all.

She pointed to her smart phone, which stuck out of her large quilted purse. "Did some research. Saw the news stories. Three days after I talked to your friend. But nothing I said could've gotten either of us in trouble."

"Either of you?"

"Oh yes. I'm always watched. In a very open and obvious way. As is anyone who might be anti-Seminar."

If that were true, it might explain the burgundy messenger bag. The guy wasn't bad at following people unobtrusively, he was purposely noticeable. It also explained Stacy meeting me wearing baggy clothes and a wig.

After giving an abbreviated version of my connection to Caleb and why I'd come to New York, I said, "You can't get an order of protection?"

"And make it harder to spot the Seminar people? No point in that. Besides, they don't get too close or say or do anything offensive. It doesn't bother me."

Despite her words, her whole self, not only her appearance, seemed different than at the conference. Her expansive gestures and smiles were gone, replaced by someone whose movements and facial expressions were minute and muted. She confined her gestures to a small area as if an invisible yet unbreakable border surrounded our seats.

"Why does Scott watch you? Because he thinks you're hostile to Seminar?"

Her eyes darted around the seating area. "I didn't say it was Scott. But I obtained a very generous settlement when we divorced. It has conditions. If I were him, I might want to make my ex feel I'd know the instant she so much as considered breaking them."

I felt doubly glad I never signed the non-disclosure agreement.

"If you're so concerned why talk to Caleb? Or me?" I said.

"Caleb, I might have miscalculated. I figured him for a spy. A way to test me. I talked to him so it would be clear I wasn't about to betray any confidences. Which I would never do."

I sat back in my chair. "I'd love to say Caleb would never

spy for Seminar, but he's very devoted. Though if that was his purpose, Scott lied to me about what he asked Caleb to do."

If Scott had lied to me, I didn't know what he hoped to accomplish by it. Other than perhaps trying to use me as an unwitting spy, but I'd been clear that I wasn't reporting to him.

"I can't imagine anyone in Seminar lying." Stacy spoke in a straightforward tone, devoid of any hint of the sarcasm I felt sure was there.

"And me," I said, "why take a chance and talk to me?"

Stacy's chin jutted forward. Her dark eyes peered out from under equally dark, carefully-shaped eyebrows. "I may not own any of it anymore, but I helped start Seminar. If it's turned into something that hurts people, I need to know."

I asked what she and Caleb discussed.

"He asked about some website I'd never heard of or seen. He thought I'd created it. To secretly profit off Seminar concepts. That would violate my agreement with Scott. My empowerment business is a specific exception and it was covered in our agreement. There's no question about that. I never designed any other website."

As she spoke, she kept scanning the entire plaza, rarely looking at me.

"He only asked about a website?"

She nodded and turned to watch a skateboarder sliding down a railing about ten yards to her left. "He wanted to know who I thought designed it if I didn't."

I found the site Lauren's client had been using on my phone. I tapped Stacy's arm to show it to her. "This site?"

She swiveled around to look at my phone. "Looks like it. Can't be positive. I viewed it on my laptop. May I?"

I handed her the phone. "Do you think it copies Seminar ideas?"

Even if it did, that wouldn't violate intellectual property

law. You can't copyright an idea, only its expression. But I doubted Scott cared much about the fine points of the law.

She scrolled through different screens and clicked on various links. "Only in the most general way. Maybe in the super-secret-sauce-type language."

"So what did you tell Caleb?"

"He asked who might have the skills to create a competing site. I'm out of touch, but I told him Frank Hernandez created the whole Internet platform for his nutritional supplement business back when you needed a lot of skills to do that. But I had no idea how to prove Frank did it. If he did."

"He wanted proof?"

"Yes. Couldn't help him."

Maybe Caleb had found some sort of proof about the website's design and that's what he wanted to talk to me about. I couldn't see why he wouldn't take it straight to Scott. Unless it had been Frank and Caleb felt sorry for him because of Zipporah's illness.

"And Caleb didn't ask you about *Give Me All Your Money*?"

"No."

My mind whirled through more possibilities. Scott lied about what he'd asked Caleb to do. Stacy was lying to me now. Caleb figured out who wrote the book and moved on to tracking down the website designer, hoping for bonus points from Scott.

"Did Caleb talk about Vincent?"

"Only to get the meeting."

"Have you read the book?" I said.

"Oh, yes. I'm not allowed to say anything negative about Scott, but nothing prevents me from reading something by someone else who does."

"So you didn't write it?"

Her shoulders hunched forward and her knees drew up a

bit toward her chest. "I'd never do that. Why would you ask that?"

"Just to be sure I covered all the bases."

"Well, I didn't write it. Don't go telling Scott I did." She wrapped her arms around her knees.

I put my hand on her shoulder. "I'm sorry I upset you. I wouldn't tell Scott even if I thought you wrote it. But I believe you that you didn't."

Her arms relaxed and she lowered her feet to the ground again, but her face still looked tense. I offered to go get her some water or coffee from the convenience store I'd seen across the street, but she said no, she just needed a moment. She apologized for getting so emotional.

"Reading that article about the hit-and-run spooked me," she said, but she insisted she wanted to keep talking.

"What did you think of the book when you read it?" I said.

I hoped it was a neutral enough question. I'd reread select parts of the book while killing time before our meeting. The more time I spent on it, the more questions I had about the author's motives.

"I thought it would have more teeth," Stacy said.

"Me too," I said. "Now that I've been through all of it, I'm not sure it would put off anyone attracted to Seminar. Most of the things that could be considered negative could also be spun to show Scott is resourceful and savvy at turning his dreams into reality."

She rested her hands on her knees. "I can't comment on what might or might not be construed as negative about Scott in the book, but generally I don't disagree with your take on it as a whole."

That sounded like the kind of statement a lawyer might have told her she could safely make. It struck me that a huge part of Stacy's life still revolved around Scott, whether she ever saw or spoke to him or not.

"But the book is marketed as if it were more controversial than it is. It makes me wonder if Scott wrote it himself," I said.

I'd been mulling over the idea in the long Uber ride. Any number of politicians had proved lately that no publicity was bad publicity. Scott might have taken a page from their strategy book.

Stacy laughed. Her whole body seemed to open up when she did. Her chest expanded and her lips widened. But the laughter had a shrieky edge. "Scott hates to write," she said. "And he's bad at it. It's part of why Seminar has no website and no written materials to speak of."

"Aren't you saying something negative about Scott by saying that?"

"Scott wouldn't see that as a negative. He's almost proud of it. Or, rather, proud he succeeded in spite of it. One of his high school English teachers told him he was a terrible communicator and that he'd never succeed in business because of it. But I still feel pleased on his behalf that he proved her so wrong."

"He could have hired someone to write it for him."

"No." She shook her head. "A ghostwriter would mean that someone else would know Scott was one of the authors. I can't see him taking that risk. He's a very private person."

I felt less sure. I could see him trusting Richard, Karla, or Frank enough. But she'd been married to Scott for over twenty years. She knew him better than I did.

"I noticed there's not much personal in the book. Nothing about his childhood or extended family. It's as if he sprang to life at twenty years old," I said.

A woman in a thigh-length leather jacket that seemed far too heavy for the weather climbed down the stairs and headed toward us. Stacy waited until she moved well out of hearing range to speak.

"I don't think he tells anyone about those things. He never told me no matter how many questions I asked." She handed my phone back to me.

I checked the time and put it in my shoulder bag. "Who do you think wrote the book?"

"Someone who spent too much on Seminar and regretted it later, but who still can't quite let go. So you get the plus/minus, love/hate aspect of the book."

Stacy suggested I leave before her and walk out onto the opposite side of the block. "You can't be too careful."

"Because of Seminar?" I said.

"I didn't say anything about Seminar. But New York is a dangerous city. Just as dangerous as Chicago."

———

Saturday, May 31, 5:32 p.m.

The man with the burgundy messenger bag sat in the hotel lobby when I got back. Though he glanced at me when I came through the revolving door, he went right back to his phone, thumbs flying over it. My different look today must have confused him.

In the hotel room, I checked my personal and law firm email. My paralegal had sent me a series of names of interlocking corporate entities involved in the office tower real estate deal. One looked familiar to me.

I longed to research the company. But Ty had texted me that he was at the hotel bar with some friends who were also business acquaintances that he wanted me to meet. He knew a lot of people who fit into both categories. I couldn't tell if it was a reflection of how well he'd integrated his life or a sign that he worked too much.

Running around all day and witnessing Stacy's ups and downs had taken a toll. To be presentable I needed a shower to wash away stress and sweat. As the water cascaded over me, I couldn't let go of the idea of Scott writing the book himself or at least having someone else do it. Richard seemed like the best prospect. Gina called him The Henchman, suggesting he'd do whatever Scott needed. Plus he was a lawyer, and a lot of lawyers like to write. Yet Caleb hadn't even tried to find out from Stacy who wrote the book.

After my shower I ironed my hair into long, loose waves, and put on an all-purpose dark red cocktail dress, heels, and the one strand of pearls I own. I thought I looked appropriate for a business/social evening. I purposely brought a vintage evening bag that was big enough to fit my phone. Maybe I'd have a chance to duck away to do a little more research.

Right before exiting the room, the company names my paralegal had sent me ran through my mind again. An image popped into my mind. I knew where I'd seen one of those companies before.

44

———

be downstairs in a few minutes have to check something

I didn't wait for Ty to answer my text, just sat at the hotel room desk and opened my laptop.

Sure enough, when I clicked the PayPal link on the website Lauren's former client had thought seemed similar to Seminar, I recognized the name of the company to whom I'd be making the payment. It was one of the parties to the real estate office tower deal. The same deal Richard handled before having his license suspended.

It took me forty minutes but I finally unwound the tangle of nested entities and discovered Frank Hernandez was the major shareholder of that company. No big surprise that the office tower deal related to someone in Seminar. It made sense that those involved with it might do business together.

But the same company, owned by Frank, running a website that competed with Seminar — at the very least, Frank was earning money from people not served by

Seminar without sharing with Scott. At worst, Frank was siphoning business away from Seminar. If Caleb had found that out, and could prove it, Frank might be willing to do anything to stop him from telling Scott.

My phone dinged with a text from Ty.

U OK? Heading to Peter Luger meet us when you can but don't cab it unless you have a lot of cash

Yes sorry be there soon

As the experience with Zipporah showed, Seminar mattered more to Frank than anything else.

There was a flaw in that reasoning, though. If Seminar mattered so much, why start a competing company and risk it all? Then again, people do self-destructive things. Maybe Zipporah's illness affected him more than it appeared.

I called Jacinda, but got no answer.

I hung up and headed downstairs to call yet another Uber.

———

Saturday, May 31, 8:25 p.m.

Peter Luger is an old-fashioned steakhouse in Brooklyn near the Williamsburg Bridge. It was a long drive, and I could see why Ty warned me not to try to pay for it in cash. Inside it's dark and smells of sizzling steak. The meat is dry aged on-site. We shared a medium-rare porterhouse and German fried potatoes for two and had a wonderful time with Ty's friends. But it took effort on my part to stop thinking about Frank and his website.

At the end of the evening, I took out my credit card to pay our share of the bill. Ty had paid for everything so far and I wanted to treat him. But it turned out the restaurant only accepted personal checks or cash. We paid at an old cashier's window, pushing bills under an iron grate.

———

SUNDAY, JUNE 1, 9:40 A.M.

The next morning Maureen texted me that although Caleb kept fluttering his eyes, he was being transferred to a different facility. Insurance wouldn't pay any longer for Northwestern, a Level 1 trauma center, when Caleb could be maintained at a less expensive facility. She wanted to know if I could talk to someone at the health insurance company when I got home. I promised I would, though I doubted there was anything I could do.

Ty had made brunch reservations for us at a crowded, noisy diner where everyone got a basket of four kinds of muffins on being seated. My phone rang while we were eating but I didn't know it until we left the restaurant. Jacinda had left a message saying she'd be free for another hour that morning.

Across the street on a small square of lawn two wooden benches sat under trees. We sat on the one with the fewest bird droppings and I called Jacinda back.

She confirmed that Frank had the skills to start a website.

"But would he be willing to compete with Seminar?" I said.

"Until you asked, I would have said no. But maybe I didn't give him enough credit for caring about Zipporah. He's sent a lot of money over the last two years. I assumed the nutritional supplement company sales picked up. But maybe it was the other site."

"Is there any chance Frank would harm someone who threatened to expose the website, assuming he started it?"

"I told you before I don't see it," Jacinda said. "But so many things over the last few years have surprised me about him. It's like he's got all these parts of himself boxed away somewhere. If he'd stick with Seminar rather than being at his dying wife's side who knows what he'd do?"

"Boxed," I said. It had triggered an idea.

Ty glanced at me, catching my tone.

"What?" Jacinda said.

"Just something I need to follow up on," I said.

"I'm not asking Zipporah about any of this. She doesn't need to spend her last time on this earth thinking that her husband might have done something horrible."

"I understand. I'm sorry I bothered you."

"It's all right. It's not so bad to need to take a moment to talk to someone else. Good luck, Quille."

———

SUNDAY, JUNE 1, 5:58 P.M.

The airport lounge had that stale inside air smell so many of them do. I squeezed into a seat near the window and called Maureen again. I'd tried her during the long ride to the airport but gotten no answer.

Ty hadn't come with me. He had another dinner this evening, this one for a smaller deal he was trying to put together. It was the main reason that justified his coming to New York with me.

Maureen answered on the fourth ring. She'd been driving earlier, which was why she hadn't answered. Caleb had been transferred today. The new facility was closer to her home. She planned to sleep at home tonight and drive to the new location tomorrow morning to visit Caleb and meet the staff. The doctors had told her not to read too much into him blinking, that sometimes it was just an involuntary reflex. But she felt sure he was starting to wake up.

"I'm sure they can transfer him back to Northwestern if that's so," I said.

"That's what Caleb's boss thought, too. He stopped by today to visit."

I asked her if, when she looked through Caleb's belongings in the row house, she checked the hidden bonus room attached to the master bedroom walk-in closet.

The idea had come to me while talking to Jacinda about all the things she didn't know about Frank. It hit me that Maureen never lived with Jack in the row house. Because of that, she might not know about the bonus room. Especially because Caleb and I had viewed it as our secret hideout and never talked about it with anyone. It seemed to me that if Caleb uncovered proof about anything important, that's where he'd keep it.

"The what?" Maureen said.

I told her about the room, and she confirmed that she knew nothing about it.

"You've got the key, so feel free to go look around. I was going to ask you to check on the plants this week anyway. I asked the neighbors, but they're out of town for the week."

I promised to check on the plants and said goodbye so that I could call Jack before the plane boarded. Fortunately he picked up right away, as I had only ten minutes left.

"The code's a four digit number," he said. "But Caleb changed it. Said it was a day he could never forget, so I'm guessing his birthday. Or Maureen's."

I took out my boarding pass. "Not yours?"

"He never remembered mine in his life. But Maureen, every year he made her a hand-drawn card. He used to send them from L.A."

The flight was delayed due to a mechanical problem, but

only for half an hour. Usually I take the Blue Line home from O'Hare, but that would take at least an hour and I'd still need to transfer to a bus to get to the row house. A car would at least give me a chance of getting there more quickly.

The taxi line was too long, and the closest Uber was fifteen minutes away. But Lyft had someone who could pick me up in seven minutes.

***

SUNDAY, JUNE 1, 10:05 P.M.

When I entered the row house, the torchiere floor lamp in the corner of the living room cast bright light across the ceiling and throughout the room. I was surprised Maureen left it on. It was an old lamp with a halogen bulb. The kind that can explode if they get too hot.

Then I remembered the timer. It probably controlled the lamp.

Sure enough, as I climbed the stairs to the second floor the lamp flipped off. The sun had set over an hour ago. With no windows in the stairwell, I was in the dark.

I used the flashlight function on my smart phone. It flashed that it was down to 20% of the battery, so I turned it off when I reached the third-floor master bedroom. The overhead light in the walk-in closet was one of the few not on a timer. I flipped it on.

The furs, long abandoned by Wife No. 2, gave off a mothball smell and the evening gowns kept falling in my way as I typed Caleb's birthday into the keypad. An angry electric buzz told me I was wrong. I tried again in case I'd typed the numbers incorrectly, but no luck.

Maureen's birthday also didn't work. Neither did Jack's, which I tried despite his comments. Caleb's graduation date from high school also wasn't it. I stopped to think. I felt

certain Caleb had said something to me since we reconnected that would give me a clue as to the code. It might be
his college graduation date, but I didn't know when that was.

I was about to text Maureen to ask for it when Jack's
words sounded in my mind again. A date Caleb said he'd
never forget.

That was it.

45

I typed in the opening night of the play Caleb and I had been in together.

A faint, high-pitched beep and click rewarded me. I inched my hand to the right and, once I felt the seam in the wall, pressed. The door creaked as it opened and I stepped into the recording room.

The furs and gowns had swung back over the doorway, making it too dim to see very much. Using the flashlight function on my phone I made my way to the floor lamp and turned it on, then switched off my phone. It was down to 10%. It'd be zero in a matter of seconds.

Everything looked the same as it had the night I'd sat here talking to Caleb after the Celebration. Except for one thing — a stack of typed pages on top of one of the orange crates filled with record albums. I sat on the floor, my back against one of the foam-covered walls, with the massive document. It was a draft of *Give Me All Your Money* with handwritten notes in the margins. Based on the impressions the letters made on the paper, it had been typed with a typewriter. At least two thirds of the notes started with a capital SG and a colon. Those notes were scribbled, as if written in a hurry. The others were printed more clearly, but all the writing looked like it had been done by the same person.

I had never seen Scott's handwriting or printing. I'd also never seen Richard's.

But I had seen Frank Hernandez's on the whiteboard during the breakout group. It was bold and thick with definitive slashing lines. In contrast, the handwriting on the manuscript was slightly wavy and sloppy. Not being a handwriting expert, I couldn't be positive, but I felt pretty certain it wasn't Frank's. Which meant, if I were right, that while he might have created the competing website, someone else had written the book.

The SG must mean those comments had come from Scott Gary. I couldn't think what else the letters would stand for. The rest were probably the author's own notes on reviewing the draft.

The recording room was the safest place to leave the manuscript, but I wanted to have some proof with me in case the book related to the attack on Caleb. I folded the first three pages and put them into my jeans pocket. I planned to return to Detective Beckwell. Between the hit-and-run, Scott's request that Caleb find the book's author, and this manuscript, the detective would take my concerns about the danger to Caleb seriously.

I shut off the lamp and stepped out of the room. As I did, I thought I heard a rattling sound from directly beneath me. I froze, but relaxed when I remembered how everything from the row house next door sounded as if it was happening here. It had added an element of fun and frightening tension when Caleb and I had told ghost stories to each other late at night.

Away from the furs and gowns, though, the sounds were

much louder. It hit me that Maureen had said the neighbors were out of town.

She'd gone home to LaGrange. Jack had said he was in Woodstock. No one else had a key.

Heart pounding, I eased off my shoes. Avoiding the floorboards that I knew from experience creaked, I slid in my stocking feet toward the open closet door. I held still and listened.

The sounds I heard now made me certain the intruder was in the office, which was right below the master bedroom closet. Slaps and thunks must be books and papers hitting the floor.

A moment later, footsteps started up the stairs.

SUNDAY, JUNE 1, 10:23 P.M.

I shut off the overhead light and turned on my phone as I inched toward the back of the closet. The phone blinked off immediately, out of juice. The row house had landline service. Another thing Jack hadn't changed. But the only phone was an old wall mounted one in the old-fashioned phone nook on the landing outside the office. It had a phone with a long cord that ran from the base to the handset. Caleb had often stretched it all the way out into his bedroom, which was next to the office, driving his dad crazy.

Getting to it meant going down the staircase the intruder was ascending.

My safest bet was to get into the hidden room and wait it out, though I'd never find out who was searching through the house. But if it was the same person who had run down Caleb, hiding was definitely the better option.

A centimeter at a time I eased the closet door shut. In the

dark, I retraced my steps. I hadn't shut the door to the bonus room.

Moving slowly and quietly, I stepped inside, then took off my blazer, stretched it out, and tucked it under the door. It should block any sounds I made if the intruder came into the master bedroom.

I pressed against the wall next to the orange crates. I wanted to be able to hear what was happening. That wall had no soundproofing and it was adjacent to the master bathroom. The master bath was fairly small with only a long narrow shower and no tub, suggesting the bonus room had been carved out of it.

Something banged, and I struggled not to react, remaining still and quiet. It sounded as if someone were in the room with me shoving things around and dropping them on the floor. Some of the sounds were softer than others, and I guessed the linen closet was being rifled through.

I tried to breathe evenly and quietly, counting breaths in my mind the way I did when I meditated to try to ease migraine pain.

Muffled footsteps clomped across the floor, likely from the master bedroom. A moment later I thought I heard metal hangers jangling. It was hard to tell from inside the room, and somehow the darkness made discerning directions harder. The keypad was fairly well hidden. Had I not known about it, I would never have thought to push aside the gowns and furs to look for it.

My hips, back, and knees ached from holding myself so still. I couldn't think why someone had come to the row house now, just as Maureen had vacated it, though I supposed Scott could have had someone watching. Then I remembered her saying Caleb's boss had visited the hospital today. I couldn't imagine Scott making it so obvious he'd broken in, though. It seemed much more his style to have persuaded Maureen to let him in and take him on a guided tour.

Finally, the footsteps and sounds moved away. For a few moments I didn't hear anything, and then creaking came from the direction of the staircase. I heard slamming a few minutes later. Maybe one of the outside doors, or maybe one inside.

With no light and no phone to tell me the time, it seemed like the moments stretched into hours. At last I bent my legs and eased to a standing position. Carefully and quietly I opened the door. Though I heard nothing, I felt uneasy. I stared into the darkness, afraid I was missing something about the situation. But I couldn't stay in the recording room forever. And I'd heard the outside back door slam, making the row house shudder.

After shutting the door behind me to keep the manuscript safe, I inched through the closet.

I realized my mistake as I reached the stairs just beyond the master bedroom. I'd left my coat hanging over the back of an armchair in the living room. It could easily have been seen in the light through the picture window from the streetlamps outside.

It was too late. A shadowy figure darted up the darkened stairwell and flew toward me.

46

———

I turned and raced into the bedroom, slamming the door behind me. The intruder ran into it and shouted in pain. I hit the button to lock the door. The low groans suggested it was a male. If it was Frank Hernandez out there the bulky man might very well be able to barrel through the door on the next try.

The master bedroom was on a corner. The windows fronting the street had a decorative balcony outside. The kind that has a railing across it with window boxes for flowers but is too narrow for chairs. But it was wide enough to stand on. Caleb and I used to climb out the window at night when Jack left us alone to watch cars driving by on the street below.

The floor below had a wider balcony off of Caleb's bedroom, which was across the hall from the phone nook. The problem was, there was no ladder or convenient trellis from this floor to the second floor balcony. And if the intruder climbed out after me, he'd be far more likely to throw me to the ground than the other way around.

I shut my eyes, thinking back to childhood. Jack had kept

so many things the same, there must be something that could help.

Footsteps sounded in the hall and there was a huge bang and yell as the intruder slammed into the door. It shuddered, but there were no cracking sounds, so it had probably held.

I didn't take time to turn on the light. In the dark I at least had the advantage of knowing my way around the house. I dropped to the floor and felt around under the bed.

The heavy cardboard box was still there, and still taped shut. The old tape tore off easily. Inside was a folded fire escape safety ladder. Never used.

After I yanked the window and the screen open, I dropped the ladder onto the narrow balcony and climbed out. In the light from the streetlamps I unfolded the ladder. It had rubber rungs and didn't look nearly as long as it ought to for a three-story building.

I scanned the sidewalk below, but saw no one walking by. The cars in the street would never hear me if I screamed or shouted, and I'd give my location away. The only way out was down the ladder.

The metal balcony railing was far too shaky to anchor the ladder there. I fastened the hooks over the window sill and pulled down the window to help wedge the hooks in place. When I yanked as hard as I could on the ladder it stayed fast. I draped it over the metal railing.

More banging came from inside the room. Holding my breath, I maneuvered onto the ladder and started down.

With each step the rubber rung gave a little under my foot and the whole ladder swung out away from the house. I clung to the rope sides as it swayed, doing my best to shut out everything else and concentrate on holding on.

47

I risked a look down. My feet were about a yard above the second-floor balcony and there were only a few rungs left of the ladder.

My breath caught in my throat. The ladder had been sealed in its original packaging. Jack and his wife probably never realized they bought a one-story ladder for their three-story home.

When I landed on the balcony and felt sure of my footing, I yanked on the ladder, trying to pull it down. I wrenched my right shoulder doing it, and the ladder remained secured above me. I considered trying to dangle myself over the balcony railing, then jumping the rest of the way down. But the railing's shakiness and my throbbing shoulder convinced me that attempt would probably result in a one-story fall onto the brick patio below.

Broken bones wouldn't help me. I was better off going for the phone. Especially because the intruder almost certainly didn't know it was there.

I tried the glass door to Caleb's room. It was locked. I

fumbled for the key ring Jack had given me. The third key worked, and I burst inside. I heard cracking and thumping sounds above me.

As in my neighborhood, response times for police tended to be good in the Gold Coast. The station wasn't far away, and there weren't many calls. All the same, it wasn't instantaneous. I had no hope the police could get here before the man upstairs attacked me. I needed to call and get out of the house.

I darted through Caleb's room and into the hallway where I felt my way to the landing and the phone nook. The intruder sounded like he was running around the master bedroom and bath. I felt for and found the large button at the base of the handset. Pressing it down so as not to take the phone off the hook, I pulled the handset with me down the stairs. I got three steps from the bottom before the cord pulled taut.

As I dialed 911, footsteps sounded on the staircase. I squatted down so that the cord would stretch across the hallway inches above the floor, putting it in the best possible position to trip someone who wasn't expecting it even if he turned on the light.

When the operator answered I said in a voice just above a whisper, "Intruder. Come quick." I rattled off the address though the system ought to pick it up. I started to give the cross streets, but the cord jerked. Something thumped above me, and the receiver was yanked from my hand. It banged against the wall. I bolted out the front door and down the steps.

I skipped the row house next door that I knew was empty and ran across the lawn and up the concrete stairs of the next one in line. The porch light flipped on, triggered by my movements. My stockinged feet, damp from the grass, skidded on the middle step. I grabbed the railing to steady myself. At the top of the steps, I banged on the front door. No one answered. I pounded again, conscious that I stood in a glow of light, making it easy for the intruder to spot me.

Still no answer.

From the corner of my eye I saw the motion detector lights in front of the Jacksons' house blink on. Someone raced out.

I turned, rushed down the steps, and headed for the next row house in line. Muffled, quick footsteps sounded on the grass behind me. As I neared the narrow sidewalk between houses the intruder hit the back of my knees with what felt like his whole body.

I plunged forward, hands out.

My palms slapped the sidewalk, sending stinging waves up my arms. The lawn smelled like grass and mud. I rolled, kicking wildly, dimly aware of sirens and screeching brakes. They sounded far away, though, drowned out by my own ragged breaths and those of my attacker. My foot connected with flesh and he let out a groan.

I maneuvered onto my back and got a quick impression of skinny arms reaching for my shoulders to pin me down.

A spotlight blinked on.

"Freeze." The police officer's voice rang through the yard.

Richard Messerly, face bruised and bloody, grabbed my shoulders.

48

Two officers pried Richard off of me. He collapsed on the grass and rolled into a ball.

Paramedics helped me to a waiting ambulance as police cuffed Richard. After he was taken away, I told the officer in charge about the manuscript in the recording room. I'm not sure how much sense I made, but I gave him the code and he took it away with them.

One of my ankles had twisted, my shoulder was sore, and I had bruises all over, but I was otherwise all right. Lauren stayed overnight with me. Though she lived only two floors away and I told her I was fine, I felt grateful for her sleeping on the other side of the king bed. I knew Richard was in custody and couldn't come after me, but I couldn't stop shaking for a long time.

Ty was at my door by nine a.m. the next morning, having gotten an earlier flight home.

I texted Maureen a link to Richard's law firm website with a photo of him. She called me and confirmed that he was the person who visited Caleb the day before, claiming to be

Caleb's boss and asking how Caleb was doing. When she filled him in on Caleb's condition, she mentioned moving back home to LaGrange, so he'd known the row house would be empty.

Maureen told me the police had found a dark gray SUV in Richard's garage. It belonged to his cousin who was visiting from Indiana. The cousin told police Richard had claimed he'd run into a concrete pillar in a parking garage and that he was saving up money to get the repairs done.

———

SUNDAY, JUNE 6, 2:30 P.M.

Caleb's eye blinking had been a good sign. By the end of the week he'd progressed to saying a few words and was back at Northwestern for a visit with a neurologist. Though he was weak, he was pronounced out of danger and sent to a rehab facility.

The doctor asked us not to question him about anything that had happened just yet. So far, he didn't remember the hit-and-run and knew only that he'd been in an accident. Maureen and Jack worried that this was due to permanent brain damage, but the doctor assured them that amnesia surrounding the accident wasn't unusual.

On Friday afternoon, while Caleb was napping, I went into the waiting room. Scott was walking away from the nurse's counter and toward the exit. He wore dark washed jeans with a striped button-down shirt open at the collar.

When he saw me, he reversed course. "Quille, I'm told Caleb's parents don't want me to see him. Can you help me out?"

"No." I pressed A12 on the vending machine for a Hershey's dark chocolate bar. My head was pounding and I thought the sugar might help.

"You blame me. Blame is a wasted emotion."

The candy bar clanged on its way down the machine. "Then I'll waste it."

Scott rested a hand on the side of the vending machine. "Richard made his choices. So did Caleb. Each has a part in what happened between them."

I hit the door at the base of the machine hard. It swung back against my hand as I grabbed the Hershey bar, making my knuckles sting. "Did you ask Richard to write the book? Were you the one commenting on the draft?"

He shrugged. "I already told the police. Yes. Richard wrote it. At my request. As Seminar grew people asked more and more questions about me. I wanted to control how the answers came out. And create interest. People like to read something scandalous. It's far more interesting than a biography. Or, worse yet, an autobiography."

"And you used paper to make it harder to trace to you." As old-fashioned as paper is, it's much easier to limit its distribution and control who sees it than a digital file.

"Of course. I didn't want a trail. That's why I only gave Richard comments verbally, and we passed the paper manuscript back and forth until it became absolutely final."

"So why ask Caleb, and then me, to find out who wrote it when you already knew?"

"If Richard did what I specifically instructed him to do and destroyed all copies, he would've had nothing to worry about. I was checking to see whether he followed my instructions. He didn't, and now he'll suffer the consequences."

"Prison," I said.

"Perhaps. More important, he's finished in Seminar. He proved he can't be trusted."

Stacy Vance had told me Scott liked to test people.

49

———

Monday, June 15, 11:07 a.m.

"I asked the prosecutor not to press charges against Richard," Caleb said.

We sat in the sun porch at the rehab center, me on the couch, him in a wheelchair. A bright purple cast encased his right leg to the hip. The crutches, which he was using a little more each day, rested against the wall behind him. His sweatpants bagged at the waist and his T-shirt hung loose at the shoulders. His face looked less pale, though, and he'd combed his hair into smooth, shiny waves.

"I don't understand," I said.

"It was an accident," Caleb said. "You always told me to pay attention. I was looking down at my phone. Crossed against the light."

There were long pauses between each phrase. The doctors said it might be as long as a year before he processed language as quickly as he once had.

"That's not what the witnesses said." I sat on the couch near him, my feet flat on the floor, my hands on my knees. "And your mom said you didn't remember what happened."

"I thought about it. I realized I did."

"Before he stopped talking, Richard admitted that the day before the hit-and-run you told him that you had proof he wrote *Give Me All Your Money*."

"Because I'd created this narrative. In my head. How Richard was scheming against Scott. He wasn't. He was working for Scott. He had no reason to hurt me. No one in Seminar does."

Once Caleb had been aware enough to make his own decisions, he'd insisted on having Scott visit him. This change had to be the result of those visits, and I wanted to argue with him more. But we were all supposed to keep from upsetting him.

"He still broke into the row house," I said.

"The door was broken open when he got there. He went in because he saw there must be an intruder. When he came upstairs, you'd laid a trap for him and you attacked him."

"You believe I attacked him?"

"Because you were scared. You both thought the other one was a burglar."

Our voices had raised, and Maureen appeared in the doorway. She'd been in the cafeteria. "Quille, this isn't good for Caleb."

————

Monday, June 21, 3:15 p.m.

Frank Hernandez sat across from me in an armchair in front of the bookshelves at Café des Livres. I chose that location because I wanted to be on what felt like home turf without inviting him to my condo or my office. I didn't trust anyone from Seminar enough to do that.

I told Frank that I figured out he created the website, telling him the trail I'd followed.

He sighed. "I did it for the extra money. Zipporah's and my premiums and out-of-pocket medical each year are over thirty thousand dollars. My nutritional supplement business isn't earning like it used to. There's so much competition now in the online world."

I drank some iced tea and set my glass on the round coffee table. "What about Seminar commissions? Or bonuses, I guess they're called."

"Bonuses can be exciting. But it's more a labor of love. If I divide it out I don't earn a lot more than minimum wage."

"A vocation," I said, remembering his word from the night we'd met.

"Yes."

"And Scott never figured out you're running a website?"

"The online world doesn't interest him. I got worried when Caleb started saying he was working on a project for Scott. I thought my website might be the target. But I guess it was the book."

A young woman tried to bring her labradoodle inside the café. The dog was on a long turquoise leash that allowed free roaming among the tables. Carole headed the woman off before she reached the counter, pointing to a sign in French and English advising patrons to leave animals outside.

"You're not worried about being excommunicated? Like Richard?"

Frank rubbed his chin. "It's a risk. But it matters more to me to help Zipporah. If I'm forced to leave Seminar over it, I'll survive."

"Caleb found your website," I said. "But he doesn't remember much from the weeks leading to the hit-and-run."

"I'm sorry he's struggling," Frank said. "Are you going to tell him about the site if he doesn't remember it? Or tell Scott?"

"It's none of my business."

He nodded. "Thank you, Quille."

"You don't have to thank me. I don't feel I owe either of them anything. But I'd appreciate it if you answer a question. Any idea exactly what happened between Caleb and Richard before the hit-and-run?"

He sighed again, making his body heave. "All I know is a few days before it happened Richard complained things were missing from his office. He insisted one of us had been in there, but he wouldn't say what was gone. Everything in my office seemed a little out of place once I took a close look. Nothing missing, though. Caleb claimed he thought the same thing about his office, but now I figure that was a cover. He'd been hunting through everyone's files looking for that book manuscript."

"I don't understand why Richard kept it at the office."

"He and Olivia have a tiny apartment. He probably didn't feel he could keep it hidden there, and he's got this heavy old file cabinet at work that locks. Must've never dreamed anyone would swipe his key."

"Did you tell the police all of this?"

"I did. If Richard ran Caleb over, he needs to answer for it."

"Why don't you get out of it? Seminar? You said you don't make much. The concepts kept Zipporah from getting treatment sooner. I don't understand why you want to stay part of it."

He shook his head. "It really isn't your business."

―――――

MONDAY, JUNE 23, 5:15 P.M.

A few days later, representing himself, Richard confessed to having purposely hit the gas, saying he needed to take full responsibility. He also admitted Caleb confronted him about the manuscript, accusing him of writing it and threatening to report it to Scott. Scott had instructed Richard to keep authorship of the manuscript a secret from everyone at all costs, so Richard feared excommunication. Or having to repeat years of Events to regain his Seminar position.

Supposedly, though, it was just happenstance that while driving his cousin's SUV Richard saw Caleb crossing the street. On impulse and in anger he accelerated. He said he meant to scare Caleb, not hit him. But Caleb was so absorbed in his phone that he didn't look up or stop as Richard expected. Richard tried to swerve, but he miscalculated and hit Caleb. Then he panicked and took off.

As for breaking into the row house, he admitted he was trying to find any proof Caleb might have. But he claimed he believed another burglar was in the house, maybe someone else hunting for the manuscript to cause trouble for Scott. He claimed he chased me because he didn't want an intruder to get away.

If he'd had a lawyer, that lawyer would have told him that confessing to hitting the gas intentionally and aiming for Caleb, regardless whether he meant to kill him, was confessing to attempted murder. What matters under the law is the intent to do the act that could kill someone, not the result you expect to get.

But with Caleb's revised testimony, and Richard's testimony about acting in sudden anger, Danielle said prosecutors would have doubts about whether they could convict on the most serious of the charges. Richard also had a clean record.

In exchange for a guilty plea, the prosecutors reduced the charges to attempted reckless homicide as to Caleb and leaving the scene of the accident, plus misdemeanor battery against me.

Richard's fingerprints did match partials on the rocks

thrown through my glass doors. But since he hadn't come inside or stolen anything, that offense was plea-bargained down to trespassing and a criminal property damage crime. Despite that he admitted he'd been trying to scare me away from investigating.

His sentence was six years in prison, which meant he would serve about three.

I attended court the day he entered his pleas.

50

Caleb stopped me in the hall outside the courtroom at the 26th Street and California Avenue criminal courthouse. There was no place to sit in the wide hallway, so he balanced on his crutches, holding the leg in the cast, a bright yellow one now, a few inches off the floor.

"I know I crossed a line in our friendship by lying to get you into Seminar's world. I created this narrative where it was okay because I so wanted to share Seminar with you," Caleb said. "I've missed you, and I thought it would be a way for us to reconnect."

He reached for my hand, keeping his crutch wedged under his shoulder.

I squeezed his fingers briefly and let go, not stepping any closer to him. "If you missed me all you had to do was call. I'm not hard to find."

"I take full responsibility. Please. Don't hold it against Seminar. Please let me mend the fractures in our relationship."

"What do you mean don't hold it against Seminar?"

"Don't let it stop you from finishing an Event."

"Let's leave everything fractured," I said, and walked away.

————

THURSDAY, JULY 2, 11:45 A.M.

Someone called my name as I reached the sidewalk in front of the courthouse steps. I'd killed time in the courthouse's cafeteria on the upper floor until I'd felt reasonably sure everyone connected to the case had gone.

An old but well-maintained green Corvette convertible idled near the curb. Jack waved to me. "Hop in. I'll give you a ride."

I got in. "You must have been waiting for me."

"Circled the block a few times." He pulled into the left turn lane. "Least I can do. Your statement cancelled out Caleb's and helped get that guy behind bars for a while. Though it's too bad nothing can hang Scott Gary, too. The prosecutor said Seminar's on the radar now, but I don't know how much that means."

"You've talked to Caleb more than I have," I said. "Does he really believe everything he said to the judge?"

Part of me wanted to think Caleb drew me into Seminar solely to try to make more money. The idea that he'd fallen for Scott Gary felt somehow sadder.

"I've never understood him," Jack said. "Should've tried harder because now — I don't know. All I can do is try to be there for him. And hope when he recovers, he'll see this Seminar thing for what it is." He squeezed my shoulder. "But thank you. No one else will say it, but I will. It means a lot. Everything you tried to do for Caleb. It means a lot."

I cried when I got home.

———

Thursday, July 4, 9:12 p.m.

The night of July 4th it finally felt truly warm out. Lauren, Joe, Ty, and I sat on my deck. There are too many buildings in the way to see many of the fireworks the city sets off at Navy Pier. But each year a few are shot at just the right angles so that they burst in a blaze of color in one of the few gaps in the skyline. Ty had made us both whiskey sours with fresh lemon juice and egg white, exactly how I like them. Lauren had opened a bottle of spicy Shiraz for her and Joe.

"At least I'm done with him," I said.

"As in you're never talking to him again?" Ty said. "Not that I'm suggesting that you should."

"She shouldn't," Joe said. "If you knew him like I do, you'd think so too."

"I'm not planning to talk to him," I said. "I mean, if I saw him somewhere, I wouldn't ignore him —"

"I totally would," Lauren said. "He knew exactly what he was doing when he lied to you."

"But I'm done being his friend. And feeling like he abandoned me because without theater I just wasn't exciting or interesting enough for him to want to be my friend."

"Quille, there is no way you were ever not exciting enough," Ty said.

"And because we're sure we can't convince you to stop leading such an exciting life, we all chipped in and got a present for you." Joe gestured to Lauren.

She reached into her purse, an emerald green Dolce and Gabbana, and took out a small box wrapped in brown paper.

I unwrapped it. Inside was a brand new rose gold iPhone.

"No more phones running out of batteries," Ty said.

"Thank you. All of you. You know I was going to get one this fall."

"Sooner is better," Lauren said.

The smell of lilac from the neighbors' potted flowers drifted over on the breeze. Ty linked his hand with mine and raised his glass with his free hand. "To a quiet summer."

I raised mine, too. "To summer."

ABOUT THE AUTHOR

In addition to the Q.C. Davis series, which includes *The Worried Man*, *The Charming Man*, and *The Fractured Man*, Lisa M. Lilly is the author of the *Awakening* supernatural thriller series. The series, which has been downloaded over 80,000 times, consists of *The Awakening*, *The Unbelievers*, *The Conflagration*, and *The Illumination*. Her stories and poems have appeared in numerous publications.

A resident of Chicago, Lilly is an attorney and a member of the Alliance Against Intoxicated Motorists. She joined AAIM after an intoxicated driver caused the deaths of her parents in 2007. Her book of essays, *Standing in Traffic*, is available on AAIM's website.

Visit www.LisaLilly.com to join Lisa M. Lilly's email list and receive Free Q.C. Davis short stories, a monthly e-newsletter, and updates on sales and new releases.

ALSO BY LISA M. LILLY

Q.C. Davis Series

The Worried Man (Q.C. Davis 1)

The Charming Man (Q.C. Davis 2)

The Fractured Man (Q.C. Davis 3)

No Good Deeds (Short Story for e-newsletter subscribers)

No New Beginnings (Short Story for e-newsletter subscribers)

The Awakening Series

The Awakening (Book 1)

The Unbelievers (Book 2)

The Conflagration (Book 3)

The Illumination (Book 4)

The Awakening Series Complete Supernatural Thriller Series Box Set/Omnibus

Other Fiction

When Darkness Falls (a standalone supernatural suspense novel)

The Tower Formerly Known As Sears And Two Other Tales Of

Urban Horror

As L.M. Lilly:

Happiness, Anxiety, and Writing: Using Your Creativity To Live A Calmer, Happier Life

Super Simple Story Structure: A Quick Guide to Plotting and Writing Your Novel

Creating Compelling Characters From The Inside Out.

The One-Year Novelist: A Week-By-Week Guide To Writing Your Novel In One Year

How The Virgin Mary Influenced The United States Supreme Court: Catholics, Contraceptives, and Burwell v. Hobby Lobby, Inc